# Out Are The Lights

# The Lights
## And Other Tales

Richard Laymon

HEADLINE
*FEATURE*

First published in 1993
by HEADLINE BOOK PUBLISHING

A HEADLINE FEATURE paperback

'Out Are The Lights' first published in Great Britain
in 1982 by New English Library

'Bad News' first published in Great Britain in 1991
in BEST NEW HORROR, ed Jones and Campbell,
Robinson Publishing

10 9 8 7 6 5 4

ISBN 0 7472 3581 3

Printed and bound in Great Britain by
Cox & Wyman Ltd, Reading, Berkshire

HEADLINE BOOK PUBLISHING
A division of Hodder Headline PLC
338 Euston Road
London NW1 3BH

# CONTENTS

# OUT ARE
# THE LIGHTS

Out - out are the lights - out all!
   And, over each quivering form,
The curtain, a funeral pall
   Comes down with the rush of a storm,
While the angels, all pallid and wan,
   Uprising, unveiling, affirm
That the play is the tragedy 'Man',
   And its hero the Conqueror Worm.

Edgar Allan Poe, *The Conqueror Worm*

# PROLOGUE

'You sure it's not haunted?' Ray asked.

The weathered, Victorian house cast a shadow over its weedy yard and Ray's Trans Am.

'Wouldn't that be rich?' Tina said. 'I've never seen a ghost.'

'This may be your big opportunity.' Ray reached for the door handle, but hesitated and looked again out the windshield. He gnawed his lower lip.

'Would you rather not stay here?' Tina asked. 'I mean, just because Todd offered to let us use it, we aren't *obliged* to stay. We could go someplace else if you want. A motel or something.'

'I guess this is all right,' Ray said.

'It's just old. He told me not to expect too much. He bought it as a fixer-upper.'

'When's he planning to start?'

Tina smiled. 'It might be wonderful, once we get inside.'

'I don't like those bars in the windows.'

'He's had a few problems with vandals. So remote, out here . . .'

'I hope there's not a fire. An old place like this, it'd go up like paper. And those bars . . . I don't know, Tina. The place rubs me wrong.'

3

'You've seen too many movies, that's your problem.'

'Think so?'

'Let's at least have a look inside.'

'Why not.'

They climbed from the car. In the shade, the breeze from the ocean felt chilly on Tina's bare skin. She pulled the back of the seat forward, and leaned into the car.

'Let's just leave the groceries and stuff till we've had a chance to look around.'

'I'm getting my blouse,' Tina said. She found it wadded behind the picnic basket they used at the beach, and tugged it free.

Ray made a mocking pout as she put it on.

She grinned. 'I don't want the ghosts to see me in my bikini,' she said.

'Nothing worse than a horny ghost,' Ray agreed.

As she buttoned the blouse, Ray slipped a hand inside the seat of her bikini shorts. Her skin was moist from the damp swimsuit. His warm, dry hand felt good.

He started to take it out.

'Oooo, don't stop.'

He removed his hand, and patted her rump. 'Tempis is fugiting. Let's have that look inside, and get going. It's a long drive to the nearest motel.'

'Maybe you'll just love it here.'

'Well, the price is certainly right. Have you got the key?'

'Right here.' She lifted her handbag off the car floor, and slung the strap over her shoulder.

They started across the overgrown yard.

'I think it's rather quaint,' Tina said.

'It is that, I suppose.'

They climbed half a dozen stairs to a roofed porch that extended along the entire front of the house. As Tina reached

into her handbag, she saw the door's heavy brass knocker –
a skull.

'That's Todd for you,' she said, grinning. 'It's no wonder
he bought the place. It's so *him*.'

Ray didn't look amused. 'What's Todd; a ghoul?'

'He's really rather nice.'

'Is he?'

She hunted for the key, face toward the door to hide her
grin. Ray could be so childish, sometimes. It was fun to bait
him, but she knew she'd better back off. If she went too far,
he might start his silent treatment.

She found the key. 'Ready?'

'As I'll ever be.'

She pushed it into the keyhole, and turned it. A bolt clacked
back. She pushed the door open, enjoying the groan of its
hinges.

'Naturally they squeak,' Ray muttered.

'We oughtta spray this sucker with WD-40 before we go.
That's fix his wagon.'

That brought a grin from Ray.

It's all right now, she thought.

She stepped into the dim foyer, glimpsed someone beside
her, and lurched back. She collided with Ray.

Laughing, he caught her in his arms. 'So who's the nervous
one?' he asked, and nodded toward the wall mirror. 'Jumping
at your own reflection.'

She snapped the waistband of his swimming trunks.

'Big deal,' she said. Then she turned away from him, and
looked around. 'The place is rather dismal,' she admitted.

Ray flicked a switch. A ceiling light came on. 'At least there's
electricity.'

Tina moved to the front of the staircase. The steps were
narrow and steep. At a landing, halfway up, they angled to

5

the right and vanished. 'The bedroom's probably up there,' she said.

'You go ahead, I'll wait here.'

'Ha, ha, ha.'

'Do you want me to lead the way?'

'If you please.'

He shut the front door, and started up the stairs ahead of her. 'Watch out,' he warned. 'Mirror ahead.'

She yanked his trunks.

'Don't!' He grabbed them at his knees. 'Want me to trip?'

'Then don't be such a wiseguy.'

'Sorry, sorry,' he said, pulling them up.

'Nice ass,' Tina remarked.

'Thank you.'

'Cracked, though.'

At the top of the stairs, they came to a narrow hallway. The only windows, at each end, were hung with heavy red drapes.

'Charming,' Tina said.

'Your friend's a great decorator.' Ray found a light switch. Dim bulbs came alive in sconces along the walls.

He tried a door. It was locked. 'Great,' he muttered.

'Hope that isn't the john.'

He tried a door on the other side of the hall, and glanced at Tina as the knob turned. He pushed the door open. The room was bare.

Tina shrugged. 'He's got an austere taste in furniture.'

'I'll say.'

They found two more empty rooms, then the bathroom.

'We're in luck,' Tina said.

They stepped inside. When she saw the enormous tub, she smiled with delight. 'Oh, this is great.'

'No shower.'

'But look at the size of that! Look, it's even got legs. Must be a real antique. Boy, I can't wait!'

'You don't really want to *stay* here!'

'Let's see if there's a bedroom.'

'If there's no bedroom, can we leave?'

'Then we can leave.'

They left the bathroom. Tina hurried ahead of Ray, and opened the last door on the right. '*Voila*!'

'Shit,' Ray muttered. He came up the hall, and looked in.

'Now this isn't so shabby, is it?'

'It's all right,' Ray admitted.

Tina kicked off her sandals and walked across the soft thickness of the carpet. 'Ain't shabby at all.' She hopped onto the king-sized bed and marched on its mattress, surveying the long dresser, the armoire, and her own image in the big wall mirrors.

Ray watched her, a grin slowly coming to his face.

'I think this'll do just fine,' she said. 'Don't you?'

'It's not bad.'

'Better than some dippy motel, right?'

'Right.'

She flopped backwards and sprawled on the mattress. Smiling languidly, she opened the buttons of her blouse.

'Maybe we'd better take a look downstairs,' Ray said.

'Right now?' Slipping off the blouse, she rolled onto her belly. She pressed herself against the soft quilt. Reaching back, she untied her bikini top.

'Right this moment?' she drawled.

And grinned at the warm touch of Ray's hands.

Tina eased away from Ray's warm, sleeping body. She was reluctant to leave the bed, but the room was nearly dark and she was hungry. Ray would probably wake up famished. It'd be nice if she had supper on the stove when he got up.

If there *is* a stove.

She slipped out of bed, picked up her blouse, and stepped silently over to a window. Through the grill-work, she looked down at Ray's car. She could just bring in the grocery bags, and let the luggage wait.

They'd better bring in the suitcases soon, though.

A thick, gray bank of fog was rolling in from the coast. It already hung in the trees near the highway. When it got here, they would want heavier clothes.

She stepped away from the window and glanced at Ray. He was still asleep, his tanned back dark against the white sheets. She slipped into her sandals. Carrying her blouse, she went to the door.

Before stepping into the hallway, she looked both ways. She caught herself doing it, and rolled her eyes. What'd she expect, for Christsake, *traffic*?

She started down the hall toward the stairs. Ray had left the lights on. The candle-like bulbs in the wall sconces weren't very bright. They made a menagerie of dim shadows as she walked down the hall, shadows within shadows, over-lapping and chasing one another along both walls. Watching them, she flapped her arms and twirled. The shadows went crazy. She kicked and spun, swinging her blouse wildly over-head.

A low, moaning sound jerked her to a stop. She stood motionless near the stairway, listening.

The sound, she thought, had come from behind the door – the first door at the top of the stairs, the one they'd found locked.

Feeling suddenly timid and vulnerable, she put on her blouse. She buttoned it, her eyes fixed on the door.

Her hand tightened around the knob.

*What if it's not locked now?* she thought.

She pulled her hand away.

She backed up, watching the door, a tightness clutching her stomach as she half expected it to swing open. Then she turned from it and rushed to the bedroom.

'Ray?' she called into the darkness. Her hand searched the inside wall for a light. 'Ray!'

'Huh?'

She found it, and snapped it. A bright light came on above the bed. Ray sat up, squinting.

'What're you doing?' he asked.

She hurried forward. 'Let's get out of here.'

'I thought . . .'

'I heard something.'

He threw aside the sheet, sat on the edge of the bed, and reached for his swimming trunks on the floor. 'What'd you hear?' he asked, pulling them on.

'Sounded like a moan.'

'Jesus!'

'Could've been my imagination, I guess.'

'But what if it wasn't?'

'I know.' Flinging through the sheets and blankets, she found her bikini. She climbed off the bed and stepped quickly into the brief pants. She stuffed the top into her handbag, and hurried after Ray.

He stopped in the doorway.

'Where'd you hear it?' he asked.

'The end of the hall. By the stairs. I think it's in the room with the locked door.'

'Christ, that means we've gotta go *past* it!'

'Maybe it was nothing.'

'Let's run. We'll run right by, and down the stairs, and out.' He took his car keys from the small, side pocket of his trunks. 'Ready?'

'I guess.'

9

'Okay, let's *go*!'

He burst ahead of her into the hallway. Tina ran hard, trying to catch up, but Ray was a dozen feet in front of her when the door near the stairway flew open.

A man leaped out, black cape billowing, fangs bared.

# CHAPTER ONE

'*Heads, You Lose.* It's playing at the Haunted Palace, over near Lincoln. You know, the theater that was closed for so long. It used to be the Elsinore.'

Connie nodded. She remembered the Elsinore. She'd gone there many times, before it closed. It was an old place, built in the days long before they made theaters like lecture halls – long and low and sterile, three or six to a building. This one's interior had ivy covered walls like a castle, battlements and turrets, and a high blue ceiling speckled with stars. It had been well named. The Elsinore. Hamlet's castle.

'Can I go with you?' Connie asked.

'If you want,' Dal said. 'It's not the kind of movie you like, though. I've heard it's awfully gory.'

'Well . . .' He wants to go alone, she thought. She forced herself to smile. 'You're probably right. You go on ahead.'

'You sure?' he asked.

He wants it definite. His conscience must be bothering him, though not enough to make a difference. 'Yeah,' she said. 'I'm sure. I wanted to wash my hair tonight, anyway.'

'Well, okay,' he said, sounding reluctant.

'What time's it over?'

'I ought to be home by midnight. It's a double feature.'

He kissed her quickly, and she smelled the scent of the

cologne she'd given him for his birthday. 'You'll be the best-smelling guy at the movies,' she told him.

For an instant, he looked flustered. 'Oh yeah, that.'

'Bring me some candy?'

'Sure.'

'Good 'n Plenty.'

'Okay, if they have it. See you later.'

'Have fun. And don't get too scared.'

'Me?' He winked, and left.

Connie stood by the door, disappointed and wondering what to do with herself. It seemed strange, having to face a night alone. Strange and sad, almost like the times before Dal.

Which hadn't been so long ago, really. They'd met only six months before, and he'd moved in two months after that. They'd been together almost every night since then.

Well, he deserved a night on his own. She shouldn't mind. It's healthy to be alone sometimes.

He's with people all day long, at work. Forced to be polite to everyone, including the creeps who come into the store from time to time – creeps he told her about through taut lips, his eyes narrow with anger.

Connie had none of that. Alone in her apartment all day with her typewriter, she met only creeps of her own devising. She dealt with them ruthlessly, and enjoyed it. By three o'clock, though, she was used up. The next three hours, she spent in solitary waiting.

Waiting to see the face of another human being, the only face that mattered much in her life anymore.

She crossed the apartment to her bedroom, and began to undress for a bath.

I spend my days in solitary, she mused, while Dal's among the madding crowd. At night, we each need a different cure.

12

I shouldn't hold it against him if he wants time by himself. I shouldn't feel rejected.

But I do.

Her satin robe felt soft on her bare skin. She tied its belt, and went into the bathroom. As the tub filled, she let the robe fall away. She stepped into the water. It wrapped around her ankles, almost too hot. It stung, at first, when she sat down.

The tub filled. She turned off the faucets. With a sigh, she eased herself backwards. The water rose over her, hot and soothing, until only her face and upthrust knees remained above the surface.

This is not so bad, she thought.

She shut her eyes.

Better than sitting in a cramped, stuffy movie theater. A lot better than that.


Dal drove past the Haunted Palace, and kept on driving. The steering wheel was slick in his sweaty hands. The armpits of his shirt were soaked.

Well damn, she was worth sweating over! He'd never seen a woman he wanted so much.

When she strolled into Lane Brothers that afternoon, Dal couldn't take his eyes off her. She walked toward him, a creamy, pleated skirt caressing her legs, her breasts obviously bare under a loose, velour top that trembled, just slightly, as she moved. Lush, brown hair swung at her shoulders. It brushed the sides of a face so striking that Dal ached.

She stopped in front of him. He stared into her green, clear eyes.

'May I help you?' he asked.

'Yes,' she said, and paused as if to let him savour the liquid whisper of her voice. 'I want a man's cologne.'

'Anything in particular?' he asked.

'I want it masculine, but subtle.'

He nodded. 'Would you like to step over this way?'

Moving sideways towards the counter, he let his eyes drop to the woman's hands. She wore no wedding ring.

'We have a new fragrance called Ram. It's quite popular.'

'I like what you're wearing.'

He smiled and blood rushed to his face. 'My cologne?'

'Yes.'

'It's . . .' He cleared his throat. 'It's called Rawhide. It's new from . . .'

'Let me,' she said. Fingertips lightly touching his chest, she leaned toward him. Her face moved close to his neck. He felt her breath. 'Yes,' she said. 'This is just what I want.'

He licked his dry lips. 'Will there be anything else?' he asked.

'Yes.'

Her lips brushed his neck, and she whispered, 'You.'

Thinking back as he drove toward her house, Dal could hardly believe it had happened. It was almost like a dream.

Damn lucky I didn't faint, he thought. He laughed nervously.

All day long, he'd relived those moments with her, analyzed them, wondered at times if it was only a hideous, cruel joke. But who would pull a stunt like that?

No, it couldn't be a joke. It had to be real.

*Had* to be!

Please God, let it be real.

Waiting at a stop light, he took out his wallet and found the slip of paper with her name and address: Elizabeth Lassin, 522 Altina. He put it back.

Altina Road was halfway up a wooded hillside of the Highland Estates, a plush area north of town, an area way out of his financial range.

Not necessarily out of Connie's, though. She could easily

afford one now. If her next steamy historical romance (`rape epics`, she called them) sold like the others, she'd start looking in this vicinity.

Dal had planned to stick with her – marry her, if necessary. Until today.

Until Elizabeth.

Lovely Elizabeth. For her, he would gladly give up Connie. God, what *wouldn't* he give up, for her?

For even one night with her.

For even one hour!

He found the address, and swung into a long, circular driveway. As he drove toward the lighted veranda, he gazed at the house. It looked like a southern plantation house – scaled down a bit, but nonetheless elegant. A fitting home for a woman like Elizabeth.

He parked. He climbed from his car. He walked toward the door. He reached toward the lighted doorbell button.

And stopped.

Bet she doesn't live here, he thought. Gave me the address as a joke. Get the guy worked up, toy with him, lots of laughs.

Damn her! If she did a shitty thing like that . . . !

He jabbed the doorbell.

It rang.

God, this probably *is* her house!

He rubbed his sweaty hands on his pants legs.

She'll probably laugh at me.

Christ, why didn't I bring her something? Flowers, wine . . .

'Cause I'm a klutz.

Oh shit, why didn't I . . . ?

The door opened and she stood in the dimly lighted foyer, her bare feet on the marble floor, her body draped in a white chiffon dress that hung on her like a wispy veil, the mild breezes shifting it against her skin. Her lips were moist and slightly open, her eyes intense, almost fierce.

'Kiss me,' she said.

I'm dreaming, Dal thought, and stepped across the threshold.

# CHAPTER TWO

The line in front of the Haunted Palace moved swiftly once the box office opened. Pete Harvey shuffled forward. Brit stuck close, a hand inside the back pocket of his jeans, a breast pushing softly against his arm.

She was a bit clingy for Pete's taste, but he let her. If a gal clings, she has a reason. She's just more afraid, than some, of getting left behind.

At the ticket window, he bought two tickets from a teenaged girl with straight black hair and white make-up. Supposed to look like a vampire, he supposed. She wore a black T-shirt with the logo, BEWARE OF SCHRECK.

'Your hairdresser?' Pete asked.

The girl laughed. 'It's a wig, and itchy as hell.'

Pete moved along. He gave the tickets to a fat man in red-stained pants and undershirt, a nylon stocking over his head. His face, pale and weirdly mashed, looked grotesque enough to make Pete uneasy.

'Isn't he a charmer?' Brit whispered.

'I think he's overdoing it.'

She hugged Pete's arm. 'Scared you, didn't he?'

'He looks like someone I used to know.'

'Oh?'

Pete nodded, and wished he hadn't brought it up. 'How about

some popcorn, or Bon Bons, or something?'

'Do you think I dare?'

'You're skin and bones.'

She leaned against him, nudging him again with that breast. 'Do you prefer your women plump?'

'Plump and juicy. I'm having popcorn and a Pepsi, how about you?'

'I'll have a hot dog.'

Pete laughed. 'Are you serious?'

'A plump, juicy hot dog.' She licked her lips. 'I can almost taste it now.'

He bought the snacks from another pale girl in a Schreck T-shirt.

The auditorium was dimly lit.

'Hey, it looks like a castle,' Brit said.

'The Haunted Palace.'

'Pretty neat.'

'Where do you want to sit?' Pete asked.

'A little closer, I think.'

'An aisle seat all right? I like to stretch out my legs.' He switched to his W.C. Fields voice. 'Trip the little bastards as they toddle by.'

'Oh, you're terrible!'

'It's better than my Bogart.'

'That's not . . .' Laughing, she shook him by the arm.

'Don't rip it off.'

'Come on.' She pulled him toward a seat.

He went along with her, amused but irritated. If he saw more of her, after tonight, he would have to straighten her out on a few items. For now, though, he wouldn't try to criticize her unless she got unbearable. Dragging him like a leashed dog nearly qualified, but he held off.

'Are these all right?' she asked, once they were seated.

18

'Fine.'

She unwrapped her hot dog. 'Now, tell me. Who did the fat man remind you of?'

'He reminded me of the bird. The black bird, and a beautiful dame, and . . .'

'Right, your Bogart stinks.'

The lights dimmed, saving Pete from a reply.

On the screen, he saw a fog-shrouded forest. A terrible scream brought silence to the theater. Something moved among the trees. Slowly, the dim figure of a man appeared. He limped forward through the fog.

The fat man who'd taken the tickets.

He wore the same tan slacks, the same sleeveless T-shirt. They streamed with blood. In his right hand, he held a hatchet dripping gore. A nylon stocking distorted his face.

'Good evening,' he said. 'Welcome to the Haunted Palace.'

'Freaky,' Brit whispered.

'I am your host, Bruno Blood.'

Laughter in the audience.

'Each night, I shall bring you a feast of hideous delights, tales of horror to make you cringe and scream. You'll see all the best in grisly entertainment. Not only the latest gems of satanic morbidity, but also the great classics of the past.

'In weeks to come, I shall bring you such fare as *Halloween, Freaks, The Hills Have Eyes, Rabid, The Texas Chain Saw Massacre,* and *The Night of the Living Dead.*'

Whistles and applause greeted his announcement. He held up his bloody hatchet for silence, as if he foresaw the audience reaction.

'Plus!' he bellowed. In a soft and menacing voice, he continued. 'Plus a special treat available *only* at the Haunted Palace. Each night, in addition to the regular features, you'll

19

witness the evil, delicious exploits of Otto Schreck, the madman – a new depravity each and every week.'

The audience roared with yells, whistles, and applause. A lot of regulars, Pete figured.

'Schreck must be quite a guy,' Brit whispered in his ear.

Pete shrugged.

'And now,' Bruno said, 'prepare yourself for tonight's show. Sit back, take hold of a friendly hand, and . . .' He grinned. 'Don't look to see who is sitting behind you.'

The audience went wild as Bruno turned, and slowly limped away until he vanished in the fog.

The screen went dark.

'Is Schreck first?' asked a girl behind Pete.

'It's after the feature,' a boy whispered. '*Heads, You Lose* first, then Schreck, then *Nightcrawlers*.'

'Three?'

'Schreck's a short. Ten, fifteen minutes. Just wait, though. It'll be fabulous.'

The first movie started. Brit tossed her hot dog wrapper to the floor, grinned at Pete, and squeezed his thigh.

# CHAPTER THREE

Taking Dal's hand, Elizabeth led him down the hallway to a bedroom. She pushed the door shut.

The room was dark except for lights from the pool in back.

'Isn't it lovely?' she said. 'We'll go swimming later, if you like.'

He watched her walk across the carpet and open the sliding glass door. A breeze entered the room, stirring her gown. The lights from the pool passed through it, making the material nearly transparent. Breathless, Dal gazed at the dark, slender shape of her legs and buttocks.

'You're beautiful,' he whispered.

She looked over her shoulder, turning slightly, her breasts visible through the veil of fabric. 'Come here,' she said.

He stepped toward her.

She turned to him. 'Don't move,' she said. Slowly, her fingers opened the buttons of his shirt. Her hands slipped inside, and lightly caressed his chest.

She drew the shirt off him. Her mouth brushed his chest, kissing, licking his nipples, as her hands unfastened his pants. When they were loose, she reached inside.

Dal moaned at the cool touch.

'You're so big,' Elizabeth murmured. 'So big and hard.' She knelt, sliding the pants down his legs. Her tongue stroked the underside of his shaft. Its touch nearly set him off.

He stepped back.

'What's wrong?'

'Nothing,' he gasped. 'Nothing. It's just . . . too much. I don't want to . . . not so fast.'

'There'll be more,' she said. Reaching out, she clutched his buttocks. She pulled him forward, and licked, and sucked him deeply into her mouth.


Connie, alone in her apartment, felt restless. After bathing, she washed her hair and put it in curlers. That took little more than an hour.

She heated up coffee, carried it into the living-room, and tried to read. Though her eyes moved over the words, her mind kept wandering.

To Dal.

She felt cheated, being left alone this way. Especially on a Friday night.

Ever since high school, Friday nights had been a time for dating and fun, a time for football games, dances in the gym, parties, bowling, movies, or just bumming around with her friends on the lookout for a good time. Friday nights brought a terrible urgency for freedom after a week of confinement, a need to get out and *do* something.

Here I am, she thought.

Alone, at home, hair in curlers – stuck here on Friday night with nothing to do but bemoan my outcast fate.

She would never allow Sandra Dane such a miserable situation. Sandra Dane, the beautiful raven-haired mistress of White Oak plantation, wouldn't sit here grumbling. She'd rush out to the stables, and mount her stallion, and ride wildly through the moonlit countryside, the wind in her face.

She wouldn't go out in curlers, though.

Connie got up from the couch. Taking off her robe, she went into the bedroom.

Where'll I go? she wondered. Since I don't have a stallion . . .

A nice, long walk.

She opened a dresser drawer, and pulled out her blue warm-up suit.

Seven-Eleven's open all night.

She stepped into her pants. They felt soft and snug.

It's pretty far away, she thought, but right on Pico. A heavily travelled boulevard like Pico shouldn't be very dangerous, even at night.

She put on the jacket of her warm-up suit, zipped it halfway up, and regarded herself in the mirror.

That's how Sandra Dane would wear it, she thought.

Sandra, of course, is rape-prone.

Rape-prone. Shit. Not funny at all.

Bending down to tie her shoes, she saw her jacket bulge open, revealing her entire left breast.

No way.

She zipped it to her throat, and headed for the door. With her handbag slung over her shoulder, she stepped outside.

From the balcony, she saw that someone on the ground floor was having a party. All the other apartments, she imagined, were deserted.

People out enjoying themselves.

As she trotted down the stairs, she pulled up the hood of her jacket to hide her curlers.

Fine way to spend a Friday night, she thought.

I should've gone with Dal, whether he wanted me or not.

Elizabeth bent over the bed, and pulled back the covers. She lay down on the white sheet, her arms and legs outstretched.

23

'This time,' she said, 'I want to look at you.'

One of her arms curled toward the headboard. Directly over the bed, a light came on – a low-hanging light like those Dal had seen over pool tables. Though it left the rest of the room in shadow, it cast soft light on the bed, and on Elizabeth.

Dal climbed onto the end of the bed. He crawled slowly, sliding his hands up the smoothness of her spread legs as he looked at her. At her solemn, intense eyes, at the painful beauty of her face. At her slim neck, and the hollows above the bows of her collar bones. At breasts, so full when she was upright, now low against her chest, pulled by gravity and her arms stretched overhead. The nipples looked almost brown. He fingered the firm, rumpled skin. Elizabeth squirmed. He moved his fingers down the softness of her breasts and along her ribs, and over a pale ridge of skin.

A scar.

Six inches long, running diagonally down her belly.

Dal drew his finger gently along it.

'Operation?' he asked.

'Without the benefit of a surgeon,' she said.

'What do you mean?'

'My husband, bless his heart, opened me up with a carving knife.'

'My God,' Dal muttered.

'He thought I'd been unfaithful.' She folded her hands behind her head, and frowned toward the ceiling. 'He was such a jealous man. He was far older than me, and incredibly wealthy, so he concluded that I'd only married him for his money. Which wasn't true at all. I loved him, I truly did, even when he made my life unbearable.

'The harder I tried to convince him of that, though, the more certain he grew of my infidelity. He followed me, he eavesdropped. He saw proof everywhere, in everything I did. At one

24

point, he hired a private investigator, then accused the investigator of having an affair with me.'

'It must've been horrible,' Dal said.

'It wasn't pleasant. He beat me constantly. With fists, with his belt. His favourite whip was an extension cord.'

'Why didn't you leave him?'

'I loved him. I always believed that someday, somehow, he would finally come to realize he had no reason for his jealousy. But it didn't work out that way.'

She propped herself up on her elbows, and stared into the darkness.

'One night, he tried to kill me. It was our sixth anniversary. I'd given the housekeeper the day off, so we could be alone. I expected him home at seven. He was a lawyer, and very successful, as you can see from all this.

'I realized, sometime around six, that we had no champagne. So I threw on some old clothes and drove over to Vendome. On the way, I saw an ambulance in my rearview mirror. I pulled off the road to let it pass. The shoulder was rough and littered with debris, and I think that's where I picked up the nail.

'I drove on to Vendome, and bought the champagne. But when I returned to the parking lot, my front right tire was flat.

'One of the clerks changed it for me. By the time I got here, though, Herbert was already waiting in a rage.

'Here it was, our anniversary, and I only went out to do something nice for him, and he had the gall to accuse me of adultery.

'"Who were you fucking?"

'I'd had it. I threw down the champagne bottles so they shattered all over the foyer. Herbert slapped me, and kept yelling, "Who? Who were you fucking!"

'"I didn't catch his name," I said. "But he was young and handsome and hung like a horse."'

'Herbert turned away. I knew I'd hurt him, and I was glad.

25

He'd finally gone too far. Then I heard him crying. He was in the kitchen, sobbing like his heart was broken. I went to him. His back was toward me. I put my hands on his shoulders. Before I could say a word, he turned around and slashed me with a knife.'

Dal saw her eyes lower to the scar on her belly. She stared at it as she continued.

'I ran. He chased me upstairs with that knife, but we had pictures on the wall. Framed portraits. At the top, I jerked one down and swung it at him. The corner of the frame hit him in the face, and he fell down the stairs.

'I went to him, but he didn't move. He just lay there, staring up at me. The fall – it broke his neck.'

'Did he die?' Dal asked.

Reaching out, she took Dal's hand. She guided it to the slick wetness between her legs. 'Don't talk. Fuck me. Fuck me, now. Put your cock in me, and fuck me till I scream.'

Connie enjoyed the long walk to the Seven-Eleven. It felt good to be out in the night air, walking briskly, sometimes slowing down to look at the window display of a closed store. At times, she forgot about Dal, forgot that he had abandoned her for a couple of horror movies.

In the Seven-Eleven store, she stepped over to the rack of paperback books. She spun it, glancing at covers, until she found *Barbary Rage*, 'a lusty tale of passion on the high seas'. She flipped the front book forward, and saw only one behind it. Two left. Last week, there'd been four.

Not bad, not bad.

Someone tapped her shoulder. She swung around.

'Oh, I'm sorry,' the young man said. He had a friendly smile and a pale, almost invisible moustache.

'It's all right,' Connie said.

'I thought you were somebody else.'

'No, I'm just me.'

He laughed. 'From the back you looked . . . well, I thought you were an old girlfriend.'

'Sorry,' Connie said.

The boy shrugged.

She turned again to the book rack, and studied paperbacks for a minute. When she looked around, the boy was standing at the end of a long line, a six-pack of Michelob at his side.

Must be older than he looks, she thought.

He was still in line when she left the store. She crossed the street, and looked back. A girl in shorts and a halter top came out, a small sack in her hand.

Connie walked away.

Had the boy, she wondered, been trying to pick her up? If so, he hadn't been very persistent.

Should've tried harder, pal.

Tonight, I might have been willing. Serve Dal right.

She kept walking. Farther and farther from the apartment. With no destination in mind until she remembered the liquor store next to Safeway. She might as well stop in there, see if they'd got her book in yet.

She walked for blocks. Finally, she reached the liquor store. But she didn't go in. She stood on the sidewalk, staring across the intersection and down the next block at the lighted marquee of a movie theater.

The Haunted Palace.

Dal thrust and thrust, driving into her. She was wild under him, gasping, shoving up to meet his thrusts, fingers digging into his back. Their sweaty bodies slapped together.

They rolled, and she was on top. He clutched her breasts, squeezed and mauled them. Her face was sweaty and contorted above him. She twisted, writhed as if trying to grind his spike deeper into her slick tightness, impale herself on it, ream out her hugging sheath.

Connie glanced at the movie posters, at the grim, coloured stills above them. The girl in the ticket window was reading a paperback.

Clever, Connie thought, dressing her up like a vampire.

She looked at the posted showtimes.

A *triple* feature?

No, the one in the middle, *Schreck the Vampire*, was only a short.

She glanced at her wristwatch.

*Schreck the Vampire* should be starting soon.

Wouldn't Dal be surprised if she went in, and sat down beside him?

He might be pissed, though.

*What if he's not alone, if he's sitting with his arm around a girl . . . ?*

No. He wouldn't.

But the fear of it was enough to keep her from entering.

She looked again at the showtimes. *Nightcrawlers* would be next, after the vampire thing. Then *Heads, You Lose* came on again, at 11:20.

Give him five minutes to drive home.

So she could expect him by 11:25 or so.

As she walked away, she wondered if he would remember the Good 'n Plenty.

'Shall we go for a swim?' Elizabeth asked.

'That'd be great. I think I'll hit the john, first.'

Elizabeth smiled strangely. She sat up, and pointed into the shadows across the room.

28

'See the doorway?'

'I think so.'

'It's right through there.'

Dal climbed from the bed. He walked over the thick, soft carpet toward a patch of darkness deeper than the shadows.

'Don't trip,' Elizabeth said.

He looked back at her. The bed and Elizabeth were closer than he expected, so bright and starkly clear in the overhead lamp that he could see the red marks his mouth had left on her skin.

'I'll try not to,' he said.

He stepped into the doorway, bumped a dark shape, and lurched backwards. 'What the hell!'

'Here, let me get it out of your way.'

Elizabeth leaped from the bed. She rushed to Dal's side, patted him on the rump, and stepped past him. Leaning into the doorway, she pulled something forward.

Then she turned on the bright, fluorescent lights of the bathroom.

*'Jesus!'* Dal gasped.

The withered, bald man in the wheelchair blinked his eyes.

Elizabeth grinned. 'Dal, I'd like you to meet my husband, Herbert. He likes to watch. I know he must enjoy it.' She patted the old man's cheek. Patted it hard. 'You *do* enjoy watching us, don't you, Herbert?'

SCREAM GEMS
PRESENTS
OTTO SCHRECK
in
SCHRECK THE VAMPIRE

Near the head of the coffin, two black candles burn. They are in a statue's stone hands. Only blunt stubs remain of the candles. The hands of the statue are clotted with black. The mouth gapes with silent agony. The eye holes are empty.

Bones litter the dirt floor of the cellar. The small, fragile bones of rodents. Bigger bones. Of dogs and cats. Of humans.

In a shadowy corner of the cellar, a human rib cage trembles. A rat, inside it, waddles up the spinal column. It squeezes underneath a collar bone, pauses, then moves up the neck and climbs onto the pale, hanging jaw.

The jawbone breaks loose. The rat tumbles. It starts towards the skull again, but stops and raises its head at the faint, rumbling sound of an engine.

The engine goes silent.

In front of the house, a woman climbs the porch steps. She is young and cute, her blonde hair windblown, her legs bare under the tails of a plaid blouse.

A slim, dark-haired man follows her up the stairs.

Smiling, the woman searches her handbag and takes out a key. 'Ready?' She opens the door, enters, and leaps back against the man. He hugs her, laughing.

'So who's the horny one?' he asks.

She tugs open the waistband of his swimming trunks. 'Aren't you?'

The woman turns toward the stairway. 'The bedroom's probably up there.'

She follows him up the stairs. As they climb, she suddenly jerks his swimming trunks. They drop from his pale buttocks.

'Don't!' He clutches them. 'Want me to trip?'

'Then don't be so damned handsome.'

'Sorry, Mary.' He pulls up his trunks, and continues to climb.

'Nice ass.'

'Thank you.'

'Cracked, though.'

At the end of the upstairs hallway, she pushes open a door. *Voila!*

He hurries to join her.

'Now this isn't so shabby, is it?'

'It's all right,' he says.

Leaving her sandals on the carpet, she says, 'Ain't so shabby at all,' and leaps onto the bed. She walks on the mattress, hands on hips, turning to look at the room. 'I think this'll do just fine, don't you?'

The man grins.

Mary falls backwards, bouncing slightly as she hits the mattress. With a seductive smile, she opens her blouse.

The man steps toward her.

Out of the blouse, she rolls over and unties the back of her bikini.

The man bends over her. He strokes her back. He kisses her between the shoulder blades.

In the cellar, black gummy wax drips from the hands of the statue. The candles are nearly spent. Their flames waver and stretch, as if struggling not to die.

The rat crouches beside the coffin, nibbling a bit of raw meat.

Fingers curl around the edge of the coffin lid, lift it, and slide it aside.

The rat pauses at the sound of scraping wood.

A hand snatches it from the ground. It squeals as Schreck,

sitting upright in the coffin, raises it toward his pallid face.

'The blood is the life,' he whispers.

He bites off the rat's head, and spits it out. He raises the rat above him like a wine bottle, the blood splashing his face, spilling into his wide mouth, running in dark rivulets down his cheeks and chin.

In the dark bedroom, Mary lies awake beside the sleeping man.

The wooden steps of the cellar stairway groan as Schreck slowly climbs. At the top, he pushes open a door. His hand leaves a bloody print on the wood.

Mary climbs from bed, and steps silently across the carpet to a window. She stares out.

Schreck climbs the main stairway. When he reaches the top, he looks up the long, dimly lit hall.

Mary crosses the bedroom. She pauses in the doorway, and glances to her right.

Schreck, seeing her, slips through a door. For a moment, he watches her. She is naked. She skips and twirls, dancing down the hallway, waving her arms overhead.

Schreck silently closes the door. Leaning against it, he stares at the ceiling and runs his tongue over his dry lips. He moans.

Mary stops. She gazes at the door. Quickly, she puts on her blouse and fastens it. She reaches for the knob, then jerks her hand away and runs. She runs up the long, dim hall, bare legs flying, the tail of her blouse flapping above her buttocks.

She lunges through the bedroom door. 'Hey! Hey!'

'What?'

The light comes on. The man sits up, shading his eyes against the brightness. 'What're you doing?'

'Let's get out of here.'

'I thought . . .'

'I heard something.'

'What'd you hear?' he asks, pulling on his trunks.

'Sounded like a moan.'

'Jesus!'

'Could've been my imagination, Arthur.'

'But what if it wasn't?'

As he rushes toward the door, Mary retrieves her bikini from the mussed bed. She steps into the shorts, and stuffs the top into her handbag.

'Where'd you hear it?'

'The end of the hall. By the stairs.'

'Christ, that means we've gotta go *past* it!'

'Maybe it was nothing.'

Schreck, in the dark room, grins at the sound of rushing footsteps. He jerks open the door. Leaping into the hallway, he grabs the throat of the running man and flings him against a wall.

The terrified woman halts. She simply watches, aghast, as Schreck picks up the man and throws him over the railing.

With a smile, he walks toward her. 'You will be my bride.'

'No. Come *on!*'

'We shall wander the nights together, you and I – all the nights of eternity – feasting on the blood of the innocents.'

As he reaches for her, she throws herself through a doorway. She tries to shut the door, but Schreck blocks it with his arm. Then he punches through the frail wood, and clutches her throat. He thrusts her away. He rushes into the room for her.

He pulls her into the hallway. He tears open her blouse. Fingers plying her full breasts, he lowers his head. He licks the blood from her splinter-torn face.

He kisses the side of her neck.

He bites. Blood spurts from the torn vein, painting his face, spraying the nearby wall. He presses his mouth tightly to the wound, and swallows furiously.

33

Breathless, he raises his head. The blood, no longer shooting, throbs out. He cups his hands to catch the flow.

When the hands are full, he raises them high. 'The blood is the life,' he says. He washes his face in it.

Then he is carrying the woman's naked body down the cellar steps. Her skin is pale in the dim light.

He lowers her into his coffin.

He lights two black candles, and fixes them upright in the hands of the statue. As the eyeless, stone face looks on, Schreck climbs into his coffin. On his knees above the corpse, he whispers, 'My bride.'

## The End

# CHAPTER FOUR

The audience hissed, booed, clapped and cheered. The theater lights came on.

Pete turned to Brit. 'What'd you think?'

'Gross-out. You know what's funny though? That girl who played Mary looks just like my best friend. Best *girl* friend,' she corrected.

'Was it?'

'Guess not. The credits said her name was Wilma Payne. The voice wasn't like Tina's, either.'

'Well, they say we all have a double somewhere.'

'This was really uncanny, though. I mean, she's identical. Even the way she walked and acted – you know, her mannerisms. And the things she said, like the cracked ass. She says that kind of stuff. It was kind of spooky, if you ask me.'

'Tina isn't an actress, is she?'

'She's a history teacher at Pacifica Coast University. That's where I went, you know. We were roomies there, and she went back, after grad school, and got a job. You know, what I ought to do is give her a call, tomorrow. She'd probably get a kick out of this thing.'

'Bruno said it's only shown here.'

Brit shrugged. 'Well, maybe she could drive down, or something. PCU's only a couple of hours up the coast.'

'If she looks like the gal in the movie, I wouldn't mind seeing her, myself.'

'*You!*' Brit pounded his knee. 'Why don't you get me some Milk Duds before the intermission's over?'

# CHAPTER FIVE

Elizabeth rolled the wheelchair toward the bed. 'Help me put him in.'

'In *that?*' Dal asked.

'It's his bed.'

Dal shook his head. He felt as if he might throw up. 'We did it in *his* bed, with him watching?'

'Don't blame yourself, dear. You had no way of knowing.'

'It's sick.'

'But doesn't it excite you, now that you know?'

'I think I'd better leave.'

She smiled as if amused by his timidity. 'Won't you help me, first? You wouldn't want poor Herbert to spend the night in his wheelchair, would you?'

'You can move him alone,' he said. The words sounded nasty, and he immediately regretted them.

'Certainly I can,' Elizabeth said. 'I don't think I *shall*, however. If you want to be responsible for the poor man spending the entire night . . .'

'I'll help.'

'Herbert thanks you.'

'Where are the sheets?'

'On the bed.'

'But they're a mess! They're all wet and ucky. We can't put him down on those.'

Elizabeth patted a shoulder of the motionless man. 'Certainly we can. Herbert understands, don't you dear?'

A car slowed down, and drove alongside Connie. Heart suddenly racing, she walked more quickly. The car kept pace.

This is what I get, she thought, angry with herself in spite of her fear.

She glanced at the car. A light-colored Mustang. Its passenger window was rolled down. She saw the dark shapes, inside, of two men.

An arm beckoned to her from the window.

'Not interested,' she said.

The car sped up. At the end of the block, it turned right and vanished.

'Oh shit,' she muttered.

They'd be waiting for her. She knew. It had happened once before. On a summer night five years ago, in Tucson.

Only then, she hadn't been alone.

Tears suddenly stung her eyes, making the streetlights streak and blur.

Those bastards.

Those goddamn punk bastards.

She would never again find a man like Dave, and they . . . Two of the three had knives. She could still hear the sound as one of the boys jammed a blade into Dave's belly, a sound like a punch, then Dave's breath blasting out. It was the last sound she heard before the third punk, the one with the tire iron, knocked her senseless.

Wiping the tears from her face, she crossed the street in the middle of the block.

If they want me, she thought, they'll have to work for it.

\* \* \*

'Now can I go?' Dal asked, stepping away from the bed.

'Now you may.' Elizabeth moved close to him. Her nipples brushed his chest. She fingered his limp penis. 'Wouldn't you prefer, however, to join me in the shower? Unless you would rather take your incriminating odors home with you. Your darling Connie might be suspicious, if you do.'

'I suppose. I can't get my hair wet, though.'

'My blow-drier will take care of that.'

Connie looked at the corner across the street. A car was parked there. A light-colored Mustang. Its lights off.

With any luck . . .

She started to cross the intersection. The Mustang swung around in a U-turn and shot toward her. She ran down the street, leaping onto the curb as the Mustang bore down.

Its passenger door flew open. A teenaged boy jumped out.

Connie backed away, staring at him. At his white T-shirt, his tan work-pants, his black hair and nervous grin.

Just like the others. Like a fucking clone of the ones who killed Dave, who beat and raped her.

'Get away from me,' she said.

The other man came up behind him. This one was heavier than the first, but he wore the same uniform. 'Come on for a . . .' She couldn't make out the rest of it.

'Yeah,' said the first. 'I'm hungry. Feel like eating some pussy.'

'Your mother,' Connie snapped.

'*Puto!*' He pulled out a switchblade knife.

Connie backed into the entryway of a shoe store.

'My mother, you don't talk about her that way!'

She stopped, back to the door.

'Not here, Joe,' said the other. 'Too much traffic, man.'

'My mother, she's no whore!'

'No more than your sister,' Connie said.

Joe snarled and stabbed. Sidestepping, Connie grabbed his wrist and elbow. Her knee shot up, snapping his forearm. As he fell, she swung around and kicked. Her foot caught the other man in the groin. He dropped to his knees, clutching himself. Her next kick hammered his forehead. He fell facedown.

Connie picked up the knife.

'Who'd you steal the car from?' she asked Joe.

'Nobody! Check the registration, cunt.'

She kicked his broken arm.

He was still sobbing as she walked over to the Mustang. She climbed in, and drove away.

'Almost dry,' Elizabeth said, running her fingers through Dal's hair as she stroked it with the hot air of the blower. 'Your girlfriend will never suspect you've been copulating behind her back.'

'I hope not.'

'What would she do?'

'Ask me to leave, I suppose.'

'That would be a pity.'

'It'd be a disaster. Do you have any idea what I'd have to pay for an apartment in this city?'

'Considerable, I should imagine. If that's the worst you have to fear, however, you've little to fear.'

'Well, I don't think she's the type to stab me, if that's what you mean.'

'Does she love you?'

'Who knows? I guess so.'

'Then you'd best be careful. A woman's vengeance is often remarkably savage.'

'I noticed.'

She laughed. 'Herbert is getting no worse than he deserves. Save your sympathy.'

Connie drove the Mustang to the Seven-Eleven store. She couldn't pass the book rack without checking on *Barbary Rage*. After seeing that nobody had bought a copy in the last half-hour, she hurried on.

She bought a screwdriver, a single can of Budweiser, a quart can of charcoal lighter, and a pack of Marlboros.

The clerk dropped two books of matches into her sack.

Connie drank the beer as she drove. Illegal, she knew. For tonight, though, she was making her own laws.

'I hereby legalize the consumption of alcoholic beverages in stolen motor vehicles,' she said.

It tasted very good.

She parked in the lot of the Safeway supermarket. The store was closed, the lot deserted except for a lone VW near the far side. It looked empty.

Connie left the engine running. With the screwdriver, she punched holes into the top of the charcoal lighter can. She emptied the can, shaking fluid onto the back seat, the floor, the front seat.

Outside the car, she took a quick look around. Nobody nearby.

She ripped the cardboard flap off a book of matches. Striking a match, she touched it to the exposed heads. They flared. She tossed the flaming pack onto the front seat.

Slowly, the fire spread.

She shut the door and walked away, sipping her beer.

Red lights flashed in Dal's rearview mirror. A siren screamed.

No, please!

Jesus, a ticket. That's just what he needed. They write

41

down the date and time. If Connie sees it, she'll know he wasn't at the movies.

Then he saw that the lights belonged to a fire truck.

Thank God.

He pulled over and let it pass. Still shaking, he drove several more blocks. He parked on a sidestreet, and walked to the Haunted Palace.

'*Nightcrawlers* just started,' said the girl in the ticket window. She looked awful. It took a moment for Dal to realize she was supposed to look that way.

He gave his ticket to a fat man in bloody clothes. The man's face was twisted horribly under a nylon stocking.

'You missed tonight's Schreck,' said the man.

Dal shrugged. 'I'll catch it another time.'

At the candy counter, he bought a pack of Good 'n Plenty.

# CHAPTER SIX

Connie was in bed when Dal got home. She breathed slowly and heavily, pretending to be asleep. She didn't want to tell him what she had done.

She didn't want to tell anyone, ever.

She felt rotten about hurting the kids. Maybe they deserved it, but what if she'd injured them permanently? Or killed one? That guy she'd kicked in the head . . .

What if a fireman got hurt trying to put out the Mustang? If the tank blew up . . .

Dal climbed into bed. He lightly kissed her cheek. She moaned as if disturbed in her sleep. Dal rolled away.

Connie lay awake for a long time. She shifted to her stomach, to her back, to her side. Her pillow was sweaty so she turned it over. She flung the top sheet aside, pulled off her damp nightgown, and stared at the ceiling.

When she awoke in the sunlight of morning, she was vaguely surprised to realize she had fallen asleep.

She eased herself carefully out of bed, hoping to avoid waking Dal. She found her nightgown on the floor. A gift from him.

A 'moving in present' he'd called it. The gown reflected his taste: it was short, low-cut, and transparent. She couldn't step outside in it, not even for a moment to grab the newspa-

43

per. She put it on, anyway. Before leaving the room, she took her robe from the closet.

As she slipped into the robe, she saw a box of Good 'n Plenty on the dining-room table.

Dal hadn't forgotten.

She felt a warm rush of affection for him. It only lasted a moment. Then, her anxiety came back. She hurried to the front door, and opened it.

The newspaper lay on the Welcome mat. She quickly picked it up. She rushed inside, tugging the plastic band off the paper.

Dropping to her knees, she spread the paper on the carpet. She leaned over it, her eyes moving swiftly over the front page.

Nothing there.

Nothing about the two kids.

Nothing about the burning Mustang.

She turned the page. Another and another. She searched the first and second sections. Section three was sports and financial. She skipped that. Wouldn't be in the entertainment section, either. Only the classified remained. Feeling light with relief, she put the paper together and flung it onto the couch.

No mention of what she had done.

The kids had probably kept the incident to themselves. If they went to a hospital – which they must've done – they gave a false story to explain their injuries.

The Mustang fire must've been too routine to report. No injuries there. It hadn't blown up in someone's face, after all.

Off the hook.

With a sigh, she got to her feet. She went into the kitchen, and began to prepare a pot of coffee.

Off the hook unless she ran into those kids again.

She took the open can of Yuban from the refrigerator, and peeled off its plastic cover. Carrying it to the counter, she raised it close to her nose and sniffed. Such a wonderful odor.

She'd always loved that smell. It reminded her of being a child, of lying in bed early in the morning listening to the rhythmic slurp of coffee perking in the kitchen. She wished she could hear that sound again. Nobody hears it now. Nobody uses a percolator. Drip machines are so much quicker, more efficient. Progress.

At least coffee still smells like coffee.

She scooped it into a paper filter.

A hand patted her fanny. She jumped, spilling grounds.

'Dal!'

He grinned. 'Morning.' He pulled her into his arms, and kissed her.

'How were the movies?' she asked.

'Not bad. I've seen better, but they were okay. What'd you do last night?'

Connie shrugged. 'Washed my hair, and read.'

'Doesn't sound very exciting.'

She shrugged. 'Well, my old friend Joe dropped by and banged me a few times.'

'Oh really?' Dal asked. Though grinning, deep red filled his face.

'Hey, only kidding!'

'I know, I know.' He turned away.

# CHAPTER SEVEN

Freya pushed the button of the remote control box, and watched the television screen flash from channel to channel.

Nothing on but shit.

*Daffy Duck, Scooby and Scrappy-Doo*, an ancient rerun of *The Lone Ranger*.

Roller Derby, for Christsake.

She lifted her teacup off the *TV Guide*, took a sip, and checked the listings. Okay, not bad. Ten more minutes of crap, and something called *Monster Walks* comes on. A 1932 thriller. Rex Lease, Vera Reynolds, and Sheldon Lewis.

Might be good.

She'd rather be at the beach on a fantastic, sunny Saturday like this. So many of the mornings had been overcast, lately. Typical June weather for Pacifica Coast. But business is business. She'd be spending plenty more weekends inside if she didn't get lucky and find a new roommate.

It wasn't that easy, summer in a university town.

A glut of vacancies.

And of those gals who'd inquired during the past three weeks, so many had been unsuitable.

The doorbell rang.

Christ, you'd think they'd have the decency to phone, first.

She got up from the couch. Walking to the door, she

47

tugged at her tight, binding shorts and adjusted her slipping tube-top. She forced a smile onto her face, and pulled the door open.

'Greetings!' the girl said. She had carrot-red hair, and freckles to match. She wore thick, wire-rimmed glasses. Her blotchy cheeks bulged as if each carried an uneaten plum. She had a figure like a potato, and wore clothes to emphasize it: tight jeans and a T-shirt. The T-shirt was decorated with a leering vulture. It read, 'Patience my ass – I'm going out and kill something.' Incredibly, she wore no bra. Her breasts hung inside the T-shirt like bulging water balloons.

'Can I help you?' Freya asked.

'I'm here about the apartment. Are you the one looking for a roommate?'

'No,' said Freya. 'I'm the new roommate.'

'But this morning's paper . . .'

'I took the place last night. She didn't have time to get the ad pulled.'

The girl shrugged. 'Those are the breaks, I guess.'

'Yep. Sorry. You should've got here sooner.' Freya closed the door.

She stared at the television. Slim Claymore was on, Stetson tipped back, grinning like a moron. 'If you're in the market for a used car, come on down to Slim's Chevrolet, where you'll get courteous service and the best deal . . .'

The telephone clamored. Freya hurried into the kitchen and picked it up. 'Hello?'

'Hello.' A young woman's voice. 'Is Tina there?'

'No, she's not. Would you like to leave her a message?'

'When do you expect her back?'

'Who is this, please?'

'I'm Brit Anderson. I'm a friend of Tina's. We were roomies at PCU'

48

'Oh yes, she's spoken of you.'

'I guess you must be her present roommate, huh?'

'We've been sharing this apartment for the past couple months.'

'Well . . . Do you have any idea when she might get back?'

'She's probably gone for the weekend.'

'Oh, that figures.' Brit laughed. 'Tina was always off some-where.'

'Do you want me to have her call you when she gets back?'

'Please. I'd appreciate it.' She gave Freya her phone number. Freya copied it down. 'That's Brit what?'

'Anderson.'

'Okay. I'll be sure to give her the message. Nice talking to you.'

'Thanks. Good-bye, now.'

'Good-bye.'

Freya hung up. She hurried into the living-room. *Monster Walks* had already started. 'Damn,' she muttered, and dropped to the couch. The screen went blank for a moment.

'Howdy friends! Slim Claymore here to invite you to come on down to . . .' She changed the channel. '. . . here to invite you to come on down . . .' Same commercial, slightly differ-ent timing.

She switched again, this time to Bugs Bunny. Bugs was preferable to Slim. She watched the hare outsmart Elmer, then she turned back to the movie station.

'. . . where prices are so low you'll have a slim chance of finding a better deal.'

The movie came on.

It was nearly over, an hour later, when the telephone rang again.

'Hello?' she asked.

'Hello. I'm calling about the apartment. I saw the ad, this

49

morning, and I'm wondering if you're still in the market for a roommate.'

'I sure am,' Freya said. 'Would you like to stop by and have a look around?'

'I'd love to. When would be a convenient time for you?'

'The sooner, the better.'

'Fine. I'll be there in about fifteen minutes. My name's Nancy.'

'Very good. See you then.'

Exactly fifteen minutes passed before the doorbell rang. Freya opened the door.

'Hi, I'm Nancy.'

Nancy wore sunglasses on top of her head, resting lightly in a tuft of blonde curls. Her eyes were bright, her skin clear, her nose slightly upturned.

A cute girl, Freya thought.

She wore a short sleeved jumpsuit of pale blue. Its zipper, open several inches, showed a long V of pale throat and chest.

'I'm Freya. Come on in.'

'Thank you.'

'Are you new to Pacifica Coast?'

'I've been here a few days. I'm staying at the Travel Inn till I find a more permanent place.'

'Well, maybe this is it.'

'Maybe so.'

She showed Nancy the living-room, then the kitchen.

'Are you a student?' she asked.

'I feel like I've always been a student.'

'What field?'

'Psych.'

'Gonna be a shrink, huh?'

Nancy laughed. 'I hope so.'

'You seem . . . too mature for a freshman.'

'Oh, I'm transferring from Santa Monica College. I have to pick up three credits this summer, and I'll start as a junior.'

'Is this your first time away from home, Nancy?'

'Oh, I've gone off to camp, and stuff. You know. But I've never lived on my own before, if that's what you mean.'

'You lived with your parents in Santa Monica?'

She nodded.

'This would be your bedroom, here.'

They entered the sunlit room.

'It comes furnished, as you can see.'

Nancy wandered the room, looking into the closet, pushing down on the mattress, glancing out the windows. 'This is very nice.'

'So are you,' Freya said in a low voice. 'You're . . . very nice.' She reached out for the tab of Nancy's zipper.

'Hey!' Nancy knocked her hand away. 'No thanks. Jeez!' She shook her head. 'I'm not into that kind of stuff.'

'Ever try it?'

Blushing, Nancy shook her head.

Freya drew down her tube-top. Her breasts popped free.

'No!'

'Come on, darling, touch.'

'No!' Nancy rushed past her.

The front door slammed.

The last of Nancy.

Freya pulled up her top, returned to the living-room, and picked up the *TV Guide*.

She sighed.

Christ, she was getting tired of this.

If it's not one thing, it's another.

Sooner or later, though, the right girl would show up. A girl perfect in every way. A girl with no close family. A girl like Tina.

# CHAPTER EIGHT

Brit phoned Pete and got a recording.

'Pete Harvey, Private Investigations. I'm speaking to you, but I'm not here. If you leave a message, I'll get back to you as soon as possible. At the sound of the tone, have at it.'

The tone beeped.

'Forget it,' Brit said, and hung up.

She didn't want to wait around for him to call back. She wanted him now. She had no idea where he might be, though. So forget it. She would go alone.

Might be better, that way. If she asked Pete to go along, he might think she was getting too serious about him. He seemed a bit wary about getting involved.

With her, anyway.

Three dates already, and he hadn't slept with her yet. Well, some guys like to take it slow.

She threw a few things into her suitcase, and went down to the car.

As she drove up the coast, she had second thoughts about going without Pete. He'd be a good man to have around, if she ran into trouble. Something definitely fishy about Tina and the movie. *And* the roommate.

The farther she drove, the more nervous she grew. Finally,

she stopped at a Denny's, and used a pay phone. Pete's recording answered.

'Damn it!'

She banged the phone down.

The hell with him.

She shoved through the door and rushed across the lot to her car. She started the engine. For a moment, she considered heading back home.

That'd be chickenshit.

Besides, she was almost to Pacifica Coast. In half an hour, she'd be there.

God, she'd spent four years in that little town. Nothing to be afraid of.

Probably wasn't even Tina, in that movie. And if it *was* her, so what? It was just a movie.

They're supposed to look real, for Godsake. Look at *The Exorcist*, how they made Linda Blair's head spin around. That looked real. Look at *The Omen*, how that sheet of glass chopped off David Warner's head. That looked real too. Just as real as Tina's blood spurting all over the place.

She'd seen Linda Blair in plenty of films after *The Exorcist*. Same with David Warner. She knew, for a fact, they'd lived through those shots. Hell, it's only special effects.

*Tina was different.*

Only because I know her.

Brit left the parking lot, and headed for Pacifica Coast.

Only because I know Tina, she thought. And because the theater was creepy. And because the film had an amateur, grainy look that made it all seem rather cheap and sleazy like some of those porno films she used to see with Willy.

Weird Willy.

Liked to practice what he saw on the screen. She went along with it, too, until he got too rough. The whip was the last straw.

54

Weird Willy. His great ambition in life was to see a 'snuff movie'.

God have mercy on his girlfriend, if he ever saw one of . . .

*Snuff movies?*

The thought hit her like a punch in the stomach.

'Ridiculous,' she said aloud.

But she realised that the idea had been in her mind for a long time, lurking there, whispering its warning. That's why she phoned Tina, this morning.

That's why the voice of the roommate, Freya, had given her a chill of dread. Because, even on the telephone, she'd recognized the voice.

The voice of Mary in the film.

Tina's voice.

Brit drove through downtown Pacifica Coast, and parked in front of the police station.

Her stomach churned.

*What will I tell them?*

I saw my friend killed in a movie, and I think it might've been real. Oh, why's that? Because they didn't use her real name in the credits, and it wasn't her voice. Are you sure it *was*, indeed, your friend? I'm almost positive. She's missing, and . . . (Freya said she'd gone off with a boyfriend – but Freya must be in on it.) Can't we check?

And the police would drive her out to Tina's apartment, and Tina would open the door.

She'd better make sure.

She left the car, and walked to a service station on the next block. She dropped a dime into the public telephone, and dialed.

Her heart raced. The black phone was slippery in her hand.

'Hello?'

'Hello, Freya.'

55

'Who is this, please?'

'Brit Anderson. I called this morning.'

'Oh yes.'

'Is Tina there?'

'Yes, she is. Just a moment, please.'

Brit shut her eyes and sighed. She wiped her trembling hands on her slacks.

Thank God.

The whole thing *had* been a figment of her imagination. It *was* someone else in the movie. Not Tina, at all. A look-alike with a voice like Freya.

'Hello?' Freya's voice.

'Yes?'

'Tina's in the shower, just now. Could she call you when she's out?'

'Well . . . I'm calling from a public phone. I'm here in town, though. Maybe I could just drop over in about ten minutes.'

'Fine. I'll tell her.'

Brit parked across the street from the apartment house. She climbed from the car. The afternoon sun was hot on her face, but she felt a cool breeze from the ocean.

She walked across the street on weak legs. God, what a day! She felt exhausted, emotionally drained, but elated.

She'd felt like this, all day, after the quake of '72.

Disaster over. Friends, loved ones, and self miraculously intact.

She passed through a squeaking gate, walked alongside the deserted, glistening pool, and climbed the stairs to the balcony.

Apartment 210.

She knocked on the door.

It was opened by a lean, dishwater blonde wearing tight

shorts and a tube-top. 'Brit?' the woman asked.

'Yes.'

'I'm Freya. Come on in.'

She entered. The curtains were shut.

'I'll tell Tina you're here.'

Freya crossed the room. Her shorts were too small. Pale crescents of buttock showed beneath the pockets. She disappeared. Brit heard her knock. 'Tina, your friend's here.'

Freya came back. 'She'll be out in a minute. Christ, she takes forever in there. Can I get you something to drink? Some wine, maybe?'

'That'd be great.'

'Red or white?'

'White, please.'

She sat on the couch. Moments later, Freya returned with two glasses of white wine.

'So, you're Tina's old roommate from college days?'

'Yeah.' The wine was cold and fruity, and not too sweet.

'Do you live near here?'

'Los Angeles.'

'Oh? I used to live there. How do you like it?'

'Too many people. That's the only trouble. But lots of things to do.' Her cheeks felt numb. 'I like movies.'

'Oh, so do I. Especially thrillers.'

'Me too. That . . . That's partly why I'm here.' She heard a strange sound, like a distant roar. But it came from inside her head. 'Thought I saw Tina . . . in a film.'

Freya grinned. 'At the Haunted Palace?'

'Yeah.' She tried to set down her empty glass, but dropped it.

'Oh, you did.'

'Schreg da . . . Sch . . .'

'*Schreck the Vampire.*'

Brit realized, vaguely, that her face was about to hit the coffee table.

Then it did.

# CHAPTER NINE

On Wednesday morning, Connie went to the main branch of the Santa Monica public library. She took the bus.

Though she hated driving near buses and considered their drivers madmen intent on cutting off every car nearby, she found that she enjoyed riding inside them. Inside the bus, she could relax. She didn't have to watch the road, or dodge maniacal bus drivers.

When it reached her stop, she moved up the aisle toward the front. The aisle was clear except for a boy with a bushy Afro. On top of his shoulder, he held a radio as big as an attaché case. He grinned and turned sideways to let her by.

On the sidewalk, she watched the bus pull forward and ease to the left, ignoring the car beside it. The car's brake-lights flashed on. It stopped abruptly to make way for the bus, and was nearly rear-ended by a station wagon.

'Nice,' Connie muttered.

In the library, she found four books about Mississippi paddlewheel boats. She checked them out, not bothering to browse the fiction or even to check for her own books. At other times, she'd done both. Disappointing results. Now, she used the library only for research.

With the four books in her shoulder bag, she walked down Santa Monica Boulevard to the small mall. She spent a long time in a paperback bookstore. They carried both of her titles. After gloating, she moved on. She bought five books, and left the store.

She stared across the sunny mall at Lane Brothers, then checked her wristwatch. A quarter till twelve.

Why not?

Making a wide circle to avoid contact with a grimy panhandler, she walked to the entrance of the clothing store. She stepped inside. She spotted three young, well-dressed men among the racks, but not Dal.

One of them approached. 'How can I help you, this morning?'

'Is Dal here?'

'No, but I am. I'm Ken.'

She'd heard tales of Ken. He looked as slick and artificial as Dal described him.

'Has Dal already gone to lunch?' she asked.

'No. As a matter of fact, he didn't come in today. He's down with a bug, as they say. I'm sure that I can be of service, though.'

'Thank you,' she said, and turned away.

Outside, she walked. She gazed straight ahead. Her stomach hurt. She felt like curling up, and hugging her belly, and shutting her eyes tightly. She wanted to close out everything – the whole damn world.

First Dave.

Now Dal. She'd lost him. She knew she'd lost him because why else would he call in sick to work, and keep it a secret from her?

God, she thought they'd been happy together.

Someone grabbed her arm, jerked her backwards. A car flashed past, inches away. She turned to the man, who still held her arm.

'Are you okay?' he asked. His blue eyes looked gentle and concerned.

'Guess I'd better watch where I'm going, huh?'

'Unless you've got ambitions to be a hood ornament.'

She laughed. 'Well, I owe you one.'

'I'm ready to collect.'

'Oh?'

'What did you have in mind?' he asked. 'One what?'

'How about a Bloody Mary?'

'Accepted.'

'I'm Connie,' she said, and offered her hand.

He shook it. 'I'm Pete.'


'Come on Wednesday,' Elizabeth had told him, Friday night.

'I don't know,' Dal had said.

'Wednesday,' she repeated. 'That will give us time to miss one another.'

'But there's Connie. I can't just take off, Wednesday night, without some kind of excuse.'

'If you don't wish to arouse her suspicion, come during the day when you're supposed to be at work.'

'I only get an hour for lunch.'

'Take the whole day off. Spend it with me.'

He shook his head. 'I don't know, Elizabeth. That's . . . it's taking a big chance.'

'If you don't wish to come, don't come.' She kissed him lightly on the mouth. 'I'll be here Wednesday, waiting.'

For days, he'd thought about her offer. He didn't want to go. He had a decent job, and a good set-up with Connie. He could lose both, if he kept on with Elizabeth.

Also, she frightened him.

If a woman could enjoy screwing men in front of her paralyzed husband . . . God, no telling what else she might do, no telling what she might want *Dal* to do.

He decided, finally, to stay away. He would be much

better off if he never saw Elizabeth again.

He was pleased with his decision. He felt clean and honest and relieved.

He was halfway to work, Wednesday morning, when he changed his mind. He called Lane Brothers from Elizabeth's house. When Ken answered, he explained that he'd come down with a bad case of diarrhea.

'Don't give me that shit,' Ken had said, and laughed outrageously.

'I should be able to make it in tomorrow,' he said.

Elizabeth unzipped him.

'Have yourself a nice vacation,' Ken said.

Her hand reached in and fondled him. 'Vacation, my ass.'

More laughter from Ken.

Elizabeth freed his penis. 'Okay, see you tomorrow, Ken.' She put it in her mouth.

'See you then, buddy. Keep your shit together.'

Dal hung up. 'Mission accomplished,' he said with a trembling voice. Elizabeth moaned. As she sucked and licked, Dal stroked her soft hair. 'No audience?' he asked.

She didn't answer. Her mouth worked. Her hands unfastened his pants, and pulled them down, and clutched his bare buttocks.

He saw Herbert off to the right. Outside by the pool. Wheelchair against the glass door. Watching him with shiny, wide eyes.

Dal didn't care. Too late to care. Only Elizabeth mattered: her probing fingers, the slick tight hole of her mouth.

Herbert didn't matter till afterward.

'Does he *have* to watch?' Dal asked.

'Of course.'

'It's sick, Elizabeth.'

She smiled. 'I know. Isn't it delicious?'

They sat by the pool, Herbert facing them, and drank Burgundy. Dal wore his boxer shorts. Elizabeth wore nothing.

'Can he hear what we say?'

'Indeed he can. He hears, sees, and thinks. He breathes, swallows, and defecates. And that's about the extent of his achievements. Isn't it, Herbert?' She pinched his cheek. Her fingers left white marks that turned red.

'Could he feel that?'

'Could you, Herbert? Don't be shy, speak right up. Aw, what's the matter? Cat got your tongue?'

'Doesn't he have a nurse, or anything?'

'Heavens no. He has me. I see to his needs. It's a terrible burden, sometimes, but I feel it's the least I can do for him.'

'You ought to get him a nurse.'

'*Ought* I? Oh, I don't think so. We don't want to fritter away our fortune on such luxuries, do we? There won't be nearly as much left for me, if we do that. Herbert, after all, is not going to live forever. I hate to say this in front of the poor dear, but I think his time is limited. No, I don't imagine Herbert will be with us much longer.' She finished her glass of wine. 'Let's go in for a dip. And for Godsake, take off those silly shorts.'

'How long have you been deaf?' Pete asked.

'You noticed.'

'Is it supposed to be a secret?'

Connie swirled her Bloody Mary with the celery stalk. 'Not exactly,' she said. 'I don't broadcast it to everyone I bump into, but I get around to it pretty quickly. I can't pick up everything that's said. If people don't know I'm deaf, they might think I'm just stupid.'

'I wondered which it was.'

Connie laughed.

'It isn't every day you see a woman walk out in front of a honking car.'

'It was honking? I'm surprised I didn't notice.'

'You're not completely deaf?'

'Just about. There's still some conductive hearing. You pick up vibrations of sounds, at least if they're loud enough. Something like a car horn, definitely.'

'I suspected you didn't hear it,' Pete said. 'As we walked over here, I said a couple of things with my head turned away.'

'You ought to be a detective.'

'I am.'

'You're kidding.'

He took a business card from his wallet.

Connie sipped her drink. It was heavy on the tabasco sauce, and made her eyes water. Blinking, she read his card. 'Pete Harvey, Private Investigations.' It gave his address and phone number. 'Can I keep it?' she asked.

'Sure.'

'Never know when I might need a private eye.'

'Let's hope you don't. Not in my professional capacity, at least.'

She tucked the card into her pocket book, briefly considered giving one of her cards to Pete, and decided not to. She didn't want to start talking about her work. Not right now.

'When did you lose your hearing?' he asked.

'It's been five years.'

'An illness?'

'Accident.'

'Tough break.'

'Could've been a lot worse.'

'How'd it happen?' he asked.

'A knock on the head.'

'Some knock.'

'I'll say. I was in a coma for three weeks.'

Pete shook his head.

'Well, I came out lucky. Even being deaf – it's not as bad as it could be. At least I had twenty-one years of hearing. I know how the world sounds, and I can talk.'

'You talk just fine.'

'Thank you.'

'And you read lips like a pro. I could use a gal like you on my staff, except for one thing.'

'What's that?'

'I have a strict rule: I don't get involved with people who work for me.'

'What?' she asked, feeling heat rush to her face.

'I don't want this to end when we walk out of here.'

'Oh.' She grinned. 'Neither do I.'

## SCREAM GEMS
## PRESENTS
## OTTO SCHRECK
### in
## SCHRECK THE INQUISITOR

She is strapped to a chair in the center of a bare room, squinting into the brilliant light as if trying to see who is behind it.

Her young face is frightened.

'Who's there?' she asks. 'Please, I know someone's there. Who are you? What do you want with me?'

'I am the Grand Inquisitor. I wish to ask you a few questions.'

She groans. 'Please, what's going on?'

'You have information I need.'

'Who are you?'

He steps from behind the light. He wears a black, hooded robe.

'Oh Jesus.'

'Take not the name of the Lord in vain, heretic.'

She cranes her neck, trying to look past him. 'Ted, are you here someplace? Ted? Is this some kind of . . .'

'Who is this Ted? One of your heretic friends?'

'What's this heretic stuff?'

'Tell me about the Coven.'

'Oh God . . .'

His hand flashes out. It smacks her cheek, the heavy blow knocking her head to the side. She begins to cry. 'Tears will do you no good, witch.' Grabbing her hair, he jerks her head backwards. 'Tell me about the Coven.'

'*What* Coven?' she cries out, her voice shrill.

'Ah, you will play your games.' He raises a handful of her long, black hair. 'Do you wish to lose your precious hair?'

'No!'

He removes shears from his robe pocket. 'The names, then, of those in your Coven.'

'I don't know anything about a Coven.'

She screams, as if in pain, when he cuts through the hair. He cuts close to her scalp, and tosses great handsful into the darkness beyond the small area of light. Though she yells and pleads and flings her head about, he works feverishly and doesn't stop until nothing remains but short, choppy bristle.

Schreck steps back, and nods with approval. 'Are you prepared, now, to give me the information?'

'You *bastard!*' she shrieks. 'Goddamn you to hell, you goddamn fucking bastard!'

'You dare speak to me of Hell and damnation? You? A sister of the Devil?'

'Fucking pervert!'

A grin curls his lips.

The rage suddenly leaves her face. 'I'm sorry,' she mumbles. 'Please, I'm sorry. I'll do what you want. I'll tell you anything. Just don't hurt me. Please.'

'Tell me the names.'

'John Brown, and . . .'

'You take me for a fool?'

'No!'

'I could tear off your fingernails. Would you like that?'

'No,' she sobs.

'Perhaps you would prefer me to burn out your eyes, or snip your nipples off.'

She shakes her head, crying softly.

'There are so many ways to make you speak of your

hellish brethren: breaking bones, burning holes in your tender flesh, slicing it with a knife, shredding it with a whip, tearing it off inch by inch with my teeth. I've done it all. Crude methods, but effective. What shall we do with you?'

'Let me go,' she pleads. 'I promise, I'll never tell anybody anything.'

'You must tell *me* something, first.'

'I don't know about any Coven. If I knew, I'd tell you. Honest! I don't know anything about Covens or witches or heretics . . .'

'Then you shall suffer.'

She is on the floor, naked and spread eagled, her wrists and ankles bound to nails in the hardwood.

Schreck crouches beside her. 'See my little friends?' He holds a jar in his hand. 'Yes, they are spiders. Three dozen spiders. Do you like spiders, my little witch?'

'Please, don't.'

He slowly unscrews the lid. 'Tell me what I need to know, and I shall spare you the discomfort.'

'I don't know anything!'

'Unfortunate.'

Schreck removes the lid. He shakes out spiders. The girl shuts her eyes tightly and shakes her head as they drop onto her face. They fall, floating down like dark flakes, dotting her pale throat, her breasts, her belly. They creep over her tangle of pubic hair. They scurry on her thighs.

The girl screams and writhes.

Schreck, crouching beside her, watches with bulging, wet eyes.

'I shall leave you now, and give you a few hours to enjoy your playmates.'

'*No!* Get them *off* me! Get them *off!*'

He leaves the room.

A small, black spider crawls along the girl's forehead. It climbs the ridge of her eyebrow. She shakes her head wildly, trying to dislodge it. It halts as if to hang on. When she stops shaking her head, it moves down onto her eyelid.

Her scream is interrupted by the crack of a gunshot.

A man rushes into the room. He drops to his knees beside her. 'My God, Susan.'

'*Get them off!*'

The man sets his revolver on the floor. His hands work quickly, flicking and brushing the spiders away.

When they are off her face, she opens her eyes. 'Oh, thank God. I thought I'd . . .'

'It's all right. Schreck's dead. You're safe, now.' Taking out a pocket knife, he begins to cut the cords.

'Oh Ted, how did . . . how did you find me?'

'I'll tell you later.' He finishes cutting her loose, and helps her up. 'Here, take this.' He removes his shirt.

Susan puts it on.

'Did you talk?' he asks.

'About what?'

'The Coven.'

'I don't *know* anything about any Coven. I kept trying to tell him that, but he wouldn't listen. I don't know what's going on. How did I get here? Who is that awful man? He . . . oh Ted, take me out of here! Please!'

'You didn't tell him the members of the Coven?'

'Damn it, I don't know about a Coven! If I knew, I would've told him right away, before he . . . Look what he did to my hair! And those . . . those *spiders!* I'd have told him anything.'

The man turns away from her.

Schreck enters the room.

'She doesn't know,' Ted tells Schreck. 'I'm sure of it.'

Dropping to her knees, Susan grabs the revolver. She aims at Schreck and fires. The roar of the blast fills the room, but Schreck doesn't fall. Instead, he walks toward her. His lean, bony face wears a terrible smile. Susan shoots again and again.

'Blanks, heretic.'

She looks to Ted, who grins at her and shrugs. 'I'm afraid he's right.' Ted walks slowly from the room, leaving her alone with Schreck.

'I have no more use for you,' Schreck says. He holds a leather switch. He flicks it, cutting the air with a sound like a whistle. 'We shall make your death slow and agonizing, as befits a foul toad such as you.'

Whirling away, Susan rushes to a window. She hammers it with the revolver. The glass bursts. She grabs a long, jagged shard. 'Stay back! I'll kill you!'

Schreck laughs with disdain as he approaches. 'If you're so fond of glass, perhaps you would like to eat some. I can arrange that. I can arrange many delights featuring glass.'

With both hands, she suddenly presses the shard to her throat and tugs it sideways, ripping a deep gash across her skin.

Schreck steps closer. Her blood sprays his face and robe. 'I had such plans for you.'

He stomps his foot, splashing blood.

'You spoiled them!'

He raises the switch.

Before he has a chance to strike, Susan drops to her knees. Schreck steps out of the way as she falls forward. Her face thuds the floor.

'Spoiled them!' Schreck yells.

**The End**

# CHAPTER TEN

On Friday, Connie waited in agony for Dal to come home from work. She had wanted to tell him before, but couldn't. Now, time was running out.

No more delays.

God, if only there was some way out of it!

Finally, the front door opened.

She went to Dal. 'How was your day?' she asked.

'Not bad, not bad.' He tossed his sport coat onto the couch and turned to her, expecting a kiss.

She kissed him quickly.

'How'd you do today?' he asked.

'Not as well as I'd like.' Her writing had gone badly because of her worries. Rather than let the day go to waste, she spent most of her time typing without trying to force herself to concentrate.

She followed Dal into the kitchen. He mixed a batch of martinis for himself. While he worked on that, Connie made a vodka gimlet. 'Want some potato chips?' she asked.

'Sure. What's for dinner?'

It's *coming!*

She breathed deeply. She felt numb. 'I thawed out a steak for you.'

'Yeah? What are you having?'

'I'm . . . going out for dinner.'

Dal looked confused.

'I have a date,' she explained.

His face went red. 'A *date?*'

'I'm sorry, Dal. I meant to bring it up earlier . . .'

'With a man?'

She nodded.

'What are you talking about?'

'I met him Wednesday. At the library. He asked me to have dinner with him tonight.'

'Well *Jesus Christ!*'

'I'm sorry, Dal.'

'What am I supposed to do?'

'Have the steak.'

'Oh, that's what I need, funny answers. You think this is funny?'

'Not at all.'

'Boy, I thought . . . Never mind. *Jesus!* Well, go out and have a ball. Want to bring him back here, later, for a little slap 'n tickle?'

'Dal, please.'

'It's a little short notice for an eviction, don't you think?'

'You don't have to go.'

'But it'd be nice if I would.'

'I didn't say that.'

'Well just exactly what *are* you saying?'

'I don't know. It's just a date, Dal.'

'Yeah, my ass.' He turned away.

'Dal!'

Ignoring her, he picked up the martini pitcher and left the kitchen. She followed him into the living-room. He opened the front door.

'Dal, don't run off.'

He glanced back at her. 'Have a ball,' he said.

'Where are you going? Dal!'

He stepped outside, and jerked the door shut.

Connie felt the impact of its slam.

The door opened. Elizabeth looked up at him with deep, green eyes, and smiled.

'Martinis, anyone? asked Dal.

She pulled the glass pitcher down to her lips, and sipped.

'Mmmm. We must have olives, though. Come along. Herbert's out by the pool. Why don't you join him? I'll get glasses and olives.'

He watched her walk toward the kitchen. Her feet were bare. He could see through the thin, white fabric of her caftan. She wore nothing under it. For a moment, he considered following her into the kitchen, raising the caftan above her waist, and stroking the firm smooth curves of her buttocks.

But she had asked him to join Herbert at the pool. Best do as she asked. Plenty of time, later on, for the other.

He went out to the pool. Herbert's wheelchair faced the table, almost as if it hadn't been moved since Wednesday. He wore a different shirt, though. A bright red, flowered shirt. It made him look like a Hawaii vacationer.

A withered, paralyzed tourist. More corpse than man.

Dal turned away from the staring eyes. The pool was still in sunlight. He thought back to Wednesday, and the slick feel of Elizabeth's skin as they grappled under water.

'Having a nice chat?' she asked, coming out with a tray. On the tray were two long-stemmed glasses, a jar of green olives, and a cheese board with Brie and crackers. Her breasts jiggled slightly as she walked. Their tips were dark through the fabric. She sat down beside Herbert.

'So,' she said, 'how did you slip away from Connie?'

'We had a little quarrel.'

'How clever. You picked a fight, and walked off in a huff.'

'Something like that.'

'Nothing too drastic, I hope. You didn't tell her about us?'

'No.'

'That's fortunate. You wouldn't want to spoil such a fine opportunity.' She plucked olives from the jar, and dropped them into the empty glasses.

Dal poured the martinis.

They picked up the glasses.

'To you and Connie,' said Elizabeth.

'Why should we drink to that?'

'Because you're going to marry her, of course.'

'I am?'

'Certainly.'

'You're joking.'

'My dear, I have expensive tastes, you would be completely incapable of satisfying on the meager salary of a sales clerk. If you're interested in pursuing this relationship, you simply must be able to afford me.'

'But you're rich.'

'Herbert is. I'll be rich when, alas, he passes on. That, however, doesn't relieve you from the necessity of seeing to my needs, once we're together.'

'But marrying Connie . . . Her money wouldn't be mine.'

'Half of it would, I believe. Think it over.' She again raised her glass. 'To you and Connie, and wealth.'

'I don't know . . .'

'You want me, don't you?'

'More than anything.'

'In that case, your decision shouldn't be difficult.'

Dal hesitated, then clicked his glass against Elizabeth's. They drank.

\* \* \*

'So, how did you get to be a private eye?' Connie asked.

'I started out with the L.A.P.D.'

'I should've guessed.'

'How's that?' Pete, across the table from her at Victoria Station, grinned as he sliced into his prime rib.

'Oh, you all have that clean-cut, Steve Garvey look.'

'Just like Reed and Molloy.' He took a bite of beef.

'When did you leave the force?'

He chewed for a moment, and started to answer.

'I can't hear you,' Connie said. 'If you talk and chew at the same time, it comes out gobble-dee-gook.'

Pete laughed. After swallowing, he said, 'How's this?'

'Just fine. I'll eat while you talk.'

'Thanks!'

'So, how come you left the police?'

'We had a disagreement. Well, no, not really. My beef wasn't with the department. More with the public. We'd been under a lot of pressure about officer-involved shootings. This was a couple of years ago. I was cruising along Sunset, one fine night, and saw this black woman running up the middle of the street with a knife. She was chasing a kid. My first thought was that the kid had snatched her purse, or something. But he came right to my car, yelling for help. I got out, and the kid sort of ducked behind me. "She crazy, man," he says. And the gal is yelling too, about cutting off the kid's private parts. I'm between the gal and the kid, though, and she keeps coming. She doesn't obey my command to stop. It's this wicked-looking hunting knife, you see. So I draw down on her, and she ignores it and keeps coming, and I'm thinking about all the heavy times I'll get from the bleeding hearts if I drop this gal. I mean, she's black, she's female, and she's unarmed except for a harmless little knife. So I hold off firing. And in the meantime, she throws the knife. I dodge it, and it kills the kid. The kid, it turns out, is her homosexual son.'

'*You're* the one,' Connie said.

'I'm him.'

'You cuffed the gal to the body . . .'

'Yeah.' He grinned. 'I cuffed both her hands to both the dead guy's hands, and walked away.'

'I wondered what kind of a man would do that.'

'Now you know. Here he is, Dirty Pete in the flesh.'

'Pleased to meet you, Dirty Pete.' She reached a hand over the table and shook his. 'Better eat, now, before your dinner gets cold.'

'Okay. I'll eat and you do the talking. How did you get to be an author?'

'It all began with a rotten social life.'

'It's quite simple, really,' said Elizabeth. 'Haven't you ever proposed before?'

'No.'

'That surprises me, I must say. You seem so impulsive. Be a dear, and push me off.'

Her air mattress had drifted, footfirst, against a side of the pool.

Dal, sitting on the end of the diving board, got to his feet. He turned around carefully, and walked, the board springy under his feet. He climbed down. The concrete was still warm, though the sun no longer hit it. He liked the feel of the breeze.

And he liked what it did to Elizabeth. It was the breeze, he assumed, that made her nipples stand rigid.

He glanced at the martini glass she balanced on her belly.

'Would you like a refill, while you're beached?'

'I would adore one.' She lifted the glass, tipped it to her mouth, and sucked in the olive.

Dal pulled her mattress alongside the wall, and took the glass from her. He retrieved his glass from the end of the diving board, and carried them to the table. 'Fix you one, Herbie?' he asked.

He smiled, realizing that the man's silent presence no longer unnerved him.

'Herbie,' he said, 'you're a good fellow.'

'He was never that,' Elizabeth called.

Dal finished pouring the drinks. He returned to the pool. He climbed down the tile steps at the shallow end, and waded out to Elizabeth.

He placed the glass on her belly. 'Thank you, dear,' she said.

'Think little of it.'

'Now, pretend I'm Connie.'

'Why'd I do that?'

'You're going to propose to me.'

'Huh?'

'You said you've never proposed before. Here's your chance.'

'Oh, I don't know.'

Elizabeth raised her head slightly off the inflated pillow, sipped her martini without spilling, and rested the glass on her belly. 'You start by taking her to a nice restaurant. Have a few drinks.'

'Ply her with liquor.'

'Precisely. Have a marvelous meal. Lobster, perhaps.'

'I can't eat seafood.'

'Then steak. Châteaubriant would do nicely. When you're done, order after-dinner drinks. Cognac . . .'

'Connie likes Irish Coffee.'

'Fine. Have that. And now, it's time. You're both full, slightly high, and happy.'

'Okay.'

'I'm Connie.'

She started to drift away. Dal caught her by the foot, and pulled her back to him. 'Connie, I want to marry you.'

'Marry me? Oh, Dal! Are you sure? Why would you want to marry someone like me?'

''Cause Elizabeth told me to.'

'That won't do at all.'

# CHAPTER ELEVEN

They stepped out of the restaurant. 'That was very nice,' Connie said. 'Thank you.' She took Pete's hand.

'The night's young. Anything special you'd like to do?'

'Yes, as a matter of fact.'

'Shoot.'

'Let's go to a movie.'

'A *movie?*' He looked at her, grinning, as if he thought it a fine, rather childlike idea. 'Anything in particular?'

She shrugged. 'I don't care. Just so it's dark.'

'Do you like scary films?'

'Do you?'

'They're my favorite. I know just the place. I don't know what's playing there tonight, but it'll probably be good.'

'Bet I can guess. The Haunted Palace.'

'You've been there?'

'Not since it changed hands. It used to be the Elsinore.'

'It's a far cry from that, now.'

In the darkness of the car, they didn't try to talk.

Connie fastened her seatbelt. She thought it would be nice to open it, and scoot across the seat, and snuggle with Pete. She hadn't done anything like that in years. Tonight, though, she felt as eager and daring and uncertain as a teenager. She hesitated. Pete might think she was acting silly, or possessive.

On the other hand, she felt so far away from him, strapped into the seat way over on this side of the car.

With a trembling hand, she unfastened the safety harness. Pete looked at her, and smiled. She slid across the seat. He put an arm around her. Connie snuggled against him, and rested a hand on his thigh.

A block from the Haunted Palace, Pete eased his car to the curb. They walked to the theater, holding hands.

On the marquee, Connie saw that *Dracula, Down Under* was showing with *The Town that Dreaded Sundown*.

The girl in the ticket window smiled at Pete. 'How are you, tonight?' she asked.

'Not bad. I see you haven't found a new hairdresser.' He handed her the money.

'*The Town that Dreaded Sundown* is just starting,' she said. 'Too bad you didn't get here half an hour sooner. You missed tonight's Schreck.'

'He's a little tacky for my taste.'

The girl laughed. 'Oh, you'd have *loved* this one, *Schreck the Inquisitor*.'

'Sounds charming.'

Inside, Pete gave the tickets to a fat man in bloody clothes.

'Evening, Bruno.'

Bruno growled through the nylon stocking he wore over his face.

'Do you hang out here?' Connie asked.

'Only been here once,' Pete said. 'Last week.'

'It *is* a little tacky.'

'So are most of the movies. Fun, though.'

'Yeah. Like a carnival.'

'Popcorn?'

'I couldn't eat a thing, at the moment. Maybe a drink, though.'

The auditorium of the theater was just as Connie remembered it: the castle walls, the battlements and turrets, the ceiling like a starlit sky.

She had spent a lot of time in movie theaters, after the Tucson incident. Too much time. First in Tucson, then in Los Angeles.

Hardly a day passed that she didn't find herself alone in a dark theater, eating popcorn and hot dogs and Good 'n Plenty, staring at a screen where silent people struggled through tragedy, fought to survive, laughed, and fell in love.

She went to the movies, though she knew she shouldn't. She should be writing more pages than the two or three she managed daily. She should be reading. Most of all, she should be out in the world, *doing* something, meeting people, not hiding in the darkness of a movie house.

One day, two years ago, she went to a noon showing of *The Island*. When it was over, she stayed in her seat and watched *Jaws II*, though she had seen it before. When that ended, she went out to the lobby to leave. Beyond the glass doors, the afternoon looked sunny. A young couple strolled by, holding hands and happy.

Her throat tightened. Her eyes filled with tears.

After buying a Pepsi and a fresh bucket of popcorn, she returned to her seat. She watched *The Island* again. She watched *Jaws II* again. When *The Island* started for a third time, she stayed in her seat.

She felt sick with herself. Cowardly and self-destructive. But she couldn't force herself to walk out.

Finally, a man sat down beside her. He smelled strongly of sweat and onions. He put a hand on her knee.

She was wearing a skirt.

The hand moved under its hem.

She lifted the hand. The man smiled at her. His lips moved, blowing stench into her face.

She broke his forefinger, and walked out of the theater.

The next day, she didn't go to a movie. Nor the next day. She was certain, if she went back even once, she would fall again into the pattern. She was like an alcoholic, afraid to take a single drink because it would lead to another and another.

She read voraciously.

She finished her novel, *Bayou Bride*, in three months.

She took a course in self-defense from a tough, scarred ex-Marine who claimed to be a mercenary – and proved it to Connie's satisfaction by disappearing one day. She assumed he'd gone to Rhodesia. She never saw him again.

One of the men in the class dated her, and she found that she could go to movies safely as long as she didn't go alone.

Then she met Dal. He took her often. He knew how she loved movies, though she never told him about her bad years as an addict.

It was really mean of him, leaving her home last week when . . . She didn't want to think about Dal.

Not tonight.

She could worry about him later – how to tell him . . .

She took Pete's hand, and didn't let go.

When *The Town that Dreaded Sundown* ended, the lights came on.

'How'd you like it?' Pete asked.

'I'll probably have nightmares.'

He smiled. 'You up for another one?'

She glanced at the clock. Nearly eleven. Dal was probably back at the apartment, waiting for her. She didn't want to face him. She wanted to stay here with Pete, holding his hand, and never leave.

'Sure, let's stay,' she said.

'Ready for some popcorn now?'

'That'd be great.'

*Dracula, Down Under* began soon after Pete's return.

It was an Italian film about a vampire among the Australian aborigines.

'Oh no,' Connie said.

Pete looked at her.

She shook her head. 'Nothing,' she whispered, and took a handful of popcorn from the tub on his lap.

It was enough, being with him.

It didn't matter that the movie made no sense. She ate popcorn, and drank her Pepsi, and paid little attention to the screen.

She leaned closer to Pete.

He put his arm across her shoulders.


'Could we see each other tomorrow?' Pete asked outside her apartment door.

'I'd like that.'

'We could go to the beach.'

'Great. I'll make a picnic lunch.'

'I'll bring the beer. Or would you prefer wine?'

'Beer.'

They held each other tightly, and kissed.

'I had a wonderful time,' Connie said.

'Me too.'

'I'd ask you in, but Dal . . .'

Pete shook his head. 'On the first date, I only kiss.'

'That so?'

'It's a lie, actually.' He pulled her close, and kissed her again. His hand gently went to her breast.

She sucked in a sharp breath. 'Oh God, Pete.'

'Goodnight.'

'Goodnight. See you tomorrow.'

'Around ten?' he asked.

85

'Great.'

'Goodnight.' He kissed her once more.

'Goodnight.'

They didn't part for a long time.

Then Connie went inside, alone. She leaned against the door, too weak to move, hurting in a strange way that made her want to cry and laugh.

A long time later, she searched the apartment. Dal wasn't there, thank God.

She put the guard chain on the door.

Then, feeling guilty, she took it off.

Then she put it on again. If Dal came back in the middle of the night, she didn't want him crawling into bed with her.

Not tonight.

Not ever again.

Pete Harvey had her now.

Dirty Pete.

With a squeal of delight, she hugged herself and twirled across the room.

# CHAPTER TWELVE

Another Saturday going to pot. Freya sat in front of the television with her tea, and stared at Popeye.

The pits.

Sunday, for Christsake, was better than this.

Ha! Sunday, for Christsake. A funny.

But it was true. Sunday morning TV had a parade of weirdos. A real circus. Some of those evangelists put on a better show than Loony Tunes. Especially the healers. Christ, the way they slapped folks around, and grabbed canes out from under cripples, and stuck their fingers in deaf people's ears! *Out, you devils! Out, Satan!* Be a kick, some morning, if the guy's finger came out of an ear with a big yellow glob of wax.

Well, shit, nothing good like that on Saturday morning. Just a bunch of feeb cartoons and reruns of crap she saw twenty years ago.

Nothing decent till 10:30. *Phantom of the Opera*. The Claude Rains version from '43. Nowhere near as good as the Lon Chaney, with those boobs trotting around the tunnels with their fingers in the air so the phantom couldn't drop nooses around their necks. 'The phantom's loops are quick!' they kept saying. What a gas! Well, the Rains version couldn't hold a candle to that, but it sure beat watching *Heckle and Jeckle*.

The N-double A-C-P must've got down on Heckle and

Jeckle. She'd swear those magpies used to talk like Amos and Andy.

The doorbell rang, startling Freya so she slopped tea onto her bare leg. She brushed it away with her hand, and got up. Her leg was still wet as she crossed the room. She rubbed it again. She adjusted her tube-top, and opened the door.

'Greetings.'

'Oh, hello,' Freya said. She forced a smile.

'Remember me?'

'I remember. I see you changed your shirt.' The vulture T-shirt had been replaced by one that read, 'Don't get mad, get even.'

'I saw the ad in the paper,' she said. 'I thought I'd come back.'

Like a bad penny, Freya thought. 'Well, I'm afraid the apartment is still not available.'

'Why not?'

'It's already taken.'

'That's the story you gave me, last week.'

'It's just as true, today.'

'Then why was there an ad in today's paper?'

'It must be an error,' Freya said.

'No, I don't think so. I think you just decided you don't want me for a roommate. Isn't that right?'

'That's right.'

'Because I'm a gross slob, right?'

'That's right.'

'Suppose I make it two-fifty.'

'You're awfully eager.'

'This place is only a block from campus. Besides, I like your style.' She gave Freya a brash grin. 'Now, how about showing me around?'

'I admire your persistence,' Freya said, loathing the girl more each second. 'What's your name?'

'Chelsea.'

'I'm Freya. Come on in.'

The girl entered, and wrinkled her nose. 'You need some light in here,' she said, and opened the curtains. 'That's better.'

Freya cringed.

'Are you from around this area?' she asked.

'No.'

'Where are you from?'

'What does it matter?'

'I'm just curious. If we're going to live together, don't you think we should know more about each other?'

'Does that mean you'll take me?'

'I'm thinking about it.'

'Well, if you really want to know, I'm from Oakland.'

'Ah. Home of the Hell's Angels. Did you live with your folks?'

'What are they?'

'You don't have parents?'

'No, I was hatched. Can't you tell?'

'I was only wondering.'

'Well don't. Just show me the apartment, okay? If I wanted a third degree, I'd set myself on fire.'

'As you wish,' said Freya. She showed Chelsea the kitchen, the bathroom, and the spare room.

'When can I move in?'

'As soon as you pay me.'

'Two-fifty.'

'Six hundred,' Freya said.

'Come again?'

'First and last month's rent. That's five hundred.'

'I can count.'

'Plus a hundred deposit for breakage.'

'You're a doozy.'

'I'm only protecting myself.'

'You think I can't come up with six hundred, right?'

'Oh, I hope you can,' Freya said.

She meant it.

'Is a check okay?'

'Cash.'

'This is Saturday.'

'Then you can move in Monday after the banks open.'

'You're trying to pull something.'

'Not at all. If you can come up with the cash today, you can move in today.'

'How about fifty down, and the rest Monday morning?'

'And you move in today?'

'Yep.'

'No thanks. Monday will be plenty soon enough.'

'You're a pal.'

'Shall we plan to see each other Monday morning, then?'

'We shall count on it,' Chelsea said, mimicking her.

When she was gone, Freya made a telephone call.

'Hello?'

'Good morning, darling.'

'Princess!'

'I have one for you,' she said.

'Marvelous!'

'This one's a bit different.'

'How so?'

'She's a pig.'

'A pig?' he asked, the lightness leaving his voice.

'I know you want beauties, darling, but this gal's wonderful. She's ugly, gross, and obnoxious.'

'This wasn't part of our plan, princess.'

'Wait'll you see her.'

'She's disgusting and repulsive?'

'Very.'

'Hmm.' He paused for several seconds. 'Perhaps we *can* fit her in. Let me work on it, and get back to you.'

'Great.'

'In the meantime, keep looking for a beauty. Tina was absolutely marvelous. Someone like her.'

'I'll keep the ad in the paper.'

'Yes. Do that. And come over tonight, if you can.'

'You got another one?'

'Oh, indeed I did. Unfortunately, it has two female voices. I'm not quite sure how to handle the dubbing of that, but I'll try to think of something before you arrive.'

'What time?'

'Oh, eight o'clock.'

'Great. See you then, Todd.'

# CHAPTER THIRTEEN

Dal stopped at Conroy's, and bought a dozen red roses in a vase. He carried the vase out to his car. Holding it in place on the passenger seat, he headed for the apartment.

The roses had been Elizabeth's idea.

'She'll be touched by your thoughtfulness and generosity,' Elizabeth had told him. 'She'll forget all about your little spat.'

Naturally, he hadn't explained the real cause of his trouble with Connie. It was too humiliating. Not only that, but Elizabeth would recognize Connie's date for what it was – a sign that she had lost interest in Dal, a sign that marriage was probably out of the question. He didn't want Elizabeth to know that, so he made up a story to satisfy her curiosity.

'She burnt dinner,' he'd said. 'We had these two beautiful sirloin steaks, and she left them in the broiler too long. Completely forgot about them. By the time she remembered, they were charcoal black. I said, "You don't expect me to eat this, do you?" Then I chewed her out. I told her I'd been working my tail off, all day, and how I came home looking forward to a nice meal, and the least she could do is not fuck it up.'

'You sound positively abhorrent.'

'She pissed me off.'

'Will you yell at me, that way, if I burn your food?'

'Never.'

'Why not?'

'Because I love you.'

'And you don't love Connie?'

'She's all right. I don't love her, though.'

'You must learn to act as if you do. Make her feel that she is the whole world to you, that your life would be a pit of ashes without her.'

'I'll try.'

'You must do better than try. You must succeed. I want you to marry her within the month.'

'My God, that's only three weeks away!'

'I'm sure you'll find a way.'

That was the time to mention Connie's new boyfriend. He couldn't force himself to tell her, though. Not enough nerve.

Three weeks. Impossible.

Unless . . . Who knows, maybe she ended up hating the guy who took her to dinner, last night.

Not much chance of that.

He drove up the alley behind the apartment house, and carefully parked the car in its stall. He carried the vase of roses into the courtyard, and up the stairs to the door of the apartment.

He unlocked the door.

The guard chain snapped taut.

'Shit!'

He kicked the door. The chain flung it back at him, slamming it with a bang. Embarrassed, he looked around to see if he was being watched. He saw no one.

He felt like kicking the door down.

That would get him inside, but further from his real goal.

So he pushed the doorbell, instead. It didn't ring; it lit bulbs in every room. He jabbed the button, again and again, to make the bulbs flash.

The chain rattled. The door opened.

'Dal.'

Though she smiled, her eyes looked troubled.

'These are for you.'

'Oh, they're beautiful. Thank you.'

'May I come in?'

'Of course.'

Of course? Then why the chain? 'Are you alone?' he asked.

'Sure I am.' Connie took the flowers, and set them on the dining-room table.

Dal watched in silence. She wore a wrap-around skirt. Her white blouse was tied in front, leaving her midriff bare. Her beach outfit.

She came back to him.

'About last night,' he said. 'I want to apologize. I acted like an ass.'

'You had a right to be upset, Dal.'

She stepped toward the bright window, and he turned to face her. She wants the light on my lips, he realized. She's always maneuvering for that.

'I should have been more reasonable,' he said. 'I mean, I don't own you. You have every right to go on a date. It's just that I was . . . hurt, I guess. The thought of you being with another man . . . It was just unbearable.'

'I'm sorry,' she said.

'Forgive me?'

'There's nothing that needs forgiving. You wouldn't have felt badly, if you didn't care for me. I can hardly fault you for that.'

'I more than care for you, Connie. I love you.'

She blinked as if slapped. 'No you don't.'

'I do. I've loved you since the first moment I saw you.'
He reached for Connie. Shaking her head, she grabbed his
wrists, and pushed his arms down.

'Don't.'

'Connie!'

'I'm sorry, but . . . We've had . . . I do like you, Dal, and
I'll always be grateful for the times we've had. But I think
they're over, now.'

'No.'

'Yes. I want you to find a place of your own, now. You don't
have to move out today, or anything, but the sooner you get
your own apartment, the better off we'll both be.'

'Connie, you can't mean it.'

'I do mean it.'

'You must've had a damn good time, last night.'

She looked up from his lips, and met his eyes. 'If things
had been better between you and me, I never would've accepted
the date. In fact, I would never have *met* him. I stopped by
Lane Brothers, Wednesday morning.'

The words made his bowels suddenly ache.

'I thought we might have lunch together, but you weren't
there.'

'I . . .'

'You don't have to tell me where you were. I know.'

'What?'

'You were with a woman.'

'I was *not*.'

'You don't have to lie. It doesn't matter anymore.'

'I was not with a woman.'

'You were with her last Friday night at the movies, and all
day Wednesday, and probably last night.'

'That's a lie!'

*How could she know?*

'It's the truth. I walked out to the theater, Friday night. I thought I'd surprise you. But I was the one who got the surprise. I saw you sitting with her, with your arm around her.'

*It's all a bluff,* he realized. She doesn't know anything. She's only guessing.

'That was a good trick,' Dal said. 'If I was sitting with a girl, it's news to me. If you want to believe it, though, go ahead. I'm sure your conscience feels better if you can convince yourself that I'm the one at fault. I was alone in that theater. I was alone Wednesday, unless you want to count the clerks I talked to while I was shopping for this.'

He reached into his pocket, and pulled out a small jewelry box. He opened it.

Connie stared at the diamond ring. Tears filled her eyes. 'Oh Dal,' she muttered.

'I was planning to . . . last night . . .'

'Oh Dal, I'm sorry.'

He took the ring from the box, and held it out to her. 'Try it on.'

She shook her head. 'I can't. I'm sorry. I . . .' She sobbed and turned away.

Dal put a hand on her shoulder.

She shrugged it off, and faced him. 'It's over, Dal. It's over. I'm sorry. I still want you to move out.'

'But why?'

'It's Pete.'

'The guy you were with last night?'

She nodded.

'I've been aced out, huh?'

'I'm sorry.'

'Okay. I'll move out, like you want. I don't want to pressure you. In case this Pete doesn't . . . Well, the ring will still be waiting.'

97

Nodding, Connie wiped the tears from her face.

'Guess I'd better go apartment-hunting.'

'I'm sorry.'

Dal turned from her. He stopped outside. The door shut.

He slipped Elizabeth's engagement ring into its box, and headed for the stairs.

# CHAPTER FOURTEEN

Freya hated driving this time of the evening. The sun hung low over the Pacific, blinding her. Sunglasses helped, but not nearly enough. Most of the time, she could barely see the road ahead of her. She blocked the sun with her hand. That wasn't easy, though. After a few minutes, her upraised arm felt as if it were being dragged down with lead weights.

The stretch along the Coast Highway seemed endless. Finally, she came to the turnoff. She didn't notice the unmarked road until she was beside it. She hit her brakes, swung onto the highway's shoulder, and backed up.

She read the sign. PRIVATE ROAD. KEEP OUT.

She drove forward. The road curved into a thickly wooded area. She stopped at a metal gate, opened its padlock, and swung the gate wide. After driving through, she shut the gate and snapped its lock into place.

The one-lane road left the pine trees behind, and snaked across low hills to the house.

Freya gazed at the house as she drove toward it. She loved the house. She loved its weathered siding, its bay windows, its gables, its single, peaked tower.

So marvelously creepy!

It looked like dozens of other old, dark houses in dozens of old, spooky movies.

Soon, it would belong to her.

She could hardly wait!

She had such visions of how it would be, of wandering its halls on stormy nights, candle flames throwing weird shadows on the walls. No electric lights. She would get rid of all those, and use electricity only for the television and refrigerator and such.

It would be glorious.

So incredibly creepy, the greatest spook-house of all time – and *hers*.

She climbed the porch steps. As she aimed her key at the lock, the door groaned open.

'Todd.'

'Princess.' He kissed her cheek. 'You're looking lovely tonight, as usual.'

'Thank you.'

He gestured for her to follow, and started upstairs. 'I hope you had a pleasant drive.'

'I survived it.'

'Traffic wasn't too bad?'

'No. Traffic was fine. It was the damn sun that nearly killed me.'

'I'm sorry to hear that. I have some news to cheer you, though. I found a solution to our problem.'

'Another woman?'

'Yes. She's waiting in the control room.'

'What did you tell her?'

'I explained that she would be perfect for a voice-over in a short suspense show I'm producing.'

'Is she safe?'

'She's a streetwalker.'

'Can she read?'

'Oh, I do hope so.'

Todd opened a door at the top of the stairs. A slim, black woman was sitting on a bench at the control booth, leaning back, her elbows resting on the blank screens of two video monitors. Her ankles were crossed. She wore boots, and tight shorts, and a vest held loosely together in front by laces.

'Freya, this is Tango.'

'Pleased to meet you,' Freya said, staring at the girl's glossy, dark skin. The vest was open wide enough to expose much of her breasts.

'Pleasure's mine,' Tango said. Leaning forward, she held out a hand to Freya.

The hand was warm. It lingered in hers, and slid away.

'All set?' Todd asked. 'Let's run through the tape once with the audio, then I'll give you some time to familiarize yourselves with the scripts before we do the dubbing.'

Freya nodded.

'Whatever you say,' said Tango. 'You're the bossman.'

They turned to the main television screen.

'Get the lights, Freya, if you please.'

Reluctantly, she reached for the light switch. Darkness wasn't necessary for viewing, but Todd always insisted on it. For atmosphere, he said.

Maybe it's best, Freya thought. With the lights on, she wouldn't see much of the tape. Her eyes, she knew, would be on Tango.

'I believe I'll call this *Schreck the Ax-man*.'

'Why not *The Ax-man Cometh?*' Tango suggested.

Todd laughed politely. 'I'm afraid not, darling. Too much levity spoils the soup.'

The two young women sit close to their campfire, as if they believe its bright flames will keep them from harm.

The one in the plaid flannel skirt tilts her head back, and

squirts a stream of wine into her mouth from a leather bota.

'Don't you ever miss?' asked her friend, who has obviously missed often. The front of her gray sweatshirt is wet and red-stained.

'Takes practice, Lynn.'

She passes the bota to Lynn, who raises its spout to her lips and starts to squirt.

'Hello, young ladies.'

They both jump. Lynn shoots the stream off into her nose and eyes, and the man laughs. 'Sorry,' he says. 'I didn't mean to startle you. I saw your fire.' He walks close to it. He is a stout, red-bearded man. 'My name's Jim.'

'I'm Kristi. This is Lynn.'

'Mind if I join you?'

Kristi glances at Lynn, then smiles at the man and says, 'Help yourself.'

He steps closer to the fire, where the girls are sitting beside each other on a six-foot log. 'You can use our table,' Kristi suggests, sweeping her arm toward the stump standing upright beside her.

'Thanks,' he says, and sits on it.

He wears tight, faded jeans. The sleeves have been cut off his denim jacket at the shoulders, and his tanned arms look thick and powerful. 'Can I have a taste of that?'

Lynn shrugs, smiling nervously. She glances at Kristi, as if for permission. When Kristi nods, Lynn passes the bota to her, and she hands it to the man. He squirts a long stream of wine into his mouth, and doesn't spill a drop. He gives the bota back to Kristi. 'Where you girls from?' he asks.

'San Diego.'

'Long way from home.'

'Are you from around here?' Kristi asks.

'Me? I'm from Scottsdale.'

'Arizona?'

'California. She's a little burg just the other side of Sunny Lake.'

'Where's that?'

'Just the other side of Loon.'

'And that's just the other side of *this* lake,' Kristi adds, nodding her head toward the shoreline down the slope from the campsite.

'I canoed in, saw your fire.'

'Probably the whole world can see our fire,' Lynn says, and laughs nervously.

'Pretty near. Can I have another taste of that? It's Zinfandel, right?'

Kristi laughs. 'Fantastic! A wine connoisseur in the middle of the forest primeval!'

'Not a connoisseur, just a drinker.' He tips back his head, and squeezes the sides of the bota. When he is done, he passes the leather sack to Kristi.

'I wanted to talk to you about this fire,' he says. 'It's a warm night. You don't really need one.'

'We like it,' Kristi says.

'Sure. I know how you feel. She's bright and cheery, and keeps the darkness at arm's-length. Gives you a good feeling. Helps you forget you're alone in the woods, with god-knows-what prowling around and watching you.'

'You're not helping the situation,' Kristi says, and contorts her face in an exaggerated expression of fear. Lynn grimaces, looking very nervous.

'I'm serious, now. You ought to douse your fire. After dark, it's like a neon sign, tells folks you're here. If they're the wrong kind of folks, and come snooping, you could be in big trouble.'

'We can take care of ourselves,' Kristi tells him.

Lynn, who doesn't look so sure of that, chews her lower lip.

'Even if you have guns, which I doubt, it's still no guarantee. The way you're dressed, Kristi, I can see you're unarmed unless you've got some dinky thing way down in one of your jeans pockets.' He aims a finger at Lynn. 'You might have a pistol concealed under that bulky sweatshirt, but I'd bet you don't.' Smiling, he pulls a knife from the sheath on his belt. 'Now, I'm sitting here with a knife. You're there without guns. What're you gonna do?'

'Why don't you put that away?' Kristi says. Her voice, so confident before, is trembling slightly.

'Scared?' Jim asks.

'Put it away, all right?'

'I just want to put a little fear into you. You need it. You're both vulnerable as hell, and don't seem to realize it.' He slides the knife into its sheath.

'I'll bet you haven't heard about our murders. If you'd heard, you wouldn't be out here at all, much less with a roaring fire.'

Kristi and Lynn glance at each other. Lynn shakes her head.

'That's what I thought,' Jim says.

'You want to tell us?' asks Kristi.

'Five murders in the past two months, all of them within a few miles of here. The first was a fourteen-year-old girl. She went out alone on Sunny Lake to do some night fishing, and never came back. They found most of her body a week later in an abandoned boat house. Someone had used an ax on her.'

Lynn groans.

'Is this really true?' asks Kristi. 'Or are you just trying to scare us?'

'It's true, all right. The next two victims, just a month ago, were Randy Wilson and his wife. Randy owned the hardware store in Scottsdale. He and Mary used to do a lot of hiking. They were camped about a mile from here the night they were killed.'

'With an ax?' Lynn wants to know.

'Same as the girl. Same as the two teachers we found last week. Those gals were camping over by Loon. Chopped up like cordwood.'

'You don't have to be so graphic.'

'I just want you to understand the danger you're in.'

Lynn makes a sickly smile.

'We're here now,' Kristi says. 'What do you want us to do? Just pack up, right now, and pull out?'

'Wouldn't be a bad idea.'

'Except for one thing. Our car's about seven miles from here. We're not about to hike seven miles in the dark. We'd probably break our necks.'

'I can give you a lift in my canoe,' Jim offers.

'Our car's *away* from the lake.'

'I don't mean to your car. I'll take you over to Scottsdale. We can drive over and pick up your car in the morning. What do you think?'

'I don't know,' Kristi says, and gets to her feet. She gestures. Lynn stands up. 'Give us a couple minutes to talk it over.'

Jim nods. He picks up the bota, and begins shooting a stream of wine into his mouth.

Kristi walks away from the fire, twigs and pine cones snapping under her white sneakers. Lynn follows. They stop in the darkness just beyond the area of light cast by the fire.

'Should we go with him?' Kristi asks.

Lynn shrugs.

Kristi brushes hair away from her eyes. 'What about these

murders?' she asks. 'Have you heard anything about them?'

'Not a word,' Lynn says.

'Me neither. Of course, I don't read the papers.'

'Neither do I. Five murders, though. Wouldn't something like that make the six o'clock news?'

'You'd think so,' Kristi says. 'This is really boondocks, though. Maybe they're keeping it quiet.'

'I don't know.' Lynn steps close to Kristi. 'I think . . .'

'Whew! Didn't you bring any deodorant?'

Lynn sniffs the armpits of her sweatshirt. 'Isn't me: Anyway, look. Maybe this Jim-guy made it all up.'

'What for?' Kristi asks.

'Who knows? Maybe he wants to get us dependent on him, so we'll let our guard down. Maybe he wants to get our equipment in his canoe, and steal it. Hell, maybe he gets his kicks drowning campers . . .'

'You've got a wild imagination, Lynn.'

'I'm just thinking of the possibilities.'

'Look, we've got to make up our minds.'

'You decide for us.'

'No! You can't put it all on me. Give me a yes or no. Come on, Lynn. Do you want to pack up and go with him in his canoe, or not?'

'A yes or no?'

'Right.'

Lynn shakes her head, and pushes a hand through her short, bristly hair. Turning, she looks for a long time at Jim. He is drinking more wine. 'Okay,' she says, her voice whiny with defeat. 'No.'

'Are you sure?'

'I'm sure,' she says reluctantly. 'Maybe he's telling the truth, but I don't want to go with him. Not in a canoe, I can't even swim.'

'All right, it's settled.' Kristi turns away.

'Wait.'

'Yeah?'

'What if he won't leave?'

Kristi frowns. 'Did you have to say that?'

Then they both return to the fire. Kristi makes it brief. 'We decided to stay here.'

'I was afraid of that.'

'Thank you for the offer, and for warning us, but . . .' She shrugs.

'You decided to take your chances,' he finishes for her.

'That's about it.'

'Well, thanks for the wine.' He stands. 'I'd better be on my way. I saw another fire, down at the south end. I'd better let *them* know. Good luck, ladies.'

Without another word, he walks into the darkness. Kristi and Lynn wait for a few seconds, then quietly follow him. They stand close together. Looking down the slope, they watch him climb into his canoe, and shove off. They watch for a long time, until the sound of his paddle dipping into the water disappears in a whisper of wind.

Then they return to the fire, and sit down.

'Maybe we ought to put it out,' Lynn says, looking tense.

Kristi shrugs. 'Why bother? If the ax-man's around, he already knows where to find us.'

'Don't say that!'

'Let's have some more wine, and forget about it, okay? That guy was probably just some kook who gets his laughs scaring people.'

'Geez, I hope so.'

Kristi lifts the bota and squeezes a long, thin stream of wine into her mouth. As she passes the leather bag to Lynn, a shape moves silently among the trees behind them.

Lynn raises the bota. She squirts into her mouth.

The shape moves into the shimmering light of the fire. It is a man. He wears black, leather pants. His bare chest is shiny in the firelight. A black hood covers his head. His eyes glisten through holes in the hood. In his hands, he holds a double-bit ax.

'I think I'm ready to hit the sack,' Kristi says. 'One more for the road.' She reaches out for the wine bag.

Lynn holds it out to her.

With a grunt, the man swings the ax in a swift, sideways blow. It chops through Lynn's neck. Her head flies, tumbling. It rolls into the campfire.

For an instant, she sits there headless, still holding out the bota to Kristi as blood spouts from her neck stump and rains down.

Kristi screams.

The bota drops. The body topples forward, shouldering into the campfire, scattering flaming branches across the ground.

Kristi screams and screams as she jumps to her feet and tries to run. The man grabs her shirt collar. He throws her to the ground.

On her back, Kristi gazes up at him.

He laughs, and pulls away his hood. His face is gaunt, his wet eyes bulging, his mouth writhing with a terrible grin.

'I am Schreck,' he says.

He raises the ax high overhead, and brings it down.

It knocks through Kristi's upthrust hands, and splits her face.

Todd turned off the machine.

Freya flicked on the lights, and saw his wide grin. She turned to Tango, who wore a smirk.

'Well ladies, what do you think?'

'That's one baaad dude,' said Tango. 'Wouldn't want to mess with him.' She laughs. 'No sir, no way.'

Todd looked amused. 'What about you, Freya?'

'Fantastic!'

'I thought you might enjoy it.'

'How'd you do that?' Tango asked. 'I mean, how'd you do that with the head?'

'Just chopped it off.'

Tango laughed. 'I know, it's a trade secret. I'll lay odds you used a dummy.'

'Very astute, young lady.'

'Sure looked real.'

'I appreciate the compliment.' Todd removed three scripts from a manila folder, and passed them out. 'I've underlined your parts. Tango, you're Kristi. Freya, you're Lynn. I, of course, will play myself. Take a few minutes to look them over.'

After glancing through her script, Freya spent the remaining time looking over Tango. The girl knew she was being watched, and seemed to approve. As she read, she casually loosened her vest. She twisted in such a way that a nipple appeared in the laces.

Todd paid no attention.

She was doing it for Freya alone.

'Ready?' Todd asked.

'Ready when you are,' Tango said. 'How come we're doing this? You know what I mean? I'm just curious, is all.' She fluttered the script. 'This looks like just what they said except for their names and a couple things. Maybe I'm just ignorant, but it seems kind of funny to me.'

'Their voices simply aren't what I want,' said Todd.

She shrugged. 'It's your dime, honey.'

'Let's begin.'

# CHAPTER FIFTEEN

They walked along the balcony to the door of Connie's apartment. She pushed her key toward the lock, but Pete stopped her hand.

'Let me,' he said.

'I didn't catch that,' said Connie. 'The light's off.'

Pete shook his head. He took the key from her, and opened the apartment door. No lights were on inside, either, so he didn't bother to speak. He stepped into the room, ahead of her, and found a light switch on the wall. A lamp beside the couch came on.

'You're certainly acting mysterious,' she said.

'Just careful. Some guys, when they're dumped, they do crazy things.'

'Dal's never been violent,' she said.

'That you know of.'

'I don't think he'd do anything to hurt me.'

Pete shrugged. 'If he bought an engagement ring, he's serious enough to be a threat. I ran into a guy once, he threw his fiancée out a fourteenth-story window because some fellow sent her flowers for her birthday. Turned out, they came from her brother.'

'You're full of grim stories,' Connie said, smiling as if she wanted more. 'Would you like a drink?'

'Ah, a libation,' he said, doing his Fields voice. 'Nothing I'd rather partake of, my dear.' It was out of his mouth before he realized she probably wouldn't understand his distorted lip movements. He didn't have time for embarrassment to set in, though.

'Come up and see me sometime,' she said.

He laughed. 'You're remarkable.'

'When I'm bad, I'm better.'

He took hold of her hands. 'Very true,' he said. 'You were very, very bad this afternoon.'

Her face, still flushed from a day in the sun, turned a deeper red. 'You were pretty bad, yourself. Now, what would you like, a beer?'

'Great.'

They went into the kitchen and Connie took two bottles of Budweiser from the refrigerator. 'Want a glass?' she asked.

'The bottle's fine. I think I'll use the facilities first, though.'

'Right through there.' She pointed.

Pete used the toilet, but didn't return immediately to the living-room. First, he stepped into another room and turned on the light. Connie's office. He stepped past cluttered, metal bookshelves and opened a closet door.

'What're you doing?'

He turned to Connie. She stood in the doorway, frowning slightly.

'Just snooping.'

'You're looking for Dal. You think he's hiding somewhere, just waiting for you to leave so he can jump out and cut my throat.'

'It happens.'

'You worry me, Pete, you know that?'

'Can't be too careful.'

'I think you *can* be too careful. If you have to spend your life looking over your shoulder, always afraid there might be some terrible villain back there just waiting for you to let your guard down so he can jump you . . . Yeah, I think you can be too careful. Where's the fun, if you're always on your toes for disaster to strike?'

'Oh, I have my share.'

'Shall I show you the bedroom, or have you already checked it out?'

'Not yet.'

He followed her into the bedroom, and grinned as she rushed to the bed, dropped to her knees, and peered under the draping coverlet. 'What on *earth?*' She reached into the space beneath the bed. 'I wonder what that . . . *aaah!*' Her body lurched forward. Belly down, she twisted and kicked. She clutched the bedframe as if to keep herself from being pulled under.

Pete ran to her side. He reached down for the bedframe, ready to fling it aside, when Connie grabbed his hand.

He saw her smile.

'That wasn't funny,' he said.

'Yes it was.'

She pulled him down to her, and kissed him.

When his hand slid under her blouse, he was surprised to feel the smooth, bare skin of her breast. She must've taken her bikini off while he was in the bathroom. He pulled the blouse up. The nipple was rigid in his mouth, and had a slightly salty taste.

He moved a hand under her skirt. Up her thigh. Her bikini pants were also gone.

'You're a darling,' he said.

She didn't answer. Of course not. His mouth was on her breast.

He raised his head. Connie's eyes lowered to his lips.

'You're a darling,' he repeated.

With a smile, she reached both hands inside his shorts, and held him.

'Would you like your beer now?' Connie asked.

'It's probably warm.'

'We'll make believe we're in Ireland, drinking lukewarm Guinness in a pub.'

'I'd rather be here,' Pete said.

'Back in a jiffy.' As she climbed off the bed, Pete patted her bare rump. She walked to the bedroom door and looked back at him. He lay on the sheets, hands folded under his head, his limp penis lying against his thigh. 'Have you no modesty?' she asked.

'A little late for that.'

'True,' she said.

There'd been plenty of modesty, that afternoon, when he took her into his house near Venice beach. A lot of drinking on the couch, a lot of talking until the right moment came and he took her into his arms. They wore only their swimsuits. Hands stroked exposed skin, moved hesitantly over the fabric, and finally explored beneath the swimsuits. At last, they were naked against each other, slick from suntan oil and sweat, gritty with sand, and they made love on the couch.

They showered together.

They ate hamburgers.

They made love again, this time on the fresh sheets of Pete's bed.

After all that, Connie realized, she still felt modest in front of him. To go for the drinks, stark naked, seemed slightly daring, slightly naughty, as if she were flaunting her nudity to arouse him.

Still in the doorway, she stared at his penis. She lowered

114

her hands, and caressed her thighs.

Pete shook his head, grinning. 'What're you up to?' he asked.

'Oh, nothing.'

Her thumbs slid against her groin, and she watched his penis rise.

'Forget the beer,' he said.

'Can't. We've got to replenish our vital fluids.'

She turned from him. She felt sexy and silly and bold – and happier than she'd been since . . . No, don't think about Dave.

Too late.

But the memory didn't hurt, the way it always had. Strange. Very strange.

She stepped into the living-room.

'Having fun?' Dal asked. He was on the couch, sitting with both feet on the floor and his back straight.

Connie slapped her hands to her breasts and spun away. She hurried into the bedroom.

Pete was already up.

'Stay here,' Connie said. 'I'll take care of it.' She jerked her robe from its closet hook, and put it on as she rushed into the hallway.

Dal still sat on the couch. 'You couldn't even wait for me to move out,' he said.

'I . . . I didn't expect you.'

'Where'd you think I'd be – at my *girlfriend's* house?'

'Dal, please.'

'Our bed.'

'It's my bed.'

'Christ, you should've heard yourselves carrying on.'

'You shouldn't have listened.'

'You're my girl, Connie.'

'Not anymore.'

'You'll always be my girl. I love you. Just remember that,

when he dumps you. He will, you know. Once he's tired of you, he'll dump you. I've seen his type. Jaguar, beach house, rugged good looks. I give you about a week.'

'Get out of here.'

'A week, and you'll come running to me, you'll come begging.'

'Come back at noon tomorrow. Your belongings will be outside the door waiting for you.'

'You'll come begging,' he said again. Then he left.

# CHAPTER SIXTEEN

'Okay, ladies, that wraps it up.' Todd took out his wallet, and paid Tango with twenty-dollar bills – ten of them.

'Don't you get paid?' she asked Freya.

'I'm a partner.'

'Ah, so.'

'You go on ahead, Todd, I'll drive Tango home.'

'Far be it from me to stand in the way of true romance. Be sure to lock up when you leave.'

'I will.'

When Todd was gone, they left the control room. Freya led Tango by the hand. They entered a room at the end of the hall, and Freya turned on the lights.

'You're so beautiful,' she said. She reached for the laces of Tango's vest.

'Ah-ah. No freebies, honey.'

'How much?'

'Depends what you want.'

Freya opened her purse. Her hands shook as she drew out her billfold. She counted the cash. To her dismay, she found only a ten-dollar bill, and three ones.

'For that, honey, you get diddle-shit.'

'I . . . I have plenty more at home. I thought I had . . .'

Tango smiled. 'That's all right. You just take me to where

the money is. This old house is a bit too haunty for my taste, anyhow.'

'I want you here, Tango.'

'No money, no fuckee.'

Freya sighed. 'Well, let's go to my apartment, then.'

They left the bedroom, and walked down the narrow hallway. Freya watched their strange, faint shadows on the walls. She remembered how Tina had danced and twirled as if fascinated by those shadows. Oh, how she would love to see Tango doing that . . . If only she had brought more cash along. Another night, maybe.

They descended the stairway. Neither spoke. The wood creaked under their weight.

They crossed the foyer.

Freya reached for the doorknob.

It didn't turn. Alarmed, she glanced at Tango.

'Let me try.' Tango struggled with the latch and knob. 'Shit, lady, that sucker's locked.'

'There's a back way out,' Freya said.

'There better be.'

She led the way, turning on lights as she went. They passed through a dining-room with a chandelier hanging over a large, mahogany table. Crystal goblets glimmered on the shelves of the highboy. Freya paused to admire them. Someday, they would all belong to her.

'Move,' Tango said. 'I want *outa* here.'

Freya pushed through a swinging door to the kitchen. She turned on the light, and stopped so abruptly that Tango bumped her.

She stumbled forward.

The man in the white apron and chef's hat clutched her arm, and flung her aside.

'I want dark meat,' Schreck said.

118

Swinging around, Tango threw herself at the door. She wasn't quick enough. He grabbed her hair and jerked her toward him. Hooking an arm around her throat, he lifted her.

Tango squirmed and kicked. Her boot heels thudded against Schreck's shins, but had no effect. Veins stood out on her face and her eyes bulged from the pressure of his grip. Her struggles, frantic at first, became feeble.

She was carried to a counter.

Freya got to her feet, watching.

'Stay out of the shot,' Schreck muttered.

He lifted Tango onto the counter.

Freya spotted the camera on a swivel mount near the ceiling. Todd had made no attempt to hide this one. He must've installed it this afternoon. It was directly above the counter where Schreck had placed Tango.

'Cut the laces,' Freya said.

'Shut up.'

'Come on, do it.'

'Leave,' said Schreck.

'I want to watch.'

'You want to watch?' He picked up a meat cleaver and swung around. 'Out!' he roared.

'It's all right with Todd if I . . .'

Schreck suddenly grinned. 'Come here.'

Her skin pricked. She shook her head.

'Come here! You want to watch.'

'No. That's . . .'

'Come here, or I kill you.'

She hesitated, wondering if she should try to run. She didn't dare. With slow, unsteady steps, she approached Schreck.

She watched his eyes. They were wet and bulging. They were somehow like spiders. They gave her goose-bumps, and nauseated her.

119

He gripped her arm.

'Watch,' he said.

Tango moaned.

Schreck put down the cleaver.

'Watch, but don't touch.'

'Help me,' Tango whispered.

Schreck picked up a knife and two-pronged carving fork.

Freya's fear turned to excitement as he sliced through the laces and opened Tango's vest.

The woman raised her head. She looked at Freya. 'Please . . .'

'Head down,' said Schreck, and plunged the fork into her eye.

Freya spun away. She doubled over, vomiting. Before she was done, Schreck jerked her upright by the hair.

'You want to watch,' he explained. 'Mustn't miss a moment.'

# CHAPTER SEVENTEEN

After Connie insisted he leave, Dal headed for Elizabeth's house. Halfway there, he changed his mind. If he went to her, he would have to admit defeat; a temporary set-back, at least. Elizabeth wouldn't like that.

He might lose her.

Rather than chance that, he decided to spend the night in a motel. He found a room at the Palm Court, just off Pico. It was a tiny room, but clean.

The television picture had shadows.

The bed had Magic Fingers, but Dal had no quarter.

He felt very depressed as he climbed into bed. For a long time, he couldn't sleep. All so damned complicated. He only wanted Elizabeth. To get her, though – to keep her – he had to marry Connie.

Not necessarily.

He only had to get rich.

*Only.*

If it were easy to get rich, he'd have done it long before now.

He could think of only one way to do it: marry money. Must be plenty of rich gals around town. But he only knew one.

Damn, he was halfway to home base before this Peter stuck his nose into the picture.

Sure, his nose. Stuck in more than that, the bastard.

Look on the bright side, though: maybe he *will* dump Connie. Could happen.

Especially with a little help.

Dal lay with his eyes shut, oblivious to the noise of cars passing just outside his window, and thought about ways to help.

In the morning, he woke up feeling good. He took a long, hot shower. Then he went for a walk. He ate a breakfast of sausage and eggs at Sambos. At a Drug Mart down the street, he brought an injector razor, a can of shaving cream, and roll-on deodorant.

Couldn't face Elizabeth looking like a bum.

Grinning, he returned to his motel room. He shaved, rubbed the sticky ball on his armpits, and checked out.

He practiced his story as he drove to Elizabeth's house.

She opened the door, looking as radiant as Dal felt. She wore a silken robe that matched her green eyes. It was belted loosely shut. It barely hung low enough to cover her groin.

'You look beautiful this morning,' Dal said.

'Don't stand there gawking. Get in here and kiss me.'

He gladly obeyed. As he kissed her, his hands roamed down the slick robe and under it. He squeezed the cool skin of her rump. He pressed her tightly against him.

'I don't have much time,' he said. 'Connie's at church. I just had to stop by, though.'

'Did it go well?'

'It went great. Unbelievable.'

'Tell me.'

'Later,' he said, grinding his hardness against her.

'Now,' she said. She pushed herself away, and walked ahead of him into the living-room. She sat on a white daven-port, and put her feet up.

Dal sat by her feet. 'I did just as you suggested. I bought

her flowers, on my way home yesterday.'

'And did she like them?'

'She loved them. Absolutely loved them. She cried, and apologized for the way she burnt dinner, and wanted to know where I'd spent the night.'

'What did you tell her?'

'That I'd spent most of it just driving around aimlessly, in a daze. And that I'd finally parked on a quiet street, somewhere, and gone to sleep on the backseat.'

'Lovely,' Elizabeth said. Her foot patted his thigh.

'Oh, Connie ate it up. I've never seen her look more guilty.'

'I hope you quickly moved in for the kill.'

'You'd have been proud of me.'

'Would I?'

'While Connie was crying and full of remorse, I took her into my arms and said, "Why don't I take you out for dinner, tonight, and we'll have a good time and forget all about our little quarrel."'

'And did you?'

'We did.'

'Bravo.'

Dal patted the lightly tanned top of her foot, and moved his hand up her shin. 'We went to a quiet, French restaurant . . .'

'Which one?'

'Henri's.'

'Ah, lovely.'

'And I proposed to her.'

'Did she accept?'

'How could she refuse?'

Dal slipped his hand beneath her upraised leg, and caressed the smoothness of her calf.

'She did accept?'

'Of course. And I gave her the ring.'

'Did it fit?'

'It was a bit tight. We'll take it to a jeweler, next week, and have it expanded.'

'She liked the ring?'

'She was flabbergasted. She said, "It's magnificent." I think she was a bit shocked to think I would spend that kind of money, but I didn't hear her complain.'

'So, you are now an engaged man.'

'Yep.'

'When's the big day?'

'July thirty-first.'

Elizabeth grinned. She swung her leg upward, and propped it on the back of the couch. 'Let me be the first to congratulate you, dear.'


'I don't want to,' Connie said.

'It won't take long,' Pete told her. 'I'll give you a hand. Both hands, if you prefer.'

'I'd really rather not. Let's just go somewhere. He can come in and get the stuff, himself. If I put it outside, I'd be worried someone might take it.'

'That'd be too bad.'

'I'm the one who'd feel guilty about it.'

'You aren't afraid he'll come in and tear the place up?'

'Dal? No. He's basically pretty timid.'

'Those are the kind who go haywire when things get rough.'

'Really, Pete, you worry too much.'

'You keep telling me.'

'Because it's true.'

'Even paranoiacs have enemies.'

She smiled. 'I know. And a broken clock is right twice a day. More coffee?'

'I'll get it.'

Pete left her. Alone on the private, rear balcony, she moved her lawn chair closer to the railing so her face would be in the sunlight. She sat back, and took a deep breath. The morning breeze was cool, the sun hot. She wondered if she had ever felt this good before.

Sure. Yesterday. And Friday night.

Being with Pete.

It was like being reborn – young and fresh and happy, the day ahead full of promise.

He came back, and handed her the coffee mug. He sat down on the chair facing her.

'How about going to the Marina for a champagne brunch?' he asked.

'Great!'

# CHAPTER EIGHTEEN

Freya stayed home from work Monday morning. She called in sick. Though she felt fine as she dialed, her heart began to race and her stomach suddenly hurt when Dr Eginton answered the phone.

Sheila Eginton, Dean of Women, the condescending bitch.

'I do hope it's nothing serious,' she said.

'I do too,' said Freya, making her voice tight as if holding back a groan of pain. 'I . . . I'm going to the doctor this morning.'

'I see. We'll do our best to forge along without you.'

'Fine.'

'Do take care of yourself.'

'I will.' She hung up.

Well, she wouldn't have to put up with bitch Eginton much longer. If everything went as planned, she'd be kissing the job good-bye at the end of the summer quarter.

Too bad she couldn't get Edgy out to Todd's house. She'd love to see her in Schreck's hands. The dean was too big, though; her disappearance would cause a stink.

So far, their caution had paid off.

Only the disappearance of the camping girls got any play in the news. Todd had been a bit careless there. Overconfident, maybe. But he assured Freya that he would hang onto that tape,

127

not even send it to the lab for conversion to 35mm, until the thing had blown over.

Then there was the business with Tina. That should've worked perfectly; neither Tina nor her boyfriend had living parents to miss them. Tina moved out, ran off with the guy, and left no forwarding address. That was supposed to be the story if anyone asked. Freya should've stuck to it when the roommate called. That'd been a dumb mistake. But who would think the gal'd keep pushing it?

Well, they took care of that little problem. Nobody had popped up, yet, asking about her. A good sign. Maybe she hadn't even been missed. Could be trouble, though, when they showed the film.

Good old Brit might have friends who frequent the Haunted Palace.

Shit, why worry? With the over-dub and dyed hair, who would recognize her?

Should've dyed Tina's hair. Couldn't, of course, the way it was shot. Probably wouldn't be able to do it with Chelsea, either. The gal has to be under control, for that. Like what's-her-face in the *Inquisitor* film. Or that moronic hitchhiker Todd picked up for his first one, *Schreck the Executioner*.

A small change of appearance, like that, was probably enough to keep folks from recognizing their friends.

If she could think of a way to disguise Chelsea . . . What the shit, Chelsea's from Oakland. That's a long, long way from L.A.

Freya poured herself a cup of tea, and glanced at the kitchen clock. Seven-thirty.

Banks open at ten.

Chelsea the Pig should arrive by eleven.

Plenty of time to kill. She went into the living-room, turned on the television, and switched the channel to *Good Morning, America*.

At 10:32, the doorbell rang. Freya got up, tugging at her tight shorts, and opened the door.

Chelsea, a cheerless smile spreading her cheeks, waved a handful of green in Freya's face. 'Six hundred bucks,' she said. 'Didn't think I'd be here, did you?'

'I never doubted for a moment.'

Today, her T-shirt read, 'Save a tree – eat a beaver'.

Freya took the money. She stood in the doorway, counting it. Six hundred dollars, in fifties.

'Receipt, please.'

'Of course. Come on in.' As she filled out a receipt, she said, 'Are you always this obnoxious, Chelsea?'

'When it suits me.'

'Suppose we call a truce? I'll help you bring your stuff up, and I'll even take you out to dinner, tonight, to celebrate.'

'You'll pay?'

'Of course.' She waved the six hundred at Chelsea. 'I just came into a lot of money.'

'You're a doozy.'

They went down to the street. Freya saw a dull, gray van plastered with bumper stickers: NUKE IRAN; PLEASE TAILGATE – I NEED THE MONEY; I NEVER HAD IT; I BRAKE FOR MIDGETS; STILLBORNS HAVE MORE FUN, and half a dozen others.

'Your van, I presume.'

'How'd you guess?'

As they unloaded it, Freya appraised the goods. Not much looked promising. The stereo, portable television, and typewriter might bring in a few bucks, but everything else looked like junk.

'Where you taking me for dinner?'

'It's a lovely restaurant up the coast.'

'Up the coast? How *far* up the coast?

129

'Only about fifteen minutes,' Freya said.

'There's gotta be someplace closer.'

'Nothing this nice. It has a lovely view of the ocean.'

'Do I have to dress up?'

'Is it possible?'

'Now who's obnoxious?'

'You look very nice,' Freya said when Chelsea came out of the bedroom in a dress that looked like an old table cloth.

'I pass inspection?'

'With flying colors.'

They went down to Freya's car.

'Fifteen minutes?'

'About that. Maybe a little longer. The place is worth it, though. Best food you've ever tasted.'

'Hope they serve plenty,' Chelsea said. 'I could eat a horse.'

'They don't serve horses.'

'You said fifteen minutes.'

'We're almost there,' Freya said. The sun was higher above the ocean than last time, and made the driving easier.

'Lot of trouble to go through for a dinner.'

'This place is special.'

'So you say.'

'Wait till you see it.'

When Freya swung onto the turnoff, Chelsea said, 'You've got to be kidding. There's no restaurant up there.'

Fortunately, Todd had remembered to leave the gate open. That would've really aroused Chelsea's suspicion. So far, she didn't seem worried – only curious.

When Chelsea saw the house, she shook her head. 'That's it?'

'That's it.'

'Is this a joke?'

'It's a restaurant. The finest restaurant for miles.'

'I'll believe it when I see it.'

A single car, a blue Plymouth, was parked in front. Freya pulled alongside it.

'If this place is so great,' Chelsea said, 'why's there only one car?'

'It's very exclusive.'

Freya climbed from the car. Chelsea opened her door against the Plymouth, and squeezed out. 'Couldn't park any closer to it, could you?'

Freya smiled. 'Don't be a spoilsport.'

'This is sport?'

They headed for the porch stairs. As they started up, the front door opened. Todd stepped out, wearing a tux. He held the door wide.

'Ah,' he said. 'Young ladies, we've been expecting you. Welcome to Hillside Manor. I am Clarence, the maitre d'.'

They followed him into the foyer.

'As you see, young ladies, Hillside Manor is a most unusual restaurant. It is the home of Rudolph Webb, noted chef and author of *Webb's Cuisine*. He opened his home to the public, fifteen years ago, as a – shall we say – testing ground for his recipes.'

They entered the dining-room. The long, mahogany table was set for three. Todd seated Freya and Chelsea across from each other near the head of the table.

'As diners here,' he continued, 'you shall be partners in the creation of an original dish. Would you care for a cocktail before dinner is served?'

'Gin and tonic,' Chelsea said.

'I'll have white wine. The house wine, please.'

'Splendid.'

Todd turned away, and disappeared through the swinging door to the kitchen.

'This is weird,' Chelsea said. 'We're guinea pigs for this chef, huh?'

'Guinea pigs never had it so good.'

'How did you find this joint?'

'A date brought me here. I was awfully nervous, at first. I didn't really believe it was a restaurant. I thought he'd tricked me, and brought me here for some kind of mischief. It is a rather creepy old house. But I was in for a pleasant shock. We had duck in some kind of marvelous wine sauce. Probably the best meal I'd ever had.'

Todd returned with the drinks. Freya raised her glass of wine. 'Here's blood in your eye.'

'Mud,' Chelsea corrected.

'Whatever.'

They drank.

Chelsea nodded toward the place setting at the head of the table. 'Is somebody going to join us?'

'Oh yes. The chef himself. He'll come out, after the food is prepared.'

'Wonderful,' Chelsea muttered.

'You'll enjoy it. He really is quite a fascinating guy.'

'The food better be good. I'd hate to barf in front of the chef.'

'Young ladies – your host, Rudolph Webb.'

Todd held open the kitchen door, and Schreck entered the dining-room. He walked stiffly to the table, his lean face solemn, and held out a hand toward Chelsea.

The girl made a sickly smile, but shook the offered hand.

'Welcome,' said Schreck. 'You are?'

'Chelsea.'

He stopped around the table. Freya shuddered as he took her hand. In his black tuxedo, he looked to Freya like an undertaker. A pallid, gaunt undertaker who spent too much time with his corpses.

132

'I'm Freya,' she said.

'Yes, I remember. Welcome again to my home.'

He sat. Todd poured red wine into his glass. He raised it to his thin lips. As he drank, a trickle slid from one corner of his mouth and dripped from his chin. He didn't seem to notice. When he emptied the glass, Todd filled it again.

'Refresh the ladies' drinks,' Schreck commanded. 'Then serve the soup.'

Todd took their glasses away.

'The first course,' said Schreck, 'will be a delicate soup of meat and herbs. I'm certain you will find it most unusual, rather like the Mexican albondigas, but more hearty.' He grinned, his lips drawing back to reveal crooked, dark teeth and pale gums.

Todd brought the drinks. Freya found her hand shaking as she raised the glass. Chelsea met her eyes, and glared.

'I eat with my guests,' said Schreck, 'so that I might have the opportunity to savour their reactions as they savour my cuisine. It is an indulgence on my part, but I believe we should permit ourselves to enjoy the effects of our creative efforts. I am, if you please, the playwright attending the opening night performance of his drama – gauging audience reaction, thrilling to the laughter and tension and applause, noting lapses where, perhaps, the script might require an adjustment.'

Todd entered, pushing a serving cart. He set a bowl of soup at each place, and returned to the kitchen.

Freya eyed the brown, lumpy liquid in her bowl. It looked identical to the soup in front of Chelsea and Schreck. Todd had assured her, though . . .

'*Bon appetit*,' said Schreck.

He dipped a spoon deep into his bowl, and brought up bits of meat along with onions and other limp vegetables. The spoon dripped as he raised it to his mouth. He chewed slowly, as if

133

probing the mixture for its subtle flavors. Then he swallowed, and sighed with pleasure.

Freya, fighting to control her nausea, took a sip of wine.

She picked up her spoon, slid it into her soup, and stirred as she watched Chelsea take her first taste.

The girl's spoon shimmered with broth. She sipped it, nodded, and smiled nervously at Schreck. 'Delicious,' she said.

Freya continued to stir. Mine's only lamb, she told herself. But she couldn't bring herself to try it. She watched Chelsea bring up a spoonful from the bottom. It was laden with vegetables and chunks of meat. It vanished into Chelsea's mouth. The girl chewed, and nodded.

Freya's stomach convulsed. Vomit came to her throat. She swallowed hard, and finished her wine.

'It's great,' Chelsea said. 'Best soup I've ever had.'

Schreck grinned and nodded.

'I normally don't care much for soup,' she continued. 'It's usually so bland.' She shoveled in another spoonful. And another. 'Have you tried it?' she asked Freya.

Freya nodded. 'Excellent.'

'Will this be in your next cookbook?'

'Most certainly,' said Schreck.

'I'd really like the recipe.' She spooned more into her mouth. As she chewed, she said, 'What kind of meat is it?'

'Can you guess?'

'I don't know. Pork?'

'No.'

She raised a spoonful, and gazed at it. With her teeth, she picked out a chunk of meat and ate it separately. She shrugged. 'What is it, rabbit or something?'

Schreck grinned. 'You're getting warm.'

She finished the spoonful, dredged the bottom of her dish, and came up with a larger piece. She studied it. 'Hey, this one's still got the bone.' With her free hand, she lifted it from the spoon and turned it over. Freya glanced at the small, shiny shield of nail.

Chelsea dropped the piece as if it burnt her. It splashed into her soup. She shoved her chair back, but Schreck grabbed her arm.

'What was it?' he asked.

'A . . . a *toe!*'

'Oh dear, you guessed correctly.' Schreck chuckled.

Chelsea gagged. She tried to struggle free from Schreck's grip, but couldn't. She threw up on herself, and began to cry.

Todd entered with the white wine. 'I hope you're enjoying your meal,' he said, smiling.

'Yes,' said Schreck. 'I believe we're ready for the next course.'

'Very good.'

'Leave the bottle,' Freya said. She filled her glass, quickly drank it all, and filled it again.

Chelsea continued to cry.

'I don't understand,' said Schreck, 'why you're so upset. Only moments ago, you were raving about its flavor.'

'You're *crazy!*' Chelsea sobbed.

'I'm sure you'll appreciate the next course even more.'

Todd brought in a platter and set it down in front of Chelsea.

Chelsea began to scream.

'A true delicacy. Lightly simmered visage over steaming linguini, topped with a delicate tomato sauce. I call it Face Marinara.'

Freya watched, disgusted and fascinated, as Schreck threw Chelsea to the floor and forced her to eat.

He pinched her nostrils shut so she had to open her mouth.

He snapped her fingers.

He tore open her dress and stabbed her with a fork.

At last, she choked on a mouthful of scorched flesh. She kicked and convulsed and turned blue and died.

Todd entered the room, clapping. 'Bravo, bravo!'

He slapped Schreck on the back.

'Satisfied?' he asked Freya.

She nodded. 'Thanks,' she said.

'Well, shall we retire to the control room, and see what Bruno got for us?'

'Todd,' Schreck said, and nodded towards the corpse.

'Certainly. She's all yours.'

As Schreck picked up the body, Freya followed Todd from the room. She grabbed his arm. 'Mine *was* lamb, wasn't it?'

'Princess,' he said, 'what kind of beast do you think I am?'

# CHAPTER NINETEEN

Connie did a lot of good work, Tuesday. The scenes filled her head as if she had become Sandra Dane. She could smell the sour breath of Sandra's stepfather as he fell upon her. She could feel his weight, and his rough hands tearing her crinoline – hear his yelp of pain as she kneed him in the groin.

The warm night air. The smell of the stable. The feel of her stallion, Thunder, between her legs as she rode him bareback over the fields. Her sudden fear as Thunder leaped a fence, and stumbled, and she flew head over heels.

The Union soldier, one of Sherman's hateful marauders, coming to help her. He had Pete's smile, and Pete's eyes. Though she'd heard dreadful tales of Sherman's army, this man seemed different. She knew she had nothing to fear from him.

A light flashed on her desk.

Damn!

She dropped her pen on the spiral notebook, and got up. Her muscles felt stiff. She stretched as she made her way to the front door.

She half expected to find Dal outside, returning for something he would claim to have forgotten when he moved out, Sunday.

But it wasn't Dal.

It was a young woman with troubled eyes.

'Yes?'

'You're Connie, aren't you?'

'Yes.'

'May I come in, please? I have to talk with you about Pete.'

'About Pete? What's . . . ?'

'I'm his wife – Sandra.'

Connie grabbed the doorknob to steady herself. 'His wife?'

'Yes.'

'That's impossible.'

The woman shook her head. 'It's quite possible, I'm afraid.'

'He would've told me.'

'Would he?'

'I've been to his house. There was no . . . He *can't* be married!'

'He took you to his beach house in Venice. That's where he always takes his . . . his women. May I come in?'

'No! You're lying! This is a trick or something.'

'I want you to stop seeing Pete. I know he . . . he can be quite overwhelming and perhaps you think you love him. He always has that effect. I've . . . I've put up with it for quite a while. God knows how many times I've thought about divorcing him. But I love him, Connie, and . . . and I've just found out that I'm pregnant. I'm going to have Pete's baby.'

'No!'

'I'm sorry. I know this must be awful for you – but think what it's like for me. My husband . . . He didn't come home, the whole weekend. He said he was on a case, but I knew it was a lie. The same old lie. So I went to the beach house, Saturday. I went in. I have a key, of course. I went in, and heard you both, and . . .' Her chin trembled. She bit down on her lower lip, and took a deep breath. 'I want my husband back, Connie. I want the father of my baby. Please. You seem like a decent person, Connie. Don't . . . don't keep my husband away from me.' She wiped tears from her eyes, and walked away.

Dal threw his necktie onto the couch, and stepped into the small kitchen area of his new apartment. He took his gin bottle from a carton on the breakfast bar. After a short search in the crowded box, he found his vermouth. He slipped a plastic cup off the end of a stack, and made himself a martini.

No olives.

Well, shit.

He opened his freezer compartment, eyed the stack of frozen dinners, and decided to eat out. No reason to eat that stuff, cramped up in this tiny apartment.

He'd taken the first furnished one-bedroom apartment he could find, on Sunday. After Connie's spacious, open place, this cubicle was enough to give him claustrophobia. Didn't even have direct access to the outside. Instead, you walk down a hallway and downstairs to get out.

He'd known, even as he carried in his few possessions, that he would hate this place.

He just had to keep reminding himself – it's not for long.

Then he met Etta, the girl across the hall, an actress, the solution to his problem.

He wondered if she'd returned yet.

Martini in hand, he crossed over to her apartment and knocked. He heard footsteps. He smiled at the peephole, and the door opened.

'Loverboy. Come on in.'

He entered admiring Etta. She was gorgeous, with a deep tan and thick blonde hair, and curves that never quit. Of course, she couldn't compare to Elizabeth.

'Did you do it?' he asked.

'Sure did, honey. Give a sip.' She took the martini from his hand, drank some, and handed it back. 'I was fabulous. You should've seen me. You? Bite my tongue. Darryl Zanuck should've seen me. Give this a listen.'

She turned on a small, cassette recorder.

For a few seconds, Dal heard the buzz of blank tape. Then came Etta's voice.

'Testing, testing, *uno, dos, tres.*'

More blank tape.

'Yes?' Connie's voice.

'You're Connie, aren't you?'

'Yes.'

He listened to all the tape. At first, the sound of Connie's voice made him ache. He wondered why he'd let himself lose her. But her shock pleased him. She really took it hard. Good. She deserved it for cheating on him. He sipped his martini. His power thrilled him – to tear apart all that trust and love by such a simple deception!

'What do you think?' Etta asked when the tape ended.

'I think you deserve an Oscar.'

'Right on.'

Dal took out his wallet. He gave her a hundred dollars, in twenties.

'If you ever need me again,' she said, 'I'll be here.'

'We'll see how this turns out.'

'Yeah, well, good luck.'

'The ring.'

'Oh! You mean I don't get to keep it?' With a laugh, she slipped it off her finger and gave it to Dal.

Briefly, he considered asking Etta to join him for supper. He decided against it, though. He didn't feel like risking a refusal. Besides, if Elizabeth found out . . .

\* \* \*

Connie felt desolate. She took a long bath, but that didn't help. Her mind replayed the conversation, went over every minute of her times with Pete, seeking unknown answers.

She wished she'd asked the woman for proof. A driver's license. Some kind of evidence to back up her awful words.

But Connie didn't want proof.

She wanted, so much, to disbelieve the woman. She clinged to the hope that it was a mistake, or a prank, or a vicious lie.

Maybe Dal put the woman up to it. For vengeance. Or to make her drop Pete.

But she knew, even as she thought such things, that she was clutching desperately at straws.

The woman had told the truth.

Pete's married.

He'd been lying to her, twisting her emotions, encouraging her to fall in love. Trickery to get her into bed.

No, she couldn't believe that.

She didn't know what to believe.

She fell onto her bed, and stared at the ceiling. Her mind was a helpless tangle.

She looked at the clock. Nearly seven. Pete should be here by now. Unless he knows. Maybe his wife confronted him today, and he'll never come again.

She covered her eyes with a pillow, then quickly flung the pillow aside. If her eyes were covered, she wouldn't see the doorbell light.

It began to flash.

Her stomach knotted. She felt as if she might vomit.

*Please, let it be Pete.*

She left the bedroom.

*Let him tell me it's a lie. Please, make it not be true.*

She opened the door, and it was Pete. He smiled, and stepped toward her. She held out a hand to stop him.

'Don't,' she said.
'What's wrong?'
'You're married.'
His face turned ashen.
'Admit it. You're married!'
'How . . . How did you find out?'

# CHAPTER TWENTY

Pete swung his foot into the doorway. The door hit it, stopped against his shoe. With his shoulder, he forced the gap wider. 'Connie, let me in. Let me in, damn it.'

She said nothing. She made whimpery, grunting sounds as she tried to hold the door shut.

Then it was open. She stepped back, shaking her head and crying.

'Listen to me. I love you, Connie. Listen to me.'

'Oh Pete, how could you? How could you do this to me, to Sandra?'

'Who's Sandra?'

'Your wife, for Christsake! She was here today. She knows all about us.'

'My wife's name is Barbara. She knows nothing about us, and couldn't give a damn what I do.'

'That's impossible.'

'It's true.' Pete took hold of Connie's shoulders. 'She left me. We were only married for two years. We lived in the beach house: Barbara and me and her brother. He was a college student. He paid a third of the monthly mortgage, and . . . the thing is, he and my wife were lovers. Apparently, it had been going on for years. It's still going on, for all I know. The only reason she married me, in the first place, was to make her arrangement with her brother look innocent. I just happened to stumble over them, one day. They thought I was going to kill them, or something, so they both lit out. That's the last I ever saw of my wife.'

'Oh Pete.' She hugged him tightly. 'I thought . . . I was so afraid . . .'

He stroked her hair, then moved back so she could see his lips. 'I haven't seen or heard from my wife in nearly a year.'

'Then who . . . ? A woman came here this afternoon, Pete. She said she's your wife, Sandra, and that she's pregnant, and wants me to stop seeing you.'

'What did she look like?' he asked.

'She was about my height, blonde, very attractive.'

Brit Anderson? That hardly seemed likely. Their relationship hadn't been serious enough to warrant such a drastic maneuver. He'd only gone out with her a few times, they'd never had sex, and he hadn't seen her for nearly two weeks. If she were so upset by his neglect, she would've been in touch with him.

Well, she did make those two calls the day after their last date. Strange calls. She'd sounded upset. He phoned her back, several times, but no one ever answered. After meeting Connie, that Wednesday, he stopped trying to get in touch with her.

'Did you notice anything unusual about her?'

'Like scars?' Connie shook her head. 'Nothing I can think of.'

'Any jewelry?' Brit, he remembered, wore a gold chain necklace with a star.

'Not that I . . . oh, a diamond ring. I did notice that. A diamond wedding ring. It looked . . .' Her face hardened. 'It looked like the ring Dal had for me.'

'Well, wedding rings all look pretty much alike, don't they?'

'This had a Marquise diamond. You know, one that's cut so it's kind of long and pointed at both ends. They're not as common as round solitaires.'

'You think Dal might've put her up to it?'

'Who else would want to? He must be trying to break us up.'

'He'll have to do better than that,' Pete said.

'A lot better,' said Connie. She moved into his arms, and pressed herself close against him. 'A lot better,' she whispered.

Pete spent the next day in his van, keeping watch on the employee parking lot of the Masters Hardware warehouse. According to a tip received by the general manager, a guy named Jesse Cook was the culprit. Every worker in the warehouse knew it, apparently, but only one had been willing to blow the whistle – anonymously, at that.

A simple operation. Cook would walk out, during lunch, and put a case of Schlage locks into his trunk. Or an electric heater, or a food processor, or whatever happened to strike his fancy.

Pete had been hired to catch Cook in the act. This was his third day on the job. So far, Cook had tried nothing.

At quitting time, the wiry little guy came out to his Firebird empty-handed, and left.

Pete reported his lack of progress to the general manager.

'Let's give it till the end of the week,' the man said. 'If he hasn't tipped his hand by then, we'll try a new tack.'

Immediately after leaving, Pete drove into Santa Monica. He left his van in a parking structure on Fourth Street, and walked to the old mall.

Lane Brothers was still open. He entered, and stepped

toward the counter. There were half a dozen people in the small, quiet store. Three of the young men looked like sales clerks. One glanced at him, and quickly looked away.

Had to be Dal.

Pete ignored him. At the counter, he asked for the manager. An older man was called from a back room. 'I'm Owen Lane. May I help you?'

'Yes.' Pete handed the man a business card for Ronald Watts, Special Assistant for Attorney General George Deukmajian. 'I'd like to question one of your employees about an investigation we're conducting.'

Owen Lane blushed. 'Of course. Who do you want to see?'

'Dal Richards.'

'Is it . . . something serious?'

'May I speak to Mr Richards, please?'

'Of course.' He turned away. 'Dal?'

Dal came forward, fastening the center button of his blazer, smiling bravely. His eyes flicked toward Pete, and quickly looked away. 'Yes, Mr Lane?'

'This gentleman is Mr Watts from the Justice Department.' To Pete, he said. 'Would you prefer to talk in my office?'

'Thank you.'

They left Owen Lane outside the door. Pete shut it, and Dal's smile fell away.

'What do you want?' he snapped.

'I'm Pete Harvey.'

'I know.'

'Yes. I figured you might. I've never met you, though. I decided, since we're both interested in Connie, that we should get acquainted.'

'Okay, we're acquainted. Good-bye.'

Pete shook his head.

146

'Look, I've got a customer out there . . .'

'He can wait.'

'What do you want?'

'That was a nasty trick you pulled on Connie.'

'I don't know what . . .'

'Sending my "wife" over.'

'You're nuts.'

'If I'm wrong, I'm sure you'll forgive me.'

'Forgive you for what?'

'Turn around, and put your hands behind your back.'

'No you . . .'

'Yes I do.' Pete spun him around and slapped a handcuff onto his left wrist.

'Hey!'

He grabbed the right hand, and cuffed it.

'Now we're walking out of here.'

'Hey, this is . . .'

'You have the right to remain silent. If you choose to give up that right, everyone in the store is going to notice you.'

'You can't do this!'

'Oh, I think I can.'

Pushing Dal ahead of him, he left the office. Owen Lane looked stunned, his face red, his mouth and eyes gaping.

'Mr Lane . . .' Dal started.

Pete shoved him forward. 'Thank you for your co-operation, Mr Lane.'

'Is he . . . under arrest?'

'I'm afraid so. Good day, sir.'

Pete steered Dal down the mall. Shoppers stared. Children on skateboards stopped and pointed. A gray-whiskered wino limped close, eyed Dal, and said, 'Trow da book at'm.'

When they reached Santa Monica Boulevard, Pete took off the cuffs.

147

Dal was crying softly. 'You bastard,' he said, 'I'll get you for this.'

'Have a nice day,' Pete said, and walked away.

SCREAM GEMS
PRESENTS
OTTO SCHRECK
in
SCHRECK THE MAD DOCTOR

'It won't be long now, my darling,' Schreck says, kneeling beside a bed. 'I have found the perfect specimen. She is so young, so vital. Soon, if the operation succeeds, you shall be heir to her vitality. You shall rise from your bed and walk as you once did, with the buoyancy of youth in your step. Once again, I shall take you into my arms.'

He lifts her hand. It is brown and withered as if the skin has been stretched over bare bones.

'Oh my darling Beatrice, we shall dance through the long, joyous hours of the night. Soon. Oh so soon.'

Leaning forward, he stares down at the face of the corpse. Its mouth is open, its teeth bared in a mirthless grin. He kisses its sunken cheek.

'Goodnight now, my love.'

A young woman lies on an operating table. Her body is covered by a white sheet. Her shoulders are bare.

Opening her eyes, she lifts her head and looks down at herself. She squirms, but can't raise her arms or legs.

The door swings open. Schreck enters, dressed in a green operating smock and cap. As he approaches, he ties a paper mask across his nose and mouth.

'How are you feeling?' he asks.

'Confused.'

'That's quite understandable, Miss Thatcher. Do you recall anything of the accident?'

'Accident?'

'The crash.'

'No, I . . .' She pauses, frowning. 'I remember *El Sombrero*. The Happy Hour. I went there after work and . . . Oh, the pier. A guy was going to take me to the Santa Monica pier. The carousel. You know, the famous carousel there? We were going to . . . He crashed?'

'Apparently, he'd been drinking heavily. He hit a telephone pole.'

She shakes her head. 'I don't feel . . . Was I hurt?'

'I'm afraid so, Miss Thatcher.'

'But . . .'

'You've been unconscious since they brought you in.'

'Wha . . . what's *wrong* with me?'

'Your legs.'

She strains to raise her head higher.

'We'll be operating shortly.'

'No!'

'We must. Otherwise, you may lose them.'

He takes a syringe from a tray of implements beside her bed.

'What's that?'

'It will help you relax.'

'But I feel fine!'

He peels back the sheet, uncovering her right arm. It is strapped to the table.

'No, don't!'

'This won't hurt at all,' he says, and sinks the needle into her upper arm.

'You . . . You can't operate without my permission. I don't give it. You can't have my permission.'

'I'm afraid you're in no condition to make such a decision,' he says, and removes the empty syringe from her arm. 'Relax now, Miss Thatcher.'

* * *

She wakes up screaming. Her head strains upward. She is naked on the table. Schreck stands beside her, arm pumping a saw buried deep in her thigh.

'Hurt?' he asks.

She keeps on screaming.

Below the tourniquet, Schreck continues to saw until the bone parts. Then he takes a long-bladed scalpel from the tray, and slices through the remaining muscle and flesh.

'Ah-ha!' he says.

He lifts the severed leg off the table, and holds it high.

'Clean as a whistle,' he says.

The woman passes out.

Her eyelids flutter open. She is lying on a bed, no longer in the stark, bare operating room.

Groaning, she raises an arm.

She pulls the sheet off her body and gazes down at two bandaged stumps where her legs should be.

She lowers her head to the pillow, and weeps.

Soon, Schreck enters the room. 'And how are we today?' he asks.

'My . . . My legs,' she says in a weak voice.

'They had to go, I'm afraid.'

'You're . . . no doctor.'

'Oh, but I am. I must say, the operation was a great success. Now, if we're as successful with the next stage . . .'

Her chin trembles. 'No,' she says.

'Oh yes.' He pats her shoulder. 'Buck up. I'm sure we have nothing to worry about. You're young and strong. With any luck at all, you'll pull through just fine.'

After he leaves, she rolls onto her belly, whimpering with pain. She drags herself to the edge of the mattress. She reaches down to the carpet, and tries to lower herself.

Her torso drops.

Her bandaged stumps pound the floor, and she faints.

She wakes up in the operating room.

'Ah, Miss Thatcher, just in time to observe the procedure.'

Her right arm is strapped to a board beside her body. A tourniquet of surgical tubing is already tied in place.

Schreck places a scalpel against the skin of her upper arms.

'No!' she shrieks.

'We came through stage two like champs,' says Schreck, grinning down at her.

She raises her head.

No arms, no legs.

She lays her head back, and her eyelids tremble shut.

Schreck slaps her awake. 'Miss Thatcher, the procedure is complete. The artificial limbs may seem a bit awkward and painful, at the outset. But you are a very lucky young lady, very lucky indeed.'

As he pulls her to a sitting position, the sheet slides away. She begins to gasp wildly. Schreck tosses the sheet to the floor.

From the bandaged stumps of her arms hang arms. Legs protrude from her bandaged thighs.

Their brown, withered skin looks as if it has been stretched over bare bones.

A waltz is playing. Schreck, in a tuxedo, dances across the floor with Beatrice in his arms. 'You have never danced better, my darling. You seem so young, so vital tonight, as if her very essence has flowed into your veins.

'Nor have you ever looked more lovely, my Beatrice. What

do you ask? Why didn't I give you a new face? How could I. This is the face that I love.' He kisses her twisted, gaping mouth.

The music changes to a tango.

'Shall we, my darling?'

Lifting one of her pale, youthful arms, he begins to dance. Her bare feet swing above the carpet, her dress billows out. Schreck spins her wildly, laughing.

He laughs, even as one of her legs drops to the floor.

'We shall dance until dawn,' he says. 'We shall dance as we have never danced before.'

The End

# CHAPTER TWENTY-ONE

'Dal, what's wrong?'

He shook his head, afraid he might cry if he tried to talk. He stepped into Elizabeth's arms. He put his hands under her loose blouse and caressed the smoothness of her back.

'You didn't break up with Connie?'

'No.'

'Why aren't you with her?'

On the way over, he'd anticipated such a question. He had an answer ready. 'She thinks I'm in San Diego. On a buying trip.'

'What's wrong, then?'

'Later.' He lifted her blouse. He took her breasts in his hands, squeezed them, pressed his face between them, kissed them, licked a nipple until it was slippery and rigid, and sucked it deep into his mouth.

Elizabeth moaned and stroked his hair.

He pulled her shorts down her legs. Squeezing her buttocks, he licked a trail down her belly. He found that she had shaved her pubic hair. He licked the smooth mound. His tongue went lower. She trembled, and her fingers clenched his hair.

'Now?'

'Okay.' Dal sat up in bed and crossed his legs. Elizabeth lay in front of him, hands folded behind her head. Hair clung to her forehead with sweat. She was still breathing heavily.

Herbert, in his wheelchair a yard away, stared at her with shiny eyes.

'Well?'

'I got fired.'

'How?'

'Pete came into the store. He was furious, apparently, because Connie told him about our engagement.'

'He didn't take the rebuff kindly?'

'He had a phony police i.d. or something, and he pretended to arrest me. He handcuffed me and marched me right out of the store.'

'Subtle bastard.'

'When I got back, Mr Lane took me into his office and fired me.'

'Didn't you explain to him?'

'Yeah, of course. I don't know if he believed me or not, but he said it didn't matter. Goddamn self-righteous bastard. He said even if I was telling the truth, that he didn't want an employee whose personal life interfered with the job.'

Elizabeth reached down and stroked his knee. 'I'm sure you can find something else.'

'Yeah. But what's to keep Pete from doing it again? He could pull that stunt every time I land a job.'

'If he posed as a cop, you might get him arrested.'

'Great. That'd *really* get him pissed at me.'

Elizabeth rolled onto her side. Her hand glided over his thigh, sending a shiver up his back. She raked the hair of his scrotum. 'Let me shave you,' she said.

Dal moaned and smiled.

'Then we'll go out and kill the bastard.'

'Pete?'

'Who else?'

'You're joking.'

'Am I? It would have to look like an accident, of course.'

'Are you serious?'

'Don't you want to?'

'I'd like him dead, that's for sure.'

'Then it's settled. Stay here. I'll get the shaving cream and razor.' She swung out of bed, patted Herbert on the cheek, and trotted into the bathroom. She returned, soon, with a wet towel, a can of Rapid Shave, and a straight razor.

'Haven't you got a safety razor?'

'Of course. But it wouldn't be half the fun.'

'Do you know how to use that?'

She knelt on the bed and looked down at her own smooth crotch. 'Does it look like it?'

'It looks great.'

'Now, we have to decide on a method that's perfectly safe. Lie back. There. How about a car accident?'

They sat in a booth at Savilli's, an Italian restaurant chosen by Connie because, in addition to good food, it catered to Santa Monica's senior citizens. For their sake, it abandoned the semi-darkness common to better restaurants and kept the place well-lit. This made it less difficult to read Pete's lips.

'I know it was a nasty trick,' he said. 'I was feeling pretty nasty when I did it.'

'That sort of thing could get him fired.'

'I hope so.'

The waitress came. Pete asked for another round of margaritas.

'What if Dal reports you?'

157

Pete grinned. 'Hell, he could sue me, get me busted, get my ticket pulled.'

'Your what?'

'Ticket. My private investigator's license.'

'My God, Pete.'

'Oh, I'm not too worried. From what I've seen of Dal, he's basically a sneak and a coward. If he wants revenge, he won't go through the legal system. He's more the type to burn down my house or poison my dog – if I had one – or maybe bribe a couple of punks to rough me up.'

Connie saw the waitress approach with fresh drinks. She finished her first margarita, tipping the glass high and sucking up the remaining froth. Pete laughed. She licked the foamy mustache off her upper lip. The waitress took her glass, and set down a full one.

When she left, Pete said, 'I'm a little worried, though, that he might try something with you.'

'I can handle him.'

'Can you?'

'My hands are deadly weapons.'

They both laughed. Then she remembered breaking the arm of the guy who attacked her, kicking the other one in the face, burning their car. Her face turned hot.

'What's the matter?' Pete asked.

'I wasn't exactly joking about my hands.'

His eyes narrowed. He looked intrigued.

'I got attacked a couple of weeks ago. Two guys jumped me, and I had to bust them up pretty badly. I sort of – I don't want to say I enjoyed it, but – at the time it was kind of exciting. I felt so *powerful*. Like I could take on the world. But later on, I just felt sick about the whole incident. I still do when I think about it.'

'You feel dirty inside.'

'Exactly.'

'You should try killing someone.'

'Thanks, I'll pass on that.'

Pete lifted his bell-shaped glass, and drank, and back-handed the foam off his mouth. 'At any rate, I think we should stay together for the next few nights. Until Dal's had a chance to cool down.'

'Do you think it's necessary?'

'It couldn't hurt,' he said.

'Couldn't hurt at all,' Connie agreed. 'Your place or mine?'

'Which would you prefer?'

'Yours. It's so rustic and romantic.'

'How would you like to move in? Just for a few days,' he quickly added.

'I'd like that. Just for a few days.'

'Or as long as you'd like.'

'When do we start?'

'How about tonight?'

When the waitress returned, Pete asked for the clams in the half shell as an appetizer. Connie, who'd never eaten them before, expected the clams to be served fried and crispy.

She stared at the wet, slimy-looking things and said, 'This isn't the way Howard Johnson does it.'

'Try one.'

'I'll try anything once.' She scooped a clam out of its shell and slipped it into her mouth. She bit into it once. Unlady-like to spit it out, she thought. So she swallowed it and managed not to gag.

'What do you think?' Pete asked.

'It's not for nothing they're called clams.'

She took a long drink of margarita. Amused, she watched Pete finish off the serving. 'I guess we don't have as much in common as I'd thought,' she said.

Pete grinned and chewed.

The rest of dinner, Connie found delicious. She ate a side dish of linguini in a delicate sauce of oil and garlic, then a full plate of veal parmesan, sipping the house rosé between bites.

'Great stuff,' Pete said as he finished.

He paid the bill. Outside, Connie thanked him for dinner and kissed him. They walked to his car, holding hands.

Dal waited in the passenger seat of Elizabeth's Mercedes. She was gone for two minutes. Then she stepped out of the shadows near the house, and started across the street.

She wore white shorts and a white halter top. By contrast, her skin looked very dark. Beautiful, Dal thought.

The car light came on when she opened the door. She smiled and climbed in and shut the door. The car went dark.

'Not home,' she said.

'What should we do?'

'Wait.'

'That could take hours.'

'What's your hurry?'

'I just want to get it over with, that's all.'

'Someone's coming. Kiss me.'

'Huh?'

'We want them to think we're lovers.'

'Aren't we?'

'Of course we are.'

He pressed his lips to her open mouth.

Pete drove Connie to her apartment house. He entered first, and had a quick look around while Connie waited in the doorway. 'It's okay,' he said.

They went into her bedroom. She knelt beside her bed. 'Did you check under here?'

'If he grabs you this time, I'll let him have you.'

'The little girl who cried wolf,' she said, and reached under the bed. As she gripped her suitcase, a hand patted her rump. 'My God, he's attacking from the rear!' She didn't move. The hand pressed against her skirt, slid lower and rubbed between her legs. 'You'd better stop him, Pete. He's getting fresh. Next thing you know, he'll be pulling up my skirt and . . .'

He did. And then he slipped her panties down.

She felt his touch. Her hand went limp on the suitcase. 'I guess I can get it later,' she said.

An hour later, wearing fresh panties and nothing else, she again knelt beside the bed. She dragged the suitcase out, and threw it onto the bed beside Pete. He took a sip of beer, and grinned.

'You look pleased with yourself,' Connie said.

'I am.'

'You ought to be.'

He drank his beer and watched her pack. She didn't pack much: toilet articles, a few changes of clothes, her swimming suit, half a dozen paperback novels, and her manuscript. 'All set,' she announced, and shut the suitcase. 'You just gonna sit there?'

'It's the best seat in the house.'

'But the show's over.' She stepped into her corduroys, and pulled a blue velour top over her head.

'Just an intermission,' Pete said. He climbed off the bed and got dressed.

He carried her suitcase to the door.

'I'd better take my own car,' Connie said. 'I'll want to come back for my mail and stuff.'

'I can bring you by.'

'Every day?'

161

'Is your mail that urgent?'

'You don't know much about writers, do you?'

'I'll never know enough about this one.'

She kissed him. Then they went outside, and down the stairway to the courtyard. They went through the gate. Pete put the suitcase into Connie's car, then patted her rump and went to his own car.

'There he is!' Dal said as a Jaguar turned onto the road.

'Down.'

They both ducked. The low grumble of the engine grew louder, and suddenly died. Dal raised himself enough to peer out the windshield. He saw the Jaguar in the driveway of Pete's house. As Pete bent over to raise the garage door, another car appeared at the end of the block. Dal hunched down. He heard the Jaguar engine start again. When he looked out, he saw a different car in Pete's driveway.

Connie's Plymouth Fury.

'Oh shit,' he muttered.

Elizabeth pushed herself up, and looked out. Across the street Pete lowered the garage door and met Connie beside her car. He took her suitcase. They walked together across the yard, and disappeared into the shadows near the front door.

'Who do you suppose *she* is?' Elizabeth asked.

Dal suddenly realized she didn't know what Connie looked like. Good thing. What would Connie, his fiancée, be doing at Pete's house – with a suitcase? 'I don't know who she is.'

'I suppose it doesn't matter unless she sees me.'

'What if she *does* see you?' Dal asked.

'Do you want to call the whole thing off?'

'You mean if she sees you?'

'I mean right now. We can't kill this guy without taking chances. A hundred things could go wrong. You've got to want it bad, even enough to cut down anybody who gets in our way.'

'But she's innocent.'

'Not if she sees me.'

'I don't know.' Dal shook his head, thinking. If they killed Connie, tomorrow's newspaper would certainly identify her. That'd finish him with Elizabeth. She'd see all his lies, know that he wouldn't be getting rich, and dump him.

By then, however, they would've committed two murders together. Maybe he should threaten to turn himself in – and tell all – unless she continued the relationship.

'What'll it be?' Elizabeth asked.

'Let's get him.'

Soon, the lights in the front windows of the house went out.

'Let's give them an hour,' Elizabeth said.

'A whole hour?'

'I don't want to kill anyone we don't have to. Give them an hour, and perhaps the lady will stay in bed.'

Dal hoped it would work that way. It just might. Connie, after all, wouldn't hear the doorbell.


Pete thought, at first, that the ringing doorbell was only part of his dream. Then he opened his eyes in the darkness and heard it again.

He glanced at the alarm clock. Nearly midnight.

Who the hell would be ringing the doorbell at this hour?

It frightened him.

Heart thudding wildly, he rolled away from the warmth of Connie's sleeping body. The room was chilly. He stepped through the darkness to the closet, and pulled his bathrobe off its hook. The doorbell rang again as he rushed down the long hallway.

Standing in darkness by the door, he turned on the outside

light. His door had no peephole.

'Who's there?' he called.

'Please,' said a woman's voice. 'My car broke down.'

Pete opened the door. The woman on the front stoop looked beautiful and frightened.

'I'm awfully sorry to disturb you,' she said. She glanced at his robe, and smiled as if embarrassed, as if she knew he was naked beneath it. 'I just didn't know what to do.'

'That's all right,' Pete said. 'Would you like to use the phone?'

She looked behind him into the darkness. 'I don't know if I should. Are you alone?'

'I'm harmless.'

'Well . . . Who would I call?'

'Triple A, I suppose.'

'I don't belong.'

'You don't have to. They'll just charge you a service fee.'

'You mean money?'

Pete nodded.

The woman chewed her lower lip. 'But I only have about three dollars.'

'What's wrong with your car, do you know?'

'I've got a flat.'

'Do you have a spare?'

'Sure. I've got a real nice one. It's right in my trunk'

'Okay. Hang on a minute while I get dressed, then we'll see if I can't change it for you.'

'Oh, would you?'

'Come on in, if you'd like.'

'Well, thank you. I'll just wait here, though, if it's all the same.'

'Whatever,' he said. Did she think he'd attack her?

He didn't want to shut the door in her face, so he left it open and returned to the bedroom. As he shed his robe in the darkness, light filled the room. He saw Connie sitting up, her arm raised to the bedside lamp. She squinted and yawned. 'What's up?' she asked.

Pete stepped into his jeans. 'I have got to go out for a minute. Some gal has a flat.'

'Gonna change a tire?'

'Yep.' He put on a gray sweatshirt, and slipped his bare feet into sneakers.

'Want me to help?' Connie asked.

'Just keep the bed warm.'

'Mmm. I'll leave the light on for you,' she said. She lowered herself onto the bed, and pulled the blanket up to her bare shoulders.

Pete went down the hall to the open front door.

'I sure do appreciate your helping me like this,' said the woman.'

'Glad to help.'

'My car's right across the street here.' She walked ahead of him, pointing to a pale Datsun. Its left front tire was flat.

Connie, warm and drowsy beneath the blanket, suddenly came wide awake.

Too damned bizarre!

In all her life, nobody ever came to the door at midnight with a story about a flat tire. And if it ever *had* happened, she would've been too suspicious to fall for it.

A set-up?

Dal!

She scurried off the bed, grabbed Pete's robe and pulled it on as she ran down the dark hallway. She jerked open the front door.

A woman in the street, Pete close behind her.

Connie looked both ways.

To the right, a car shot away from the curb. No headlights on.

'Pete! Look out!'

He jerked around, and tried to leap out of the way. The speeding car caught him in the legs and Connie screamed as she watched Pete cartwheel over the car and crumple onto the pavement behind it.

The car stopped.

The woman climbed in.

It sped away.

Connie raced to the telephone. She picked it up and dialed 0. She waited five seconds, then said, 'Hello, hello. Operator? I'm deaf. If you're there, send an ambulance to 186 Seafront Lane in Venice. A man's been hit by a car. It's a hit and run, so send the police, too.' She repeated the address, and hung up.

She ran outside crying.

'She saw it,' Elizabeth gasped. 'She was in the doorway. She saw it.'

'Oh Jesus!'

'Turn around. You've got to go back.'

'Did she see you?'

'Not close up. But she saw the car. Do it!'

'This city has thousands of gray Mercedes. We covered the license plate. There's no way . . .'

'Go back.'

He'd already turned the corner onto Pacific, but there were no other cars nearby. He made a U-turn and headed back toward Seafront. As he slowed for the turn, he saw several people down the lane. He drove on by. 'Forget it,' he said.

'We can't get them all.' With a shaking hand, he turned on the windshield wipers to clear off the spattered blood.

# CHAPTER TWENTY-TWO

A doorbell startled Freya awake. She sat up in bed, shaking, and flinched as the doorbell rang again.

She looked at her alarm clock. Twelve-twenty.

Who the hell . . . ?

The *police*?

She cringed as it rang again. Swinging herself out of bed, she turned on a lamp. She crouched at her dresser, wiped her cold wet hands on her thighs, and pulled open a drawer. The bell rang again, again.

Jesus, it had to be cops! Who else would come at this hour? They're rounding us up. Oh Jesus!

She jerked a nightgown out of the drawer, and put it on as she rushed through the apartment. The bell kept ringing. She turned on a lamp in the living-room. Turned on the porch light. Opened the door.

The chubby girl's T-shirt read, 'Save a tree – eat a beaver'. She smiled up at Freya and said, 'Greetings.'

Freya opened her mouth to scream.

She fainted, instead.

# CHAPTER TWENTY-TWO

# CHAPTER TWENTY-THREE

In Elizabeth's garage, Dal inspected the car. The only damage seemed to be a couple of small dents in the hood. There wasn't as much blood as he expected. Elizabeth filled a bucket, and he sponged the car clean. He dumped the bucket of pink water into a flower bed behind the pool.

They went into the house. Dal flopped on the sofa. He was still shaking, his heart racing.

'I'll stir up a batch of martinis,' Elizabeth said.

She left him alone. He rubbed his face. He saw Pete in front of the car, heard the thud of the impact, saw Pete tumble toward him. He shook his head sharply. He didn't want to think about it. Getting up, he went into the kitchen to be with Elizabeth.

She stood at the counter pouring gin into a beaker. Dal pressed his face to the back of her head. Her hair felt thick and soft, with a fresh outdoor smell. Reaching around, he held her breasts. They were bare under the halter top. The nipples pushed against his hands through the fabric.

'Does it excite you?' she asked.

'You always excite me.'

'Not me. What we did.'

'I don't know,' Dal said. He didn't want to admit that he felt dizzy and confused. But holding Elizabeth helped.

'I feel absolutely grand,' she said.

'It doesn't bother you?'

'Only that we let the girl live. Unless she's a complete fool, she'll know it wasn't an accident. You may find yourself a suspect when the police start snooping.'

Dal dropped his hands. He stepped away from her, and leaned back against the counter.

'They'll find out, quickly enough, about your rivalry over Connie. A little more digging, and they'll learn how you got fired.'

'My God,' he muttered.

Elizabeth poured the martinis into a pair of glasses. 'None of this would've come up, of course, if the girl hadn't seen us.'

'What'll we do?'

She handed a glass to him. 'Cheer up, darling.' She clinked the rim of her glass against his, and took a sip. Dal drank. The martini was cool in his mouth, and made a hot trail down him as he swallowed. 'I'm your accomplice, remember? I certainly can't allow the police to arrest you.'

'What'll we do?' he asked again.

'An alibi would help, of course. You told Connie you were going to San Diego?'

'Yes,' he said, though he'd told her no such thing.

'Did you say which hotel?'

He shook his head.

'That's fortunate. At least they can't catch you in an outright lie.'

'What'll I tell them?'

Elizabeth leaned against the counter beside him. She frowned at the clear surface of her drink. She took a sip. Then she smiled. 'If they ask where you were tonight, you explain – reluctantly of course – that San Diego was a lie to appease Connie.

172

Actually, you picked up a prostitute on Sunset. You went to a motel with her. You're not sure which one, but she signed in and you spent the night together. Voila! You have an alibi that can't be disproved. The cops don't have any physical evidence connecting you to the crime. You're home free.'

'Why would I go to a prostitute, though, if I'm engaged to Connie?'

Elizabeth shrugged. 'Perhaps you can say she's an old-fashioned girl who won't let you touch her before the wedding night?'

'Nobody'd believe that.'

'You're probably right. Ah! I have it! She's an old-fashioned girl who won't give head.'

'Good. That's good.'

'Okay, you have your story. They've got no evidence. We're home free.'

'God, I hope so.'

'There's just one more thing.'

'What?'

'We'll have to stay away from each other. If they connect us, they've got the car.'

'But . . .'

'It won't be forever.' Elizabeth drew her fingers over his cheek.

'How long?'

'A few weeks, I suppose.'

'I don't want to be away from you.'

'I don't like it either, darling.' She opened the top button of his shirt. 'This will be our last time together for a long while. Let's make it memorable.'

She led him into the bedroom. They took off each other's clothes. Under the bright light and the staring eyes of Herbert, they made love.

When they were done, Elizabeth straddled him and rubbed his chest. 'I have a surprise,' she said.

'Mmm.'

'Back in a minute.' She climbed off, and left the room.

Dal folded his hands behind his head, and looked at Herbert sitting motionless in his wheelchair beside the bed. The man's steady gaze made him uneasy. He pulled up the sheet to cover himself, and wished Elizabeth would hurry back. He didn't like being alone with Herbert.

Finally, she came in. She walked silently through the darkness, and into the pool of light near the bed. A dish towel covered her hands. She stepped behind Herbert, and licked her lips.

'Took you long enough.'

'I had a lot to do.'

'What's under the towel?'

'The surprise.'

She lifted the towel away.

Dal jerked upright. 'My God, don't!'

'It's time,' she said. She wrapped her hand in the towel and gripped the butcher knife and swung it down. It plunged into Herbert's throat. A spray of blood hit Dal. He rolled backwards, out of the way, as Elizabeth jerked out the knife and stabbed again.

'Oh my God,' he gasped. 'Jesus!' He scrambled off the bed.

Elizabeth, with a half smile on her face, rammed the blade again into Herbert's throat.

'My God, *stop*! For Godsake!'

She pulled out the knife. She was breathing hard. She wiped its handle with the dish towel, and stepped around the end of the bed.

Dal backed away. 'No,' he muttered.

'An . . . an intruder broke in,' she said, walking toward him.

Hair hung in her face. Her skin was slick with sweat. 'Took a knife from the kitchen. Killed poor Herbert. Beat up poor Elizabeth, raped her.'

'You're nuts!'

'Am I?'

'You can't get away with it.'

'Of course I can.'

She backed him against the sliding door. 'And you'll help me. You, darling, are the intruder.'

He thrust out his hands to ward off the knife.

Elizabeth laughed softly. She turned the handle toward him. 'Take it,' she said.

'Huh?'

'Take it. Don't worry about prints. You can wipe them off with the towel. I'll tell the police you wore gloves.'

She pressed the knife into his hand.

Dal stared at the dripping blade.

'When you're done, go outside and smash a hole in the glass. It'll look like you broke in.'

'My . . . my fingerprints are everywhere.'

'I got most of them.' She grinned. 'That's what took me so long, out there. When I tell the cops you wore gloves, though, they might not even bother to check.'

'My God, Elizabeth.''

'Don't worry. They'll never even suspect you . . . or me.' She took his wrist, and pulled him toward the bed. She sat on the mattress. Still holding his hand, she lay down. She guided his hand lower, until the knife touched her belly.

Dal jerked his hand away. 'What're you doing!'

'Cut me.'

'*Cut* you?'

'It has to look real.'

'I can't *cut* you!'

'Can you punch me?'

'I . . . I don't know.'

'Try.'

'Where?'

She tapped her cheek.

'God, Elizabeth.'

'Do it!' she snapped.

He climbed onto the bed and straddled her. He set the knife on the sheet. He raised his fist.

'Go ahead.'

'I can't.'

'You have to.'

His arm trembled. Then he was crying. 'I can't. Don't ask me to. Please.'

'Okay then.'

'I'm sorry.'

'It's all right, darling. I guess I should be flattered, huh?'

'I'm sorry.' He climbed off her.

'Go ahead and get dressed. Then break that window.'

He picked up his clothes.

Elizabeth picked up the butcher knife. She pressed its blade to her throat.

'What . . . !'

'Shhhh.'

He saw the blade slide on her skin, saw a line of blood spill out.

'*Elizabeth!*'

She carved a second cut onto her throat. She cut her right cheek, her forehead. Dal stared, cold and numb. The blade went to her right breast.

'No!' Dropping his clothes, he ran to her and grabbed her hand.

'Then hit me,' she said. 'Beat me up. Hurt me.'

176

Pinning her knife-hand to the sheet, he punched her face.

'Again,' she muttered.

He hit her again.

'Scratch me. Bruise me.'

Dal did as he was told, reluctantly at first. She sobbed and writhed under him, and urged him on. He punched her, raked her with fingernails, squeezed and twisted her slippery skin. Then he was hard and aching. He shoved himself into her, pounded, and burst with quick release.

He climbed off her, exhausted. She lay on the bed, torn and sheathed in blood. She raised her head to see herself.

'This'll do nicely,' she moaned. 'Now get dressed . . . Break that window and get the hell out of here . . . so I can call the cops.'

'Are you all right?'

'Do I . . . look all right?'

Dal started to get dressed. He was wet with blood. His clothes stuck to him. 'When will we see each other again?' he asked.

'I'll . . . phone.'

# CHAPTER TWENTY-FOUR

'Greetings again.'

Freya raised her head off the couch. She looked at the girl on the nearby chair, and shut her eyes. Her head hurt.

'You okay?'

'Yeah.'

'I was starting to worry. You bashed hell out of your head when you fell. Hit the bookcase. You been out for a goddamn hour. You always go around fainting?'

'I . . . I've been sick.'

'Yeah? You too? I just got over a case of the trots, myself. Something I ate.'

Freya opened here eyes. She sat up slowly, feeling dizzy, and touched the back of her head. A big lump. She looked at the girl. 'Who are you, anyway?'

'Who do you think?'

'Chelsea?'

The girl grinned.

'Can't be.'

'Can't?'

'She's . . . ' Freya caught herself. 'She's out of town.'

'Oh shit. Where?'

'Up north.'

'Damn it, she knew I was coming. What's she trying to pull?'

'You're her twin?'

'Right on the money. Name's Grenich.' She spelled it.

'I'm Freya.' She spelled it.

'When's *el grosso* coming back?'

'She didn't say.'

'When'd she leave?'

'Today.'

'Just in time to miss me.'

'She said it was an emergency.'

'I'll bet. Hey look, you mind if I flop here tonight?'

'No. That'd be fine.'

# CHAPTER TWENTY-FIVE

Someone touched Connie's shoulder, startling her awake. She was in the hospital waiting room, slumped in a plastic chair. She looked up at the doctor beside her.

'Mr Harvey's out of surgery,' he said.

'How is he?'

'He's stable, Miss Brent. His vital signs look good. That's about the best we can offer at this point.'

'But he will survive?'

'We can't promise anything, but I think there's a good chance of it.'

'May I see him?'

The doctor shook his head. 'Later, perhaps. Visiting hours are from four to five, and eight to nine. He'll be on the third floor, once he's out of intensive care. Now, I'd suggest you go home and try to get some sleep.'

The sun came up while she was driving home. She thought about heading over to Pete's house for her suitcase, but she didn't want to go there. Maybe later today, if she felt better.

Her neck was stiff from the hours in the waiting room. Her eyes were raw and burning. She felt tired and hollow and sick.

When she got to her apartment, she lay on her bed and covered her face with a pillow. Images twisted through her mind: Pete on the bed, grinning and sipping beer; Pete broken on the pavement; jerking her out of a car's way the day they met; tumbling through the night and crumbling to the street; Dal grinning as he aimed the car; the doctor shaking his head – 'I'm sorry, Miss Brent, but he didn't make it'; a preacher beside the grave – 'Earth to earth, ashes to ashes'; the casket slowly lowering . . .

She flung the pillow aside and sat up. She sat motionless, wondering what to do with herself. She felt like doing nothing. If she could just sleep, just shut off her mind and sleep and not wake up until it was all over . . . A bath might help.

She turned on the faucet and took off her clothes and sat in the hot shallow water, hugging her knees to her breasts as the tub filled. When the water was deep, she lay back. Her shoulders touched the cold porcelain. She flinched and quickly slid lower, sighing as she was wrapped in heat. The warmth was soothing. The water's gentle motion caressed her. She shut her eyes.

After the bath, she would make sausages and fried eggs. A whole bunch of them. Then she would go to Westwood and browse bookstores and buy a dozen books, at least. And then she would buy herself a dress, a lovely new dress for visiting Pete tonight. Maybe get him a gift. A special gift . . .

She was chilly. She sat up, the cool water sluicing down her chest. She realized she'd been asleep. She unplugged the drain, thinking she might refill the tub with hot water. Except for the cold, she felt good. If she could just return to the cozy warmth . . . But her hands were pale and shriveled. She certainly didn't need another doze in the tub.

But she was so cold.

She slid the glass door shut. Kneeling, she reached for the faucet. Moments later, hot water was raining onto her head, pelting her shoulders and streaming down her chilled skin, sheeting her in warmth. She raised her face into the shower.

It tapped her eyelids, filled her mouth. She swallowed some, and let the rest spill down her chin.

Standing, she picked up the soap and remembered the day at the beach house – only a few days ago – showering with Pete, his hands rubbing her soapy body everywhere. Then she soaping him, his skin slippery under her hands.

She started to cry. Sobs shook her body. She dropped the soap and covered her face. The water pounded on her back. It began to turn cold. She shut it off. She shoved open the shower door and climbed from the tub. She pressed her warm dry towel to her face and fell to her knees, crying harshly.

Later, she found herself lying on the bathroom rug. She'd been asleep. Sun from the window was warm on her back. She got up, feeling weak. Except for her hair, she was nearly dry.

She felt very hungry.

Rubbing her hair dry, she went into the bedroom. She put on fresh clothes, then went into the kitchen. She took a pack of sausages from the refrigerator. As she poked at its plastic wrapper, the lights flashed on and off.

Someone at the door.

She went to it and opened it.

'I thought I'd drop by and see how you are.'

She stared at Dal in disbelief. His face was somber. He looked haggard.

'I read about it in the paper,' he said.

'That's the first you knew about it, I suppose.'

He nodded. 'I was afraid you might feel that way. That's another reason I came by. I want you to know I had nothing to do with it.'

'Is that so?'

'Can I come in for a minute?'

She stepped away from the door and let him enter. She shut the door. She faced him.

'The article said the police are looking for a suspect. I suppose that's me.'

'That's right.'

He turned away and walked toward a chair. Connie opened the draperies to fill the room with light. Then she sat across from him, watching his mouth.

'You have every reason to think I was involved. I mean, after everything Pete's done to me. I lost my job, you know.'

'I didn't know.'

'Yeah. Because of that stunt he pulled. But Christ, I wouldn't try to run a guy over, no matter what he did.'

'Tell that to the police.'

'I intend to.'

'Why don't you call them now?'

He looked shocked. 'Now?'

'I know they're looking for you. It'll save time. You can use my phone, and I'll keep you company till they arrive.'

'I can't.'

'Why not? They'll find you anyway, sooner or later. You might as well get it over with.'

'I have a job interview in half an hour.'

'Do you indeed.'

'I didn't come over here to argue, Connie. I came over to offer my sympathy.'

'I don't need your sympathy.'

'How *is* Pete?'

'He'll live,' she said, praying she was right. 'And if he saw the face of the driver, you'll be in deep trouble.'

Dal grinned. The corners of his mouth trembled. 'I hope he did see the driver. Then maybe you'll believe me.'

'I know you did it, Dal.'

'Then why don't *you* call the police?'

'Last night I called for an ambulance.' The memory almost

brought fresh tears. She paused, trying to regain control. 'I called and thought I was talking to an operator . . . but I wasn't, apparently. I was talking to no one, to a ringing phone, probably . . . and I didn't even know it. If someone else hadn't called for an ambulance . . .'

'I'm sorry.'

'So I don't think I'll call the police. What I might do, I might disable you and go next door and ask a neighbour to call.'

'You're crazy.'

'Maybe. I'll tell you why I won't do it.'

He smirked. 'Tell me.'

'Because if I attack you, I won't be able to stop. I'll kill you.'

'That so?' he asked, looking pale.

'And I don't want to kill you, because then it'll be hard to find out who the woman is.'

'What woman?'

'Your friend with the Mercedes.'

He shook his head. 'You're not making any sense.'

'Yes I am.'

'I don't know any woman with a Mercedes. That's a bit out of my league.'

'That's true.'

'Look, I don't need this. I just came by . . .'

'I know. To offer your sympathy. Well, thanks anyway. But you're the one who'll need sympathy, Dal. You and your girlfriend. Something bad is gonna happen to you both.'

'Connie, for . . .'

'You tried to kill my man.'

He got up. 'I'm leaving.'

She walked to the door and opened it. Dal stepped outside.

As soon as she shut the door, she rushed across the room, grabbed her purse, and ran back to it. She opened it a crack and peered out. Dal was halfway down the stairs. She waited until he reached the bottom. When he was out of sight, she stepped onto the balcony and looked over the railing. Dal, at the end of the courtyard, was nearly to the rear gate. He'd parked in the alley: Connie's car was in front. She ran down the stairs, and out the front gate to her car.

She glanced both ways. Dal could exit the alley at either end of the block; if she chose wrong, she might lose him. She decided on the south end because it was closer.

She backed onto the road, and hit the gas pedal. With a quick spurt, the car shot to the corner. She stopped. As her eyes sought the alley's opening, she saw Dal's red VW already heading down the road. Away from her, thank God. If he'd come this way, he couldn't have missed her.

While she was stopped, a car passed. Great. It would run interference for her. She pulled out and followed it, sometimes veering to the left for a glimpse past it. They were gaining on Dal.

He turned right and disappeared around the side of an apartment house.

Approaching the corner, Connie eased off the gas. She took the turn slowly. Dal's car had almost reached the end of the block. It stopped at an intersection, then continued straight ahead. Connie sped up.

On the next block, his VW turned into the driveway of an apartment complex. Connie drove by, squinting into the darkness of the subterranean parking lot. She glimpsed his brake lights, and drove on.

If Dal knew he was being followed, he might've ducked in to lose his tail. That, Connie knew, was one possibility.

The other two were more intriguing.

She stopped near the corner. In her side mirror, she could see the driveway. She waited for Dal's car to appear.

Nearly two minutes passed. Then a station wagon came up the road behind Connie. She turned the corner to let it pass, then drove slowly along to an empty stretch of curb. She parked, and leaned her forehead against the steering wheel.

Dal, she realized, hadn't ducked into the lot to lose her. He was too impatient to wait inside for more than half a minute. So, unless he'd gone out a rear exit – if there was one – he'd entered the lot to park.

The apartment complex was his destination.

He lived there.

Or the woman did.

Connie climbed from her car and walked back to the driveway she'd seen Dal enter. Its pavement sloped into shadows. She stepped down it.

The parking lot was cool, and dark after the brightness outside. She took off her sunglasses. There were only half a dozen cars down here. She didn't see Dal's VW. She saw a dark brown Mercedes, but not a gray one.

Maybe around the corner . . .

The concrete felt slippery, as if it had been waxed. Poor footing if she was attacked.

Who would attack her, Dal?

'Those parking structures are bitches,' her self-defense instructor had warned. 'Great places to get mugged or raped. And where do you think the creep's waiting for you? He's crouched there between the parked cars. So always walk right up the middle of the driveway, so you'll have plenty of time to see him coming.'

Connie walked up the middle, her glance darting from car to car. Several times, she looked behind her. Then she came to the curve. She stepped over to the concrete wall, and peered around it.

Her heart flip-flopped.

She ducked.

Had Dal seen her? She didn't think so. He was still sitting in his car. My God, why? She'd expected him to be in a room by now.

Maybe he did know that he'd been tailed.

If that were true, he'd drive right past her once he thought it was safe to leave. She looked around. The nearest car to hide behind was yards away. Should she dash for it? Or maybe break for the sunlit entrance and try to get back to her car while Dal was still waiting?

Standing, she chanced another glance at Dal. He opened his door. She pressed herself to the wall and looked to the right at the nearby elevator.

If he walked straight to the elevator, the wall would conceal her. She could watch him in safety, as long as he didn't turn around.

She looked for floor numbers above the elevator door.

None.

Damn! She could've watched them to see where Dal got off. Without them, she'd have no idea which floor to check.

She'd have to look in the lobby. Maybe his mailbox or buzzer . . .

He walked by, moving slowly, head down, and the idea barely had time to form in Connie's mind before she rushed out. He started to turn. Her stiff open hand chopped the side of his neck. He dropped to his knees. Connie tensed, ready to kick the back of his head, but the single blow had been enough. He fell forward. His face hit the concrete.

The keys were in his hand. Connie took them. She found one with a room number. 316. She threw down the keys and jerked the wallet from his rear pocket. Should she just take the money? No, a real mugger might want the credit cards, the license, the works.

She stuffed the wallet into her handbag.

Then she ran from the parking lot.

In the heat and brightness outside, she put on her sunglasses. She walked quickly to her car and drove home.

# CHAPTER TWENTY-SIX

'Sure you don't want to come along?' Grenich asked.

No, really. I can't look food in the face before noon.'

'I was counting on you driving. Haven't got a car, myself.'

'How did you get here?'

She held up her thumb.

'Want to take my car?'

'Can I?'

'Sure.' Freya took her keys from her handbag, and gave them to the girl.

'You sure it's okay?'

'No problem. Have fun.'

'Want me to bring you something back?'

'No. Thanks.'

'Okay. Back in a jiff.'

The moment she was gone, Freya raced to the telephone and dialed. She waited nervously as it rang.

'Hello?'

'Todd.'

'Princess.'

'We've got troubles.'

'With a capital T?'

'Sure, make jokes. That's just what I need.'

'What *do* you need?'

'Help. My God! You know who's here – who dropped in last night? Chelsea's twin sister. Her *identical* twin. I tell you, I nearly dropped dead.'

'Ho! I should think so! Thought the delightful lady'd come back from the grave, eh?'

'That's exactly what I thought. And it's not funny. What'll we do?'

'What did you tell her about Chelsea?'

'I said she'd gone on a trip.'

'And so she did – a trip from whose bourne no traveler returns.'

'Todd!'

'You'll have to bring her out to the house, I think.'

'And how do I manage that?'

'Where is this lovely specimen now?'

'She headed over to the Box for a Breakfast Jack.'

'Marvelous. When she returns, simply explain that Chelsea called while she was out. She wants the two of you to meet her at a fabulous old house on the coast.'

'What if she doesn't buy it?'

'Oh, she'll buy it. You underestimate yourself, princess. You are a master of duplicity – or should I say mistress?'

'Well, I'll try.'

'We'll be waiting for you. Perhaps we can work the twin angle into the story-line. Wonderful potential. See you soon.'

'Sure.'

He hung up.

Freya heated water. She took her tea into the living-room, sat on the couch, and stared at the blank screen of the television.

'Look, I admit I ran the light. Okay? But I did not steal the car.'

'The registration . . .'

'I know,' Grenich said. 'She let me borrow it. Look officer, her apartment's only a block from here. Can't we just go back and *ask* her? Please?'

The doorbell rang. My God, back already? Must've changed her mind.

Freya got off the couch and went to the door.

*Guess who phoned while you were out.*

'Miss Jones . . .' the cop started.

She sprang through the doorway, shoved Grenich against him, and ran.

'Hey!'

Her bare feet slapped the painted concrete as she raced along the balcony. At the top of the stairs, she glanced back. The cop was running toward her.

'Stop!' he shouted.

She lunged down the stairs. Missed one. Tumbled headlong.

Like a nightmare when she falls down a long flight of stairs, and endless flight, and always wakes up before she hits.

But Freya wasn't asleep and she didn't wake up and she hit with a quick blast of pain as if she'd been smashed in the face with a sledge hammer.

'Is she dead?'

The cop nodded.

'Christ on a crutch!'

# CHAPTER TWENTY-SEVEN

Back in her apartment, Connie finished unwrapping the sausages she'd planned for breakfast. They were still cool from the refrigerator; she supposed they would be all right. She put them in a skillet and turned the burner on low.

Then she made coffee. She stared at its dark stream as it slowly filled the pot.

Now what? she wondered, watching it. Give Dal's address to the police? That's what she'd half-planned to do when she got the idea of following him. A good reasonable justification. Find out where he lives so the cops can arrest him. But that had only been half her plan. Not really what she wanted to do. Just an excuse.

So what's your *real* plan, kiddo?

Bust into his place tonight and murder him? Hell, she could've finished him off this morning, if that's what she wanted.

Stake him out, that's it. Follow him. Sooner or later, he would lead her to the woman with the gray Mercedes.

*Then* go to the police.

Maybe.

The coffee stopped steaming. It dripped a few times. She picked up the pot and filled her mug. She poked the sausages with a fork, turned them. They'd take a good deal longer.

She sipped her coffee, and went to the kitchen table. She opened her handbag. Reaching in, she pulled out Dal's wallet.

Another good reason to stay away from the cops; they might not look fondly on her methods.

Sitting at the table, she emptied Dal's wallet. Twenty-eight dollars in the bill compartment, along with assorted cards and papers. She set them aside. The wallet had slots for six credit cards. She pulled out the cards and stacked them neatly. Then she emptied the clear plastic picture holders, taking out his driver's license, Social Security card, a Red Cross card with his blood type, his high school graduation photo, and a Polaroid shot of Connie, herself, in a bikini.

He used to beg her to pose nude. She never allowed it, but one night he caught her in the shower. She chased him and tore up the photo and then they made love.

To think she used to . . .

She ripped the photo into tiny bits. She dropped the pieces onto the table. They made a nice little pile. She tore up the photo of Dal, and added it to the pile. Then his Red Cross card, his Social Security card, his driver's license.

She drank some coffee, and remembered the sausages. She got up to check them. She rolled them over. They were doing fine. She added more coffee to her mug, then took scissors from a drawer and returned to the table.

The plastic was easy to cut. She snipped up his Shell card, his Chevron card, his automobile club card, his Visa and Master Card, his Sears card. The pile of debris was growing.

Nothing left to add but the odds and ends she'd found in his bill compartment. She got up to check her sausages, then sat down again. She took a long drink of coffee. Then she tore up a post office receipt, a plumber's business card, and an old envelope corner on which he'd written Connie's address the day they met.

She wished she'd never given it to him.

She found four postage stamps. She set them aside to keep, then tore up three nondescript receipts and added them to the pile. She picked up a piece of tissue paper, the kind used at Dal's store – correction, former store – to wrap clothes before boxing them. She ripped it in half, the split nicely dividing a woman's first name from her last, her address number from her street, and dropped the pieces into the pile.

She picked them up again.

She held the pieces together.

The words were in Dal's handwriting: Elizabeth Lassin, 522, Altina.

Could be anything.

Could be *her*.

Altina, she knew, was up in the Highland Estates. A plush area where she wouldn't mind living herself someday.

Lots of fancy cars. Cadillacs, Rolls Royces, Mercedes.

'My God,' she muttered.

Then she smelled burning sausage.


Connie looked up the circular driveway. The door of the two-car garage was shut. Somehow, she had to see inside.

She walked up the driveway. The house seemed deserted, but she kept her eyes on the windows. If anyone looked out, she planned to go to the front door with a story.

*I'm a new neighbor, thought I'd drop by to get acquainted* . . . Sounded perfectly plausible.

Of course, it wouldn't work if the woman recognized her. If it's the gal who posed as Pete's wife . . . But Connie didn't think it was her. The woman last night had seemed older. Her hair was different, too: darker and longer.

She reached the garage. Standing close to its door, she couldn't see the house windows – or be seen from them.

Bending down, she gripped the handle and pulled. The door didn't budge.

A pathway led around the corner of the garage. She went to it, and looked along the side. No window.

But maybe in back.

She walked up the path, stepping lightly from one flagstone to the next. The ground was covered with redwood chips like the school playground when she was a kid. Their sweet aroma was the same. She remembered the squeak of swing chains, the yelling of kids on the monkey bars, the smell of her lunch box. All so vivid. If she closed her eyes, she could . . .

She had to keep them open.

She came to the end of the garage, and stopped. Crouching, she peered around the corner.

A swimming pool. Plenty of outdoor furniture. No people.

She took a step forward, and looked at the back wall of the garage. It had a window. Sidestepping between the wall and a row of oleander bushes, she made her way to the window. She cupped her hands around her eyes, and looked through the glass.

Except for light from the single window, the garage was dark. Off to the right, she saw the vague form of a car. Maybe a Mercedes. Maybe not. To be certain, she would need a better look.

She had to break in.

The idea made her stomach go tight and cold.

I can do it, she told herself. After a mugging, what's a little breaking and entering?

She stayed close to the garage wall, and sidestepped toward the house. As she was about to step out from behind an oleander, a movement caught her eye.

At the far end of the pool was a woman.

Connie stared, holding her breath.

198

The woman was walking slowly away, taking small steps, holding herself rigid as if in pain. She had long, dark hair like the woman last night. In the sun, it was a rich, red-brown. She wore a white, string bikini. When she turned at the pool's corner, Connie saw her front. She was matted with bandages: bandages on her face, her neck, her chest and belly, her thighs. Her skin was blotched with bruises, her face swollen and blue.

As Connie watched, she walked along the other side of the pool. She was nearly even with Connie when she stopped at a chaise longue. She untied her bikini and let it fall. Then she eased herself onto the chaise and lay back. Her head turned until she faced the house.

Connie stood motionless behind the oleander.

The woman didn't move her head. She lay on her back, arms at her sides, her skin glistening with moisture.

Asleep?

The sunglasses hid her eyes.

Connie didn't dare move.

Finally, the face turned away.

Connie waited a few seconds, then inched back along the garage wall. The woman's head remained turned. At last, Connie reached the corner. She ducked around it, then looked back once more. Apparently, the woman hadn't seen her. She still lay there, naked except for the bandages, facing the back fence.

Connie circled around to the front of the house. Hoping to God the woman was alone, she tried the front door. Locked. She checked the windows along the front of the house. All were shut.

On the far side of the house, a bathroom window stood open. She looked around. The redwood fence was close behind her; if there were neighbors on the other side, they wouldn't see her.

199

She struggled with the screen, and finally got it off. She pushed the window high, boosted herself up, and climbed in. She tiptoed across the bathroom. When she looked into the bedroom, she almost screamed. She covered her mouth, and stared at the blood-matted carpet beside the bed.

My God, what had happened here? So much blood! She thought about the woman's bandages. Had all of this come from her? It hardly seemed possible. Even the wall by the bed was splattered with it.

She wanted to get out. Fast. But she'd come this far. She needed to see inside the garage.

She walked swiftly to the sliding glass door. Stepping close to the draperies, she peeked out. The woman was still on her chaise.

Leaving the bedroom, Connie started down a hall-way. She came to other open doors, glanced into the rooms, and saw nobody.

At the rear of the living-room was an enormous picture window with a sliding door at one end. She saw the woman across the pool. On hands and knees, she crept the length of the room, staying behind furniture whenever possible. Then she was in the kitchen. She crawled across its tiles to a door at the far end.

She reached up for the knob. Turned it. Pushed the door open and looked into the dark garage.

She crawled ahead.

The garage was hot and stuffy, and smelled of grease.

She stood up. She pushed the door shut, and walked through the darkness to the car. Feeling along its side, she found a door handle. She opened the door, and the interior light came on.

A Mercedes, all right.

A gray Mercedes.

Leaving the door open for the light, she stepped to the

front of the car. She couldn't see the bumper or grill, but the shiny hood showed two small dents. They were enough for her.

She went over to the garage window to see if the woman was still on her chaise. Even as she looked, the woman flinched and sat upright, frowning toward her.

*What . . .?*

Oh God, an alarm. The car has a burglar alarm! She'd triggered it when she opened the door! She hadn't heard it, of course – but she should've, should've caught the vibrations!

The woman sprang from the lounger and rushed alongside the pool.

Thoughts darted through Connie's mind. She could make a dash for the front door. Or find the garage door opener and get out that way. Or stand and fight.

That's it. Take the woman out. Bring in the cops. Plenty of evidence now. She knew, from research for an old crime novel, that there'd still be traces of blood on the car.

She shut the car door, pressed her back to the wall by the kitchen door, and waited.

Her heart felt as if it might explode. She blinked sweat out of her eyes.

God, what if I faint?

What if she has a gun?

The door stayed shut.

What's taking her so long?

Connie wiped a hand on her corduroys, and gripped the knob. She slowly turned it. She eased the door open a crack, and looked into the kitchen.

The woman stood at the other end of the kitchen, talking on the telephone.

The telephone. That's what brought her running, not a car alarm.

She stood there naked, dripping sweat, her back to Connie. Then she turned.

Gazing at her mouth, Connie could almost hear the words formed by her tongue and lips.

'*Dal, you fucking idiot.*'

# CHAPTER TWENTY-EIGHT

'Thanks. That's just what I need after everything I've been through.'

'You weren't supposed to get in touch.'

'What can it hurt to call?' Dal asked, swiveling the seat of his stool. 'They didn't tap your phone, for Christsake.'

'What if a cop had picked it up?'

'I was ready for that. I would've pretended to be a magazine salesman.'

'Brilliant.'

'I know. Hey, look, how did it go?'

'I don't think we should discuss it on the phone.'

'That's ridiculous.'

'I'll just say that everything went as planned.'

'Fantastic! Did they check for fing . . . ?'

'Dal!'

'Okay, okay.'

'No, they didn't. By the way, mister.'

'Yeah?'

'I read this morning's paper, did you?'

He knew what was coming. It was the main reason he'd finally decided to call. 'Yes,' he said.

'The woman last night.'

'Yes?'

'Your fiancée.'

'I know.'

'What the fuck was she doing there?'

'I asked her that, myself. This morning, after I read the article. She broke down, said she was lonely with me away and it meant nothing – just a last fling with her old boyfriend.'

'And why'd you lie to me last night? Don't tell me you didn't recognize her.'

'I recognized her. I just . . . couldn't bring myself to tell you. I was in shock. I couldn't believe it was her.'

'You should've told me.'

'I know. I'm sorry.'

'Don't ever lie to me, Dal.'

'I'm sorry.'

'You can lie your head off to the rest of the world, but save the truth for me.'

'I will. I promise.'

'All right. I take it nothing is up?'

'Huh?'

'She didn't suspect anything?'

'No. She thinks it was related to his job. Someone wanted to get even.'

'Very good.'

'So everything's working.'

'Seems to be.'

'We should get together and celebrate.'

'Sure. Don't call again, Dal, unless there's an emergency.'

'When can we get together?'

'A month, maybe.'

'I don't know if I can stand it.'

'You have to. Bye, now.'

'Hey!'

She hung up.

Dal hadn't mentioned the mugging, yet. But he didn't dare call her back. He'd tell her about it another time.

# CHAPTER TWENTY-NINE

Connie watched her leave the kitchen. She waited a few seconds, then opened the door wider and looked out. No one. She stepped into the kitchen. Through the window, she saw the woman heading back to her chaise.

She hurried to the front door.

Then she was striding up the driveway, breathing deeply of the fresh warm air. She felt as if she'd spent hours caged in that house. So good to be out and free!

Once her car was running, she felt even better.

She drove down the road away from the house, and tried to piece together what she had learned.

Obviously, the woman was Elizabeth. She was the one who lured Pete out of the house, last night. Dal used her car to run Pete down. But what happened to Elizabeth? Why the bandages? Why the blood in the bedroom? Did Dal attack her? That hardly seemed likely.

The bits she'd caught of the phone conversation, with Elizabeth turned away half the time, didn't make much sense.

As she drove out of the hills, she wondered where to go next. She didn't want to return home and spend the rest of the after-noon worrying about Pete.

Go to the police? Tell them what she'd learned? What's the penalty for attempted murder? Not much. Hell, even a life term for first degree murder never amounted to more than fifteen years. So what would they get, three or four? Unless Pete . . .

No! He's got to live!

She headed for the hospital, getting more nervous with each mile. All the detective work had kept her from dwelling on Pete's condition. Now, she could think of nothing else. Her hands were wet on the steering wheel and she had trouble getting enough breath.

She imagined the worst.

'I'm sorry,' the doctor would say. Just like in the movies. 'We did all we could, but . . .'

No, no, no!

The doctor had said he was stable.

'Complications.'

Finally, she entered the parking lot. She walked into the hospital on shaky legs. The lobby smelled like floor wax. She ignored the reception desk, and went to an elevator. Her hand felt cold and numb as she pushed the up button. She leaned against the wall to steady herself while she waited.

The elevator came. It was deserted. She stepped inside, and pressed the button for the third floor. When the doors slid shut, she wanted to squat down and hug her belly. She leaned on the wall instead. Her teeth were chattering. She clenched her mouth shut.

The doors opened. She stepped out, and walked to the nurses' station.

A pink-faced woman smiled up at her. 'Yes?'

'I'm here to . . . Mr Harvey? Is he . . . ?'

'Just a moment, please.' Her eyes lowered to a clipboard.

Connie pressed her knuckles on the desktop to hold herself up.

The nurse smiled. 'Mr Harvey has been taken off the critical list.'

'How is he?'

'He's doing just fine, all things considered.'

'Oh, thank . . .' A sob broke Connie's voice and she covered her face, weeping. She was vaguely aware of the nurse getting up and putting an arm around her and leading her to a couch. The nurse sat down with her, patted her back. When she finally calmed down, the nurse brought her a cup of coffee.

'May I see him?'

'Well now, visiting hour isn't till four, and . . . Just a moment.' The nurse left her and walked down the hall. She looked into a room, then came back. 'I think it'll be all right if you just want a peek. He's sleeping, though. He shouldn't be disturbed.'

'I'll just look.'

The nurse led her to the room and opened its door.

Both legs were in traction. The head and face were bandaged. He was snoring.

Connie smiled. The nurse led her away.

'Can you tell me his injuries?'

'Well, just in general.'

'That's all right.'

'He has compound fractures of both legs, three broken ribs, a concussion, plus a roomful of lacerations and contusions. Doctor was worried most about the concussion, but it isn't real severe, fortunately. Now, you should get on home and climb in bed before you fall down.'

Connie looked at her watch. Nearly three. 'If visiting hour's at four . . .'

'You just forget about visiting hour. Mr Harvey won't be in any condition to appreciate your company. If I were you, I'd just go home and take care of myself, and come back tomorrow.'

'But tonight . . .'

'He won't even know you're here, honey.'

Back at her apartment, Connie climbed into bed. She intended to heed the nurse's advice – but only so far. She would take a little nap, then fix dinner and dress up and head out to the hospital for the eight o'clock visiting hour. Even if Pete wouldn't know she was there, at least she could sit by him, hold his hand. And who knows, maybe he would be awake after all.

She slept.

When she opened her eyes, the room was dim.

'Oh no,' she muttered. She looked at the clock. Five after eight. 'Damn!'

The hospital was a half hour drive. By the time she could get dressed and over there . . .

Forget it. Tomorrow would have to do.

She sat on the corner of the bed and wondered how to spend the evening. She felt very good. And very hungry. Putting on her satin robe, she went into the kitchen. She looked in the refrigerator. Nothing she could make a decent dinner out of. And anything in the freezer would take forever to thaw.

So I'll go out, she thought. How about the Sizzler? Then she had a better idea: she would drive over to the Safeway, buy a fresh slab of tenderloin and some other goodies, come back to the apartment and have a feast.

A regular celebration.

Hoist a few drinks to Pete's health, a few to the imminent downfall of Dal and Elizabeth.

Great idea!

She hurried into her bedroom to change.

As she slowed down for the entrance to the Safeway parking

lot, she saw the movie theater on the next block.

The Haunted Palace.

Where she'd gone on her first night out with Pete.

She drove past the Safeway.

Don't do this, she warned herself. Don't get started again. The minute something goes wrong in your life, you head for the movies.

This is different. Not an escape, like the other times. Pete is alive! We'll be together again. This isn't an escape, it's a celebration!

A celebration of my first date with Pete.

As she parked behind the theater, she hoped it had hot dogs.

# CHAPTER THIRTY

Connie paused in front of the ticket window of the Haunted Palace, and checked the show times. *The Howling* had started at 7:15. *Savage Schreck* would come on at 8:55, followed by *City of the Dead* at 9:10. If she wanted to stick around, *The Howling* would show again at 10:50.

She stepped up to the window and bought a ticket from the same white-faced girl with straight black hair who'd sold the tickets to Pete.

Bruno waited inside the door, his face twisted under the nylon stocking. His bloody T-shirt reminded Connie of the carpet at Elizabeth's house.

'Hi, Bruno,' she said, and handed him the ticket. He ripped it in half. Giving back the stub, he touched her hand. She went into the restroom to wash it.

No hurry. The less she saw of *The Howling's* finish, the better. In a different theater – one without Bruno hanging around – she would've waited in the lobby until the movie ended.

In the mirror above the sink, she saw that she didn't look as bad as she expected. A little pale. A little nervous in the eyes. Her hair could use a shampoo.

The top of her warm-up suit was open too much. She raised the zipper a couple of inches. If she'd known she would be out for more than a quick trip to the supermarket, she would've worn a bra. She felt rather exposed without it. Nothing to be done, though. She hiked up her pants and left the restroom.

The girls at the refreshment counter looked like clones of the ticket girl. The nearer one smiled with bright red lips.

'I'll have a hot dog and a large Pepsi,' Connie said. 'Make that two hot dogs.'

While she waited, she looked around. Bruno, standing by the door, was watching her.

Creepy.

Well, he's *supposed* to be creepy.

Turning away, she watched the numbers appear on the cash register. She paid the girl, and took her food to the end of the counter. There, she opened the foil-wrapped hot dogs. Steam drifted up from them. Mouth watering, she squirted mustard onto both hot dogs. She wrapped them up, grabbed a straw and a couple of napkins, and hurried into the dark auditorium.

She found an empty seat at the end of a row, but didn't want to block the man behind it. She took the next seat over.

She ate her hot dogs slowly, trying not to watch the screen. But the action drew her eyes.

What the hell, she decided. So I'll know how it ends.

She watched the rest of the movie, fascinated.

Then the lights came up. Looking around, she saw that the theater was crowded for a weeknight. Must be a couple hundred people, she guessed.

She checked her wristwatch. Ten to nine. If she'd gone to the hospital, she would just be arriving. Ten minutes to spend with Pete.

She should've gone.

Too late now.

Maybe she'd overslept on purpose. Maybe, subconsciously, she didn't want to see Pete tonight. Didn't want to see him lying there broken.

The thought made her burn with guilt. Well, she would make up for it tomorrow. She'd be there waiting at four . . .

The lights dimmed.

Words appeared on the screen, red and dripping like blood: **SCREAM GEMS PRESENTS OTTO SCHRECK IN . . .** flames curled out of **SAVAGE SCHRECK.**

It is daylight. A young woman in a dirty gingham dress makes her way down a slope, glancing nervously over her shoulder. At the bottom of the slope, she crouches by a brook. She dips her hands into the water and drinks.

Knife raised, an Indian rushes down the slope. His body is naked except for a red breechclout. Warpaint streaks his skin.

A goddamn maniac, Connie thought.

The girl continues to drink.

*Get out of there!* Connie wanted to shout.

Finally, she looks around. Fright twists her face. She throws herself into the brook, splashes to the surface, and wades through the waist-high water.

The savage leaps from the shore, black hair streaming behind him, knife clamped in his teeth, and drops onto the girl's back.

They crash into the water.

The girl breaks the surface. She is on her back, coughing, kicking, waving her arms. She seems, at first, to be floating. Then she is lifted straight out of the water. The savage raises her overhead and throws her.

She smashes through a bush near shore, hits the ground shoulder-first, and rolls.

She lies there stunned.

The savage strides through the water. Climbing the bank, he takes the knife from his teeth.

The girl is on her hands and knees, trying to get up.

*Run!* Connie thought.

215

But she can't get to her feet.

The savage kicks her in the belly.

Connie grunted as the impact lifted the girl completely off the ground.

She falls onto her back, clutching her belly, her knees upraised.

The savage crouches at her head. He twists her hair around his hand, and pulls it taut. He presses the knife against her scalp.

'Oh God,' Connie muttered.

A young man in the next row looked around at her, grinning. Connie smiled back, and shrugged.

Blood streams down the girl's face. Her eyes bulge. Her mouth is stretched open so wide she looks as if her cheeks might rip.

At least I can't hear the scream, Connie thought.

Suddenly, a revolver muzzle pushes against the back of the savage's head. He stops trying to scalp the girl.

Connie sighed with relief.

While the girl lies on the ground, crying and clutching her slashed head, a red-haired man in cowboy clothes ties the savage's hands with strips of rawhide.

The scene changes. The savage sits astride a horse beneath an oak tree. A rope hangs from a branch overhead. Its noose is around his neck.

*All right*, Connie thought.

The girl stands nearby, watching. Her head has been bandaged with a strip of fabric torn from her dress.

The cowboy smiles at her. His mouth moves. 'You wanta do the honors?'

She nods, steps to the rear of the horse, and slaps its haunch. The horse lunges away. The rope snaps taut, jerking the savage off the saddle. He swings, kicking and twisting, his face turning purple, his tongue lolling out.

The girl and the cowboy turn away and start walking.

'That's another good Indian,' the cowboy says.

'What are you gonna do to me?' asks the girl, looking frightened.

What's wrong with *her*? Connie wondered. This is the guy who saved her life.

'I'll see you safely back to the settlement,' the cowboy tells her.

They're still walking away, but the savage swinging below the tree is now straining, his arm and chest muscles bulging.

The cowboy says, 'I'm sure your folks will be mighty glad to see you.'

'Bullshit,' the girl says. 'You're gonna kill me, just like you killed Tina.'

The savage's hands burst free. With rawhide dangling from both bloody wrists, he reaches overhead and clutches the rope. He climbs it, pulling himself upward hand over hand.

'You're crazy,' says the girl. 'You're all crazy. You don't seriously think you can get away with this? You show this thing on the screen, and people are gonna see me. They'll recognize me, just like I recognized Tina.'

What's all this? Connie wondered.

'Oh, sooner or later I suppose someone will. In a few weeks, though, I'll be long gone. We'll have thirteen *Schrecks* by then. Filmworld is picking up the whole package for an even million – planning to edit them into a feature. Nice, don't you agree? You'll be a star.'

'A dead star.'

'You'll be immortalized on the silver . . .' His mouth springs wide as the savage, behind him, shoves a knife into his back.

The girl tries to run, but the savage grabs her hair and jerks her backwards off her feet. He drags her to the tree. As he props her against it, she scratches his face. He slams a knee into her belly, doubling her. Then he starts tying her to the tree.

Connie watched, totally confused. She'd seen plenty of awful movies before, but this had to be the worst. Not only vicious and gruesome, but the dialogue made no sense at all. This must be one of those crazy film-within-a-film movies that Europeans seemed so fond of making. An artsy-fart movie. Not supposed to make sense.

The savage finishes tying her to the tree.

'You bastards!' she cries. 'Let me go!'

Connie watched the savage wander through the trees, gathering twigs. As she realized what they were for, she muttered, 'Oh no.'

The man in front of her looked around again, smiling. His mouth moved, but the darkness hid his words. He might be saying anything. Connie assumed he was being friendly. Smiling, she nodded agreement with whatever he'd said. He nodded back, and turned away.

Twigs and sticks are piled around the girl's feet. The savage, several yards away, is standing behind a small fire. He slowly wraps cloth around the head of an arrow. When it is secure, he lowers it into the fire. He raises his bow. He aims the flaming arrow at the girl. It streaks through the air.

It hits the tree inches above the girl's head.

'My name if Brit Anderson,' she says. 'I'm not an actress. This is not a movie, it's real. If you can hear me out there . . .'

The savage lights another arrow. 'They'll hear whatever we like, bitch.' He shoots the arrow. It enters the kindling at her feet. Smoke rises out, then flames.

She writhes against the ropes. The hem of her dress catches fire.

'*My name is Brit . . .*'
A flaming arrow plunges into her chest.

# CHAPTER THIRTY-ONE

Connie grabbed the shoulder of the man in front of her, and he jumped. 'I've got to talk to you,' she whispered. 'In the lobby. I'm deaf. I read lips. I need light to see what you say.'

He nodded.

As they walked up the aisle, Connie glanced back at the screen and saw the girl burning – hair on fire, skin turning black.

She pushed through the door and clutched the man's arm. He frowned at her, looking puzzled. 'That girl . . . she was killed.'

'I know, but . . .'

'It wasn't fake. They *killed* her.'

'Are you out of your mind?'

'What was she saying there at the end?'

'Hail Marys.'

'No. That must've been dubbed. She was saying her name is Brit Anderson, and she's not an actress, and it's really happening. There's a phone over there. I want you to call the police.'

'The *police*? Hey, that's serious business.'

'She was murdered.'

'Maybe you should talk to the manager.'

'He might be in on it.'

'Oh for . . .' He shook his head. 'Is *everyone* in on it?'

'No, but the manager . . .'

'I've been coming here since it opened. The man may look awful in that get-up, but he seems to be a perfectly nice guy. Come on.' He crossed the lobby toward the entrance, where Bruno was taking tickets.

Connie hurried after him.

'Could we speak to you in private for a moment?'

Bruno nodded. He called to one of the vampire girls at the refreshment counter, then led the way to an office on the far side.

Connie followed both men inside. She stood near the open door.

Bruno pulled the stocking off his head. Without it, he had a pleasant, chubby face. 'Now,' he said. 'What seems to be the problem?'

Both men looked at Connie.

'The girl in that Schreck film wasn't an actress. Her name is Brit Anderson and she was murdered on camera. Actually murdered.'

Bruno shook his head. 'I'm afraid I don't understand. What leads you to think such a thing?'

'She said so. Her real words were dubbed over, but I read her lips.'

'Are you certain of this?'

'I know what she said, and I believe her.'

Bruno nodded. He picked up the telephone, and dialed O. 'Operator, put me in touch with the police. Yes, this is an emergency.' He covered the mouthpiece and said, 'They'll get to the bottom of this.' Then he took his hand away. 'Yes. I'm calling from the Haunted Palace movie theater at 8424 Pico. Would you send a car over here right away? We have an urgent situation . . . Apparently, murder has been committed . . . Yes. Thank you.' He hung up. 'That should get them here in short order.'

He stood up. 'Shall we go upstairs and seize the evidence?'

They followed him through the lobby. The carpeted stairway was roped off. A sign hung from the plush cordon: BALCONY CLOSED. Bruno unhooked one end of the cordon, and let them through.

At the top of the stairs, he stepped over to a door. He pushed a key into its lock, and opened it. 'Right through here,' he said.

The man and Connie entered.

She saw a pair of movie projectors near the side wall. One was running, its reels turning slowly, flashing pictures through the tiny window in front of it. A miniature image reflected on the pane.

Someone between the projectors.

Bruno talked to him, then picked up a film can and checked the label. 'It has to be rewound. Only take a minute. I should go down and see if the police are here yet.'

He stepped past the man.

'Excuse me,' he said, and moved past Connie. He shot an elbow into her side, knocking her off balance, and threw the door shut. Connie fell against the wall.

She saw the projectionist leap from between the two big machines. No warpaint, but she knew his face, his mad eyes.

Bruno swept her feet from under her. As her back hit the floor, she saw Schreck punch a screwdriver into the belly of the man who'd come up with her.

She flung up her crossed arms and blocked a kick Bruno aimed at her face.

Someone clutched her ankles.

'No!'

Schreck lifted her feet. He raised her off the floor until she was hanging upside down. In that position, with no leverage and her vision distorted, she was nearly defenseless. Still, she blocked Bruno's first punch to her belly. The second punch got through, knocking her wind out. She clutched her belly, and he kicked her in the head, and when she opened her eyes she was facedown on the backseat floor of a car speeding through the night.

# CHAPTER THIRTY-TWO

The car drove for a long time. Connie's head throbbed with pain. Her arms, tied behind her back, were tingly and almost numb. Somebody's feet were on her back and rump. When she tried to lift her head, once, they stomped hard. After that, she didn't move.

She had a good idea of what they planned to do with her. She was frightened, but angry too.

Angry at herself. For letting Bruno sucker her that way. Obviously, he hadn't phoned the cops. Was his phone unplugged? She should've been more careful, damn it. And she got that poor man killed: she didn't even know his name.

Now, everything she'd learned about Dal and Elizabeth was useless. She should've gone to the cops with her information. But no, she'd been too damned set on getting her own revenge. Stupid! Now they might just get away with running Pete down.

Should've.

So damned many should'ves.

She should've gone to the hospital, tonight. Now she'd never see Pete again.

It's not over yet, kiddo.

Not over yet. Keep telling yourself that.

The car stopped. Doors opened. She was dragged out by

her feet. Schreck lifted her and slung her over his shoulder. He carried her through the darkness. She felt a cool breeze on her back where the jacket of her warm-up suit had pulled up. The air smelled like the ocean.

We're near shore, she thought, and wondered what good that knowledge would do. What good would any of it do? Her martial arts training sure hadn't helped. Maybe the reverse. If she hadn't been so damned confident, she never would've waltzed into the projection room like an idiot.

Schreck carried her up a few wooden stairs. He waited a moment, then took her through a doorway. They were in darkness. He started up more stairs, his shoulder shoving into her belly with each step he climbed. The stairs seemed to go up forever. Finally, they stopped and he carried her through a long straight way. He turned. Her head brushed a wall or a door-frame. He carried her forward several steps, and bent over.

Connie fell backwards through the darkness. She landed on something soft – a bed? – with her legs hanging over the end.

An overhead light came on. Squinting in its brightness, she saw Schreck above her. He took a screwdriver from a deep pocket of his coveralls. She sucked in her belly. The blade pushed against her navel.

Bruno, behind him, said something.

'Sure, I can wait,' Schreck answered. He took the screwdriver away. He flipped it end over end, caught it by the handle, and slipped it into his pocket.

The two men sat down in chairs across the room.

'Can I sit up?' Connie asked, raising her head to see the response.

Bruno nodded.

She sat up, taking the pressure off her shoulders and numb arms. The men stared at her. 'What are you waiting for?' she asked.

'Todd,' said Bruno. 'The producer. He'll be along soon.'

'The producer?'

'Producer, writer, director.'

'The brains,' Schreck said, and smiled in a way that sent a chill up Connie's back.

'I'm going to star in one of your little productions?'

'I'm the star,' Schreck said.

'But we'd be nowhere,' added Bruno, 'without the little people.'

'I'll be recognized,' Connie said.

Bruno shrugged. 'Maybe. That'll be Filmworld's problem.'

'It'll get back to you.'

'Oh, I doubt that. Todd's the only connection, and he'll be in South America living like a king.'

'Where'll you be?'

'I'll still have the theater – a fairly profitable enterprise. I'm completely ignorant, naturally, of anything unusual about the *Schreck* films. I'm only an innocent exhibitor. And Otto, here, will undergo cosmetic surgery – he can use it, don't you think? With his new face, he'll continue as projectionist and my partner in the theater.'

'I have a lot of money.'

'Do you?'

'How much would it take to get you guys to let me go?'

'More than you have, I assure you.'

'Half a million dollars?'

'Come now.'

'I have that much in my savings account. Just untie me, and . . .'

Another man entered the room. Connie recognized him from tonight's film: he'd played the cowboy. 'Oh, she's a beauty!' he said.

'Look, let me go. I'll keep my mouth shut. You can split

up my money among the three of you.'

'Oh, we can't do that,' he told her. 'We have a film to make! The thirteenth and final *Schreck*!' Stepping close to Connie, he brushed a curtain of hair away from the side of her face. 'It's a pity they had to bang you up, but we'll make do.' He patted her bruised cheek. 'You've come as something of a surprise, unfortunately, so we'll have to work out a story-line before we commence shooting. I like to begin with the mode of death, and work backwards from there.'

'Don't strain your brain.'

He slapped her. Then he stepped right away and sat on a dresser. 'Can you see me all right? I don't want you to miss any of this.'

'I can see you.'

'Good. Now, we must find a way of dispatching you that hasn't been done to death — if you'll pardon the pun. We've already used knives, a fork, a scalpel, an axe, arrows, a chain saw. We hanged one. One unfortunate lady choked on human flesh. Schreck bit out the throat of another. Guns are out, naturally. Too mundane.'

'Let me skin her alive,' Schreck suggested.

'We don't want excessive nudity. We're doing horror, after all, not porn.'

'Film it from behind,' Bruno said.

Schreck scowled. 'All the good stuff's in front.'

'Well, we'll keep it in mind. Let's brainstorm for a bit, though.'

'Drown her in the bathtub?' Bruno asked.

'We already drowned one in the stream.'

'I'll pound nails in her.'

'*Schreck the Carpenter*,' Bruno said, and laughed.

'Bury her alive?'

'How would we film it?'

'How about I eat her?'

'*Schreck the Snatch* . . .'

'Too close to *Gourmet Schreck*.'

'Shit,' said Bruno. 'What's left?'

'We'll think of something. Genius, after all, is ninety percent perspiration.' He grinned at Connie. 'Do you have any preferences?'

'Yeah! Suppose I kill Schreck and escape? It'd give your film a nice upbeat finish. Audiences go for that.'

'Good thought, but I don't think we'll run with it.'

'We bury her alive,' Schreck said. 'But shallow. I bash her on the head, and throw the dirt on her. Only she's not dead. She digs her way out and tries to run away. I chase her down. I can take her head right off with the shovel.'

'I like it.'

Connie felt dizzy and faint. She took deep breaths.

'What do you think, Bruno?'

'Who digs the hole?'

'We'll let her do it. Good drama there, digging her own grave.'

'Just so I don't have to do it.'

'I'll take her head off last,' Schreck said. 'Chop her up some, before that.' His hands, gripping an imaginary shovel, jab the air. '*Ram* her in the back. Get her down. Take off one of her hands, maybe. Or both of them. Maybe take off her feet. Then take that shovel and . . .'

Connie threw herself sideways and vomited on the mattress.

Schreck untied her feet. He made a loop at one end of the rope, and dropped it around her neck.

'Struggle a bit,' Todd said. 'You're on *Candid Camera*.' He pointed to a mirror above the dresser. 'Bruno's in the control room getting this down, so make it look good.'

She turned to the mirror. 'My name is Con . . .'

Schreck jerked the rope, yanking her off the end of the bed. She fell to her knees.

'Lovely,' Todd said.

Schreck dragged her by the rope. She kicked and choked. Then he grabbed her hair and pulled her to her feet. 'Walk, bitch,' he said.

Todd left the room first. He pranced ahead of them down the lighted hallway.

Schreck walked behind Connie, keeping the rope taut.

'Pull,' Todd said. 'Try to get free. You're fighting for your life.'

'Fuck you,' Connie said.

The rope jerked her backwards off her feet. She cried out as she landed on her tied arms. Schreck stepped past her. He grabbed her left foot, and dragged her to the end of the hall.

He'll break my arms, she thought. If he takes me down the stairs like this, they'll both . . .

But he stopped at the head of the stairway. He leaned over her, gripped her crotch and the front of her jacket, and hoisted her overhead. He carried her down the stairs that way, holding her high, one fist like a post pounding her chest, the other clutching as if to split the fabric of her warm-up pants and claw into her.

The door at the bottom of the stairs was open. He carried her outside, and stopped.

She expected to be hurled into the night, but he simply swung her down and shoved her against the wall. Todd was standing on the lawn, smiling and nodding.

Then Bruno came out the front door with a video camera on his shoulder as if he were here to capture the event for *Eyewitness News*. He stepped down the porch stairs, turned on a powerful light, and aimed the camera at her.

Schreck punched her in the belly. As she doubled over, choking, he flung her from the porch. She twisted in midair, and landed on her side.

Schreck cut her hands free. He grabbed the back of her jacket and carried her like a piece of luggage. Her feet dragged the grass, her arms hung numb and useless. Near the back of the house, her zipper popped apart at the bottom. It skidded open, dropping her. Schreck let her fall to the ground.

She didn't try to get up. She lay there on the cool wet grass. Her arms were no longer numb. They hurt and tingled.

She tried to think, but she couldn't concentrate. Her mind seemed blurry.

Schreck jerked her to her feet. She turned her face away from the brightness of Bruno's camera light.

Bruno pushed a shovel at her.

She took it.

He pointed to the ground at her feet.

She could barely grip the shovel. She punched it at the ground. It hardly went in an inch. She jumped on the top edges of its head. Her weight forced it deeper. She pried out a wedge of dirt, and dumped it on the grass. Then she repeated the process. This time, her arms were stronger. She jumped on the shovel with more force. It plunged in deeper. She took out a larger load.

Todd, she saw, was standing close to Bruno. Schreck remained beside her.

She stabbed in the shovel, jumped on it, and removed the dirt. She dumped it onto the growing pile. Then she lunged forward.

Schreck grabbed her. He caught the hanging hood of her warm-up jacket.

Todd's mouth moved. 'Let her go! Run her down!'

Schreck let go.

231

Connie ran. Glancing back, she saw Schreck close behind her. The others followed. She ran harder, but the shovel weighed her down. If she tossed it, she might outrun Schreck.

Ahead, she saw the tree where they'd burned the girl. Beyond it would be a steep slope, the brook, and a thickly wooded area. If she could make it to the woods . . .

She glanced back.

Saw Schreck's wild face, his reaching hands.

*Bayonet roll!*

Shovel clutched to her chest, she threw herself head over heels, hit the grass, twisted around and jammed the handle to the ground. Schreck, unable to stop, ran against the shovel blade. The shaft jerked in Connie's hands. She yanked it, throwing Schreck overhead. He hit the ground and rolled. She rushed him. She raised the shovel high and crashed it down on the back of his head.

Looking around, she saw Todd and Bruno racing to catch up.

Schreck rolled onto his back.

Connie punched the shovel blade into his belly. It hardly went in an inch. She jumped on it with both feet, and it plunged in deep.

She jerked it out and whirled around. Shielding her eyes from the camera light, she saw Todd and Bruno a dozen feet away.

'Okay bastards, who's next?'

# CHAPTER THIRTY-THREE

A nurse pushed the wheelchair out the automatic doors of the hospital. 'We're going to miss you, Pete.'

'Well, we'll be back one of these days. Give us about nine months.'

'Rascal.'

Connie handed him the crutches, and he used them to push himself out of the chair.

'Now watch yourself crossing streets,' the nurse said.

'I'll be careful.'

Connie smiled. 'I don't think he has to worry about any more accidents.'

# EPILOGUE

## SCREAM GEMS
## PRESENTS
## VENGEANCE!

In the shadows at the head of the cellar stairs, the door opens. A woman in a white nightgown lunges through it. Stumbling off the top stair, she throws herself against the railing. It wobbles, but stops her fall.

The door above her swings shut.

Pushing herself off the railing, she steps up to the door and tries it. Locked.

Slowly, she descends the stairs, moving out of shadows and into light. Her nightgown is grimy and torn, exposing her right breast. Her neck and face and legs are bandaged, her face dark with bruises.

Halfway down the stairs, she stops. She gazes at something below, then hurries to the bottom.

A man lies on the bone-littered floor near a coffin – tied and gagged.

Kneeling beside him, she peels the wide strip of tape off his mouth. His mouth is stuffed with a handkerchief. She pulls it out.

'Untie me,' the man says.

'Not just yet.'

'Please.'

'Tell me what's going on.'

'How do I know?'

'How'd you get here?'

'Some guy rang my doorbell. A fat guy. I opened up, and he stuck a gun in my face.'

'Who was he?'

'Untie me, huh?'

'Who was he?'

'Never seen him before. I figured he was a cop, you know? In fact, I asked him. He grinned and said, "You're under arrest for attempted murder. For hit-and-run." He didn't read me my rights, though. Then, down at the street, he opened the trunk of his car and bashed me on the head.'

'Roll over.'

He rolls onto his side, and the woman picks at the knotted rope behind his wrists.

'That's about what happened to me, too,' she says. 'Mine was a red-headed guy. I knew for sure he wasn't a cop. I saw plenty last night, and they didn't behave like this guy.'

'Did he hurt you?'

'Yeah. The bastard knocked me around, tore my night-gown. He didn't bash my head, though.'

'Did he put you in a car trunk?'

'Fuckin' right he did.' She finishes untying his hands. He rolls over, sits up, and starts to work on the knot at his feet.

'Who do you think they are?' he asks.

'Somebody's figured it out.'

'Huh?'

'Somebody knows we did it.'

'Who?'

'Three guesses.'

He shakes his head and unwraps the rope at his feet. He rubs his ankles. 'Just tell me, okay?'

'Your adorable fiancée.'

'You're kidding.'

'Think about it. She saw us. She put it all together.'

He scowls and shakes his head. 'I guess . . . maybe so. What do you think she's gonna do?'

'I don't know, but we'd better get out of here.' She helps him to his feet. They stand by the coffin, each silently scanning the cellar.

Behind them, the coffin lid is flung off. They whirl around. Inside the coffin, a hooded figure sits up. The hood belongs to a warm-up jacket worn backwards. Ragged holes have been cut for eyes and mouth.

As the figure stands up, the man and woman back away. It steps out of the coffin, bare feet crushing the bones on the cellar's dirt floor.

'It's her,' the woman says.

The man shakes his head. He is pale and trembling.

'What do you want?'

The figure doesn't answer.

'Let's take her,' mutters the woman. 'Now!' She attacks. Alone.

The hooded one grabs her arms, pivots, slams her to the floor, and steps past her.

'It *is* you,' the man says, moving backwards. 'You think I . . .' He shrieks as a kick smashes his left knee. He drops sideways, screaming. Before he hits the floor, a second kick shatters his right knee.

The hooded one pivots and shoots knuck'es into the face of the attacking woman. The blow slams her backwards. The nape of her neck hits the coffins' edge. Her head snaps back.

She jerks and trembles as if a thousand volts are ripping through her body. Then she slumps.

Slender figures press her neck as if seeking a pulse. Then the hooded one straddles her body, grips her beneath the arms, and wrestles her into the coffin.

The man is still on the floor, whimpering.

The hooded one drags him to the coffin.

'No!' he cries. 'No, please! I'll do anything! Whatever you say!'

'Confess.'

'Okay! I did it. We both did it. There!'

'Get in the coffin.'

'No!'

Screaming, he fights as the hooded one struggles to lift him. His hands jerk open the jacket. He pounds the bare back, claws furrows in the skin. He rips at the blonde hair behind the hood. Then he falls into the coffin on top of the woman. Grabbing its edges, he pulls himself up. A fist smashes his nose, and he drops away.

The hooded one places the lid on the coffin.

Muffled screams rage inside the coffin as the lid is nailed down.

### The End

# AND OTHER TALES

ANOTHER TALES

# MESS HALL

Jean didn't hear footsteps. She heard only the rush of the nearby stream, her own moaning, Paul's harsh gasps as he thrust into her. The first she heard of the man was his voice.

'Looks to me like fornication in a public park area.'

Her heart slammed.

Oh God, no.

With her left eye, she glimpsed the man's vague shape crouching beside her in the moonlight, less than a yard away. She looked up at Paul. His eyes were wide with alarm.

This can't be happening, Jean told herself.

She felt totally helpless and exposed. Not that the guy could see anything. Just Paul's bare butt. He couldn't see that Jean's blouse was open, her bra bunched around her neck, her skirt rucked up past her waist.

'Do you know it's against the law?' the man asked.

Paul took his tongue out of Jean's mouth. He turned his head toward the man.

Jean could feel his heart drumming, his penis shrinking inside her.

'Not to mention poor taste,' the man added.

'We didn't mean any harm,' Paul said.

And started to get up.

Jean jammed her shoes against his buttocks, tightened her arms around his back.

'What if some *children* had wandered by?' the man asked.

'We're sorry,' Jean told him, keeping her head straight up, not daring to look at the man again, instead staring at Paul. 'We'll leave.'

'Kiss goodbye, now.'

Seemed like a weird request.

But Paul obeyed. He pressed his mouth gently against Jean's lips, and she wondered how she could manage to cover herself because it was quite obvious that, as soon as the kiss was over, Paul would have to climb off her. And there she'd be.

Later, she knew it was a shotgun.

She hadn't seen a shotgun, but she'd only given the man that single, quick glance.

Paul was giving her the goodbye kiss and she was wondering about the best way to keep the man from seeing her when suddenly it didn't matter because the world blew up. Paul's eyes exploded out of their sockets and dropped onto *her* eyes. She jerked her head sideways to get away from them. Jerked it the wrong way. Saw the clotted wetness on the moonlit trunk of a nearby tree, saw his ear cling to the bark for a moment, then fall.

Paul's head dropped heavily onto the side of her face. A torrent of blood blinded her.

She started to scream.

Paul's weight tumbled off. The man stomped her belly. He scooped her up, swung her over his shoulder, and started to run. She wheezed, trying to breathe. His foot had smashed her air out and now his shoulder kept ramming into her. She felt as if she were drowning. Only a dim corner of her mind seemed to work, and she wished it would blink out.

Better total darkness, better no awareness at all.

The man stopped running. He bent over, and Jean flopped backward. She slammed something. Beside her was a windshield plated with moonlight. She'd been dumped across the hood of a car. Her legs dangled over the car's front.

She tried to lift her head. Couldn't. So she lay there, struggling to suck in air.

The man came back.

He'd been away?

Jean felt as if she had missed a chance to save herself.

He leaned over, clutched both sides of her open blouse, and yanked her into a sitting position. He snapped a handcuff around her right wrist, passed the other bracelet beneath her knee, and cuffed her left hand. Then he lifted her off the hood. He swung her into the car's passenger seat and slammed the door.

Through the windshield, Jean saw him rush past the front of the car. She drove her knee up. It bumped her chin, but she managed to slip the handcuff chain down her calf and under the sole of her running shoe. She grabbed the door handle. She levered it up and threw her shoulder against the door and started to tumble out, but her head jerked back with searing pain as if the hair were being torn from her scalp. Her head twisted. Her cheekbone struck the steering wheel. A hand clasped the top of her head. Another clutched her chin. And he rammed the side of her face again and again on the wheel.

When she opened her eyes, her head was on the man's lap. She felt his hand kneading her breast. The car was moving fast. From the engine noise and the hiss of the tires on the pavement, she guessed they were on the Interstate. The highway lights cast a faint, silvery glow on the man's face. He looked down at her and smiled.

The police-artist sketch didn't have him quite right. It had the crewcut right, and the weird crazy eyes, but his nose was a little larger, his lips a lot thicker.

Jean started to lift her head.

'Lie still,' he warned. 'Move a muscle, I'll pound your brains out.' He laughed. 'How about your boyfriend's brains? Did you see how they hit that tree?'

Jean didn't answer.

He pinched her.

She gritted her teeth.

'I asked you a question.'

'I saw,' she said.

'Cool, huh?'

'No.'

'How about his eyes? I've never seen anything like that. Just goes to show what a twelve-gauge can do to a fellow. You know, I've never killed a *guy* before. Just sweet young things like you.'

Like me.

It came as no surprise, no shock. She'd seen him murder Paul, and he planned to murder her, too – the same as he'd murdered the others.

Maybe he doesn't kill them all, she thought. Only one body had been found. Everyone talked as if the Reaper had killed the other six, but really they were only *missing*.

Maybe he takes them someplace and keeps them.

But he just now said he kills sweet young things. Plural. He killed them all. But maybe not. Maybe he just wants to keep me and fool with me and not kill me and I'll figure a way out.

'Where are you taking me?' she asked.

'A nice, private place in the hills where nobody will hear you scream.'

The words made a chill crawl over her.

'Oooh, goosebumps. I like that.' His hand glided over her

skin like a cold breeze. Jean was tempted to grab his hand and bite it.

If she did that, he would hurt her again.

There'll be a world of hurt later, she thought. He plans to make me scream.

But that was later. Maybe she could get away from him before it came to that. The best thing, for now, was to give him no trouble. Don't fight him. Act docile. Then maybe he'll let his guard down.

'Do you know who I am?' he asked.

'Yes.'

'Tell me.'

'The Reaper.'

'Very good. And I know who you are, too.'

He knows me? How could he? Maybe followed me around on campus, asked someone my name.

'You're Number Eight,' he said. 'Just think about that. You're going to be famous. You'll be in all the newspapers, they'll talk about you on television, you'll even end up being a chapter in a book someday. Have you read any books like that? They'll have a nice little biography of you, quotes from your parents and friends. The bittersweet story of your brief but passionate relationship with that guy. What was his name?'

'Paul,' she murmured.

'Paul. He'll get a good write-up, himself, since he's the first guy to die at the hands of the Reaper. Of course, they'll realize that he was incidental. You were the intended victim, Paul simply an unlucky jerk who got in the way. He got lucky, then he got unlucky. Good one, huh? Maybe I'll write the book myself. He got off and got offed. Or did he? Which came first? Did he go out with a bang?'

'Why don't you shut up?'

'Because I don't want to,' he said, and raked a path up her belly with a single fingernail.

Jean cringed. Air hissed in through her teeth.

'You should be nice to me,' he said. 'After all, I'm the one making you famous. Of course, some of the notoriety may be a trifle embarrassing for you. That book I was telling you about, it'll have a whole lot about today. Your final hours. Who was the last person to see you alive. And of course, it won't neglect the fornication in the park. People read that, a lot of them are going to think you were asking for it. I suppose I'd have to agree with them. Didn't you know any better?'

She *had* known better. 'What about the Reaper?' she'd asked when the movie let out and Paul suggested the park.

'He'll have to find his *own* gal.'

'I mean it. I'm not sure it's such a great idea. Why don't we go to my place?'

'Right. So your demented roommate can listen through the wall and make noises.'

'I told her not to do that anymore.'

'Come on, let's go to the park. It's a neat night. We can find a place by the stream.'

'I don't know.' She squeezed his hand. 'I'd like to, Paul, but . . .'

'Shit. Everybody's got Reaperitis. For Godsake, he's in *Portland*.'

'That's only a half-hour drive.'

'Okay. Forget it. Shit.'

They walked half a block, Paul silent and scowling, before Jean slipped a hand into the rear pocket of his pants and said, 'Hey, pal, how's about a stroll in the park?'

*'Didn't you know any better?'*

His hand smacked her bare skin.

'Yes!'

248

'Don't you ignore me. I ask you a question, you answer. Got it?'

'Yes.'

The car slowed. The Reaper's left hand eased the steering wheel over and Jean felt the car slip sideways. It tipped upward a bit, pressing her cheek against his belt buckle.

An off-ramp, she thought.

The car stopped, then made a sharp turn.

A cold tremor swept through Jean.

We're getting there, she thought. Wherever he's taking me, we're getting there. Oh, Jesus.

'You thought it couldn't happen to you,' he said. 'Am I right?'

'No.'

'What, then? You were just too horny to care?'

'Paul would've kept on pouting.' Her voice was high, shaky.

'One of those. I hate those sniveling, whiny pouters. Take me, for instance – I never pout. That's for the losers. I never lose, so I've got no reason to pout. I make *other* people lose.'

He slowed the car, turned it again.

'I hate pouters, too,' Jean said, trying to keep her voice steady. 'They stink. They don't deserve to live.'

He looked down at her. His face was a vague blur. There were no more streetlights, Jean realized. Nothing but moonlight, now.

'I bet you and I are a lot alike,' she said.

'Think so, do you?'

'I've never told anyone this before, but . . . I guess it's safe to tell you. I killed a girl once.'

'That so?'

*He doesn't believe me!*

'Yeah. It was just two years ago. I was going with this guy,

249

Jim Smith, and . . . I really loved him. We got engaged. And then all of a sudden he started going with this bitch, Mary Jones.'

'Smith and Jones, huh?' He chuckled.

'I can't help it if they had stupid names,' she said, and wished she'd taken an extra second to think up names that sounded *real*, damn it. 'Anyway, he spent less and less time with me, and I knew he was seeing Mary. So one night I snuck into her room in the sorority and smothered her with a pillow. Killed her. And I enjoyed it. I laughed when she died.'

He patted Jean's belly. 'I guess we are two of a kind. Maybe you'd like to throw in with me. I can see some advantages to an arrangement like that. You could lure the pretty young things into my car, help me subdue them. What do you think?'

She thought that she might start to cry. His offer was just what she had wanted to hear – and he knew it. He knew it, all right.

But she went along, just in case. 'I think I'd like that.'

'That makes it an even fifty percent,' he said.

The front of the car tipped upward. Again, Jean's cheek pressed his belt buckle.

'You're the fourth to try that maneuver. Hey, forget about killing me, I'm just your type, let's be partners. Four out of eight. You're only the second to confess a prior murder, though. The other one said she pushed her kid sister out of the tree house. I sure do pick 'em. Two murderers. What are the chances of that?'

'Coincidence,' Jean muttered.

'Nice try.'

His right hand continued to fondle her. His left hand kept jogging the steering wheel from side to side as he maneuvered up the hill.

She could reach up and grab the wheel and maybe make

them crash. But the car didn't seem to be moving very fast. At this speed, the crash might not hurt him at all.

'Let's hear the one about your rich father,' he said.

'Go to hell.'

He laughed. 'Come on, don't ruin the score. You'll make it a hundred percent if you've got a rich father who'll pay me heaps of money to take you back to him unscathed.'

She decided to try for the crash.

But the car stopped. He swung the steering wheel way over and started ahead slowly. The car bumped and rocked. Its tires crunched dirt. Leafy branches whispered and squeaked against its sides.

'We're almost there,' he said.

She knew that.

'Almost time to go into your begging routine. Most of them start about now. Sometimes they hold off till we get out.'

I won't beg, Jean thought. I'll run for it.

He stopped the car and turned off the engine. He didn't take the key from the ignition.

'Okay, honey. Sit up slowly and open the door. I'll be right behind you.'

She sat up and turned toward the door. As she levered the handle, he clutched the collar of her blouse. He held onto it while she climbed out. Then he was standing, still gripping her collar, knuckles shoving at the back of her neck to guide her around the door. The door slammed shut. They passed the front of the car and moved toward a clearing in the forest.

The clearing was milky with moonlight. In the center, near a pale dead tree, was a ring of rocks that someone had stacked up to enclose a campfire. A pile of twigs and broken branches stood near the fire ring.

The Reaper steered Jean toward the dead tree.

She saw wood already piled inside the wall of rocks, ready for a match.

And she felt a quick glimmer of hope. *Someone* had laid the fire.

Right. *He* probably did it. He was up here earlier, preparing.

She saw a rectangular box at the foot of the tree.

A toolbox?

She began to whimper. She tried to stop walking, but he shoved her forward.

'Oh please, please, no! Spare me! I'll do anything!'

'Fuck you,' Jean said.

He laughed.

'I like your guts,' he said. 'In a little while, we may take a good look at them.'

He turned her around and backed her against the tree.

'I'll have to take off one of the cuffs, now,' he explained. He took a key from the pocket of his pants and held it in front of her face. 'You won't try to take advantage of the moment, will you?'

Jean shook her head.

'No, I didn't think so.' He shot a knee up into her belly. His forearm caught her under the chin, forcing her back as she started to double. Her legs gave out. She slid down the trunk, the barkless wood snagging her blouse and scraping her skin. A knob of root pounded her rump. She started to tumble forward, but he was there in front of her upthrust knees, blocking her fall. She slumped back against the trunk, wheezing, feeling the cuff go away from her right wrist, knowing this was it, this was the big moment she'd been waiting for, her one and only chance to make her break.

But she couldn't move. She was hurting and dazed and breathless. And even if she hadn't been disabled by the blow, her position made a struggle pointless. She was folded, back tight against the tree, legs mashing her breasts, arms stretched out over her knees, toes pinned to the ground by his boots.

She knew she had lost.

Strange, though. It didn't seem to matter much.

Jean felt as if she were outside herself, observing. It was someone else being grabbed under the armpits, someone else being lifted. She was watching a movie and the heroine was being prepared for torture. The girl's arms were being raised overhead. The loose cuff was being passed over the top of a limb. Then, it was snapped around the girl's right hand. The Reaper lifted her off her feet and carried her out away from the trunk. Then he let go. The limb was low enough so she didn't need to stand on tiptoes.

The man walked away from his captive. He crouched on the other side of the ring of rocks and struck a match. Flames climbed the tented sticks. They wrapped thick, broken branches. Pale smoke drifted up. He stood and returned to the girl.

'A little light on the subject,' he said to her. His voice sounded as faint as the snapping of the fire behind him.

This is okay, she thought. It's not me. It's someone else – a stranger.

It stopped being a stranger, very fast, when she saw the knife in the Reaper's hand.

She stood rigid and stared at the dark blade. She tried to hold her breath, but couldn't stop panting. Her heart felt like a hammer trying to smash its way out of her chest.

'No,' she gasped. 'Please.'

He smiled. 'I knew you'd get around to begging.'

'I never did anything to you.'

'But you're about to do something *for* me.'

The knife moved in. She felt its cool blade on her skin, but it didn't hurt. It didn't cut. Not Jean. It cut her clothes instead

– the straps of her bra, the sleeves of her blouse, the waist-band of her skirt.

He took the clothes to the fire.

'No! Don't!'

He smiled and dropped them onto the flames. 'You won't need them. You'll be staying right here. Here in the mess hall.'

Somewhere in the distance, a coyote howled.

'That's my friend. We've got an arrangement. I leave a meal for him and his forest friends, and they do the clean-up for me. None of this "shallow grave" nonsense. I just leave you here, tomorrow you'll be gone. They'll come like the good hungry troops they are, and leave the area neat and tidy for next time. No fuss, no bother. And you, sweet thing, will be spared the embarrassment of returning to campus bare-ass.'

Squatting beside the fire, he opened the toolbox. He took out pliers and a screwdriver. He set the pliers on the flat top of a rock. He picked up the screwdriver. Its shank was black even before he held it over the fire. Jean saw the flames curl around it.

'No!' she cried out. 'Please!'

'No! Please!' he mimicked. Smiling, he rolled the screw-driver in his hand. 'Think it's done yet?' He shook his head. 'Give it a few more minutes. No need to rush. Are you savoring the anticipation?'

'You bastard!'

'Is that any way to talk?'

'HELP!' she shouted. 'HELP! PLEASE, HELP ME!'

'Nobody's going to hear you but the coyotes.'

'*You can't do this*!'

'Sure, I can. Done it plenty of times before.'

'Please! I'll do anything!'

'I know just what you'll do. Scream, twitch, cry, kick, beg, drool . . . bleed. Not necessarily in that order, of course.'

He stood up. Pliers in one hand, screwdriver in the other, he walked slowly toward Jean. Wisps of pale smoke rose off the shank of the screwdriver.

He stopped in front of her. 'Now where oh where shall we begin? So many choice areas to choose from.' He raised the screwdriver toward her left eye. Jean jerked her head aside. The tip moved closer. She shut her eye. Felt heat against its lid. But the heat faded. 'No. I'll save that for later. After all, half the fun for *you* will be watching.'

She shrieked and flinched rigid as something seared her belly.

The Reaper laughed.

She looked down. He had simply touched her with the nose of the pliers.

'Power of suggestion,' he said. 'Now, let's see how you like some *real* pain.'

Slowly, he moved the screwdriver toward her left breast. Jean tried to jerk away, but the handcuffs stopped her. She kicked out. He twisted away. As the edge of her shoe glanced off his hip, he stroked her thigh with the screwdriver. She squealed.

He grinned. 'Don't do that again, honey, or I might get mean.'

Sobbing, she watched him inch the screwdriver toward her breast again. 'No. Don't. Pleeease.'

A rock struck the side of the Reaper's head. It knocked his head sideways, bounced off, scraped Jean's armpit and fell. He stood there for a moment, then dropped to his knees and slumped forward, face pressing against Jean's groin. She twisted away and he flopped beside her.

She gazed down at him, hardly able to believe he was actually sprawled there. Maybe she'd passed out and this was no more than a wild fantasy. She was dreaming and pretty soon she would come to with a burst of pain and . . .

No, she thought. It can't be a dream. Please.

A dim corner of her mind whispered, *I knew I'd get out of this*.

She looked for the rock thrower.

And spotted a dim shape standing beside a tree on the far side of the clearing.

'You got him!' she shouted. 'Thank God, you got him! Great throw!'

The shape didn't move, didn't call back to her.

It turned away.

'No!' Jean cried out. 'Don't leave! He'll come to and kill me! Please! I'm cuffed here! He's got the key in his pocket. You've gotta unlock the cuffs for me. Please!'

The figure, as indistinct in the darkness as the bushes and trees near its sides, turned again and stepped forward. It limped toward the glow of the fire. From the shape, Jean guessed that her savior was a woman.

Others began to appear across the clearing.

One stepped out from behind a tree. Another rose behind a clump of bushes. Jean glimpsed movement over to the right, looked and saw a fourth woman. She heard a growl behind her, twisted around, and gasped at the sight of someone crawling toward her. Toward the Reaper, she hoped. The top of this one's head was black and hairless in the shimmering firelight. As if she'd been scalped? The flesh had been stripped from one side of her back, and Jean glimpsed pale curving ribs before she whirled away.

Now there were *five* in front of her, closing in and near enough to the fire so she could see them clearly.

She stared at them.

And disconnected again.

Came out of herself, became an observer.

The rock thrower had a black pit where her left eye should've been. The girl cuffed beneath the tree was amazed that a one-eyed girl had been able to throw a rock with such fine aim.

It was even more amazing, since she was obviously dead. Ropes of guts hung from her belly, swaying between her legs like an Indian's loincloth. Little but bone remained of her right leg below the knee – the work of the Reaper's woodland troops?

How can she walk?

That's a good one, the girl thought.

How can *any* of them walk?

One, who must've been up here *a very long time*, was managing to shamble along just fine though both her legs were little more than bare bones. The troops had really feasted on her. One arm was missing entirely. The other arm was bone, and gone from the elbow down. Where she still had flesh, it looked black and lumpy. Some of her torso was intact, but mostly hollowed out. The right-hand side of her ribcage had been broken open. The ribs on the left were still there, and a shriveled lung was visible through the bars. Her face had no eyes, no nose, no lips. She looked as if she might be grinning.

The girl beneath the tree grinned back at her, but she didn't seem to notice.

Of course not, dope. How can she see?

How can she walk?

One of the others still had eyes. They were wide open and glazed. She had a very peculiar stare.

No eyelids, that's the trouble. The Reaper must've cut them off. Her breasts, too. Round, pulpy black discs on her chest where they should've been. Except for a huge gap in her right flank, she didn't look as if she'd been maimed by the troops. She still had most of her skin. But it looked shiny and slick with a coating of white slime.

The girl beside her didn't seem to have any skin at all. Had she been peeled? She was black all over except for the whites of her eyes and teeth – and hundreds of white things as if she had been showered with rice. But the rice moved. The rice was alive. Maggots.

The last of the five girls approaching from the front was also black. She didn't look peeled, she looked burnt. Her body was a crust of char, cracked and leaking fluids that shimmered in the firelight. She bore only a rough resemblance to a human being. She might have been shaped out of mud by a dim-witted child who gave her no fingers or toes or breasts, who couldn't manage a nose or ears, and poked fingers into the mud to make her eyes. Her crust made papery, crackling sounds as she shuffled past the fire, and pieces flaked off.

A motley crew, thought the girl cuffed to the limb.

She wondered if any of them would have enough sense to find the key and unlock the handcuffs.

She doubted it.

In fact, they didn't seem to be aware of her presence at all. They were limping and hobbling straight toward the Reaper.

Whose shriek now shattered whatever fragile force had allowed Jean to stay outside the cuffed stranger. She tried to keep her distance. Couldn't. Was sucked back inside the naked, suspended girl. Felt a sudden rush of horror and revulsion . . . and hope.

Whatever else they might be, they were the victims of the Reaper.

Payback time.

He was still shrieking, and Jean looked down at him. He was on his hands and knees. The scalped girl, also on her knees and facing him, had his head caught between her hands. She was biting the top of his head. Jean heard a wet ripping sound as the girl tore off a patch of hair and flesh.

He flopped and skidded backward, dragged by the rock-thrower and the one with the slimy skin. Each had him by a foot. The scalped girl started to crawl after him, then grunted and stopped and tried to pick up the pliers. Her right hand had no fingers. She pawed at the pliers, whimpering with frustration, then sighed when she succeeded in picking up the tool using the thumb and two remaining fingers of her other hand. Quickly, she crawled along trying to catch up to her prize. She scurried past Jean. One of her buttocks was gone, eaten away to the bone.

She gained on the screaming Reaper, reached out and clamped the pliers to the ridge of his ear and ripped out a chunk.

Halfway between Jean and the fire, the girls released his feet.

All six went at him.

He bucked and twisted and writhed, but they turned him onto his back. While some held him down, others tore at his clothes. Others tore at *him*. The scalped one took the pliers to his right eyelid and tore it off. The burnt one snatched up a hand and opened her lipless black mouth and began to chew his fingers off. While this went on, the armless girl capered like a madcap skeleton, her trapped lung bouncing inside her ribcage.

Soon, the Reaper's shirt was in shreds. His pants and boxer shorts were bunched around his cowboy boots. The scalped girl had ripped his other eyelid off, and now was stretching his upper lip as he squealed. The rock-thrower, kneeling beside him, clawed at his belly as if trying to get to his guts. Slime-skin bit off one of his nipples, chewed it and swallowed. The girl who must've been skinned alive knelt beside his head, scraping maggots off her belly and stuffing them by the handful into his mouth. No longer shrieking, he choked and wheezed.

The dancing skeleton dropped to her bare kneecaps, bent over him, and clamped her teeth on his penis. She pulled, stretching it, gnawing. He stopped choking and let out a shrill scream that felt like ice picks sliding into Jean's ears.

The scalped girl tore his lip off. She gave the pliers a snap, and watched the lip fly.

Jean watched it, too. Then felt its soft plop against her thigh. It stuck to her skin like a leech. She gagged. She stomped her foot on the ground, trying to shake it off. It kept clinging.

It's just a lip, she thought.

And then she was throwing up. She leaned forward as far as she could, trying not to vomit on herself. A small part of her mind was amused. She'd been looking at hideous, mutilated corpses, such horrors as she had never seen before, not even in her nightmares. And she had watched the corpses do unspeakable things to the Reaper. With all that, she hadn't tossed her cookies.

A lip sticks to my leg, and I'm barfing my guts out.

At least she was missing herself. Most of it was hitting the ground in front of her shoes, though a little was splashing up and spraying her shins.

Finally, the heaving subsided. She gasped for air and blinked tears out of her eyes.

And saw the scalped girl staring at her.

The others kept working on the Reaper. He wasn't screaming anymore, just gasping and whimpering.

The scalped girl stabbed the pliers down. They crashed through the Reaper's upper teeth. She rammed them deep into his mouth and partway down his throat, left them there, and started to crawl toward Jean.

'Get *him*,' she whispered. '*He's* the one.'

Then Jean thought, maybe she wants to help me.

'Would you get the key? For the handcuffs? It's in his pants pocket.'

The girl didn't seem to hear. She stopped at the puddle of vomit and lowered her face into it. Jean heard lapping sounds, and gagged. The girl raised her head, stared up at Jean, licked her dripping lips, then crawled forward.

'No. Get back.'

Opened her mouth wide.

*Christ!*

Jean smashed her knee up into the girl's forehead. The head snapped back. The girl tumbled away.

A chill spread through Jean. Her skin prickled with goose-bumps. Her heart began to slam.

*It won't stop with him.*

*I'm next!*

The scalped girl, whose torso was an empty husk, rolled over and started to push herself up.

Jean leaped.

She caught the tree limb with both hands, kicked toward the trunk but couldn't come close to reaching it. Her body swept down and backward. As she started forward again, she pumped her legs high.

She swung.

She kicked and swung, making herself a pendulum that strained higher with each sweep.

Her legs hooked over the barkless, dead limb.

She drew herself up against its underside, and hugged it.

Twisting her head sideways, she saw the scalped girl crawling toward her again.

Jean had never seen her stand.

*If she can't stand up, I'm okay.*

But the *others* could stand.

They were still busy with the Reaper. Digging into him.

Biting. Ripping off flesh with their teeth. He choked around the pliers and made high squeaky noises. As Jean watched, the charred girl crouched over the fire and put both hands into the flames. When she straightened up, she had a blazing stick trapped between the fingerless flaps of her hands. She lumbered back to the group, crouched, and set the Reaper's pants on fire.

The pants, pulled down until they were stopped by his boot tops, wrapped him just below the knees.

In seconds, they were ablaze.

The Reaper started screaming again. He squirmed and kicked. Jean was surprised he had that much life left in him.

The key, she thought.

I'll have to go through the ashes.

*If I live that long.*

Jean began to shinny out along the limb. It scraped her thighs and arms, but she kept moving, kept inching her way along. The limb sagged slightly. It groaned. She scooted farther, farther.

Heard a faint crackling sound.

Then was stopped by a bone-white branch that blocked her left arm.

'No!' she gasped.

She thrust herself forward and rammed her arm against the branch. The impact shook it just a bit. A few twigs near the far end of it clattered and fell.

The branch looked three inches thick where it joined the main limb. A little higher up, it seemed thin enough for her to break easily – but she *couldn't* reach that far, not with her wrists joined by the short chain of the handcuffs. The branch barred her way like the arm and hand of a skeleton pleased to keep her treed until its companions finished with the Reaper and came for her.

She clamped it between her teeth, bit down hard on the dry

262

wood, gnashed on it. Her teeth barely seemed to dent it.

She lowered her head. Spat dirt and grit from her mouth. Turned her head.

The Reaper was no longer moving or making any sounds. Pale smoke drifted up from the black area where his pants had been burning. The charred girl who had set them ablaze now held his severed arm over the campfire. The slimy, breastless girl was pulling a boot onto one of her feet. The skinned girl, kneeling by the Reaper's head, had removed the pliers from his mouth. At first, Jean thought she was pinching herself with them. That wasn't it, though. One at a time, she was squashing the maggots that squirmed on her belly. The rock-thrower's head was buried in the Reaper's open torso. She reared up, coils of intestine drooping from her mouth. The rotted and armless girl lay flat between the black remains of the Reaper's legs, tearing at the cavity where his genitals used to be.

Though he was apparently dead, his victims all still seemed contented.

For now.

Straining to look down past her shoulder, Jean saw the scalped girl directly below. On her knees. Reaching up, pawing the air with the remains of her hands.

She can't get me, Jean told herself.

But the others.

Once they're done with the Reaper, they'll see that bitch down there and then they'll see me.

If *she'd* just go away!

GET OUT OF HERE!

Jean wanted to shout it, didn't dare. Could just see the others turning their heads toward the sound of her voice.

If I could just kill her!

Good luck on that one.

*Gotta do something*!

Jean clamped the limb hard with her hands. She gritted her teeth.

Don't try it, she thought. You won't even hurt her. You'll be down where she can get at you.

But maybe a good kick in the head'll discourage her.

Fat chance.

Jean released the limb with her legs. She felt a breeze wash over her sweaty skin as she dropped. She thrashed her feet like a drowning woman hoping to kick to the surface.

A heel of her shoe struck something. She hoped it was the bitch's face.

Then she was swinging upward and saw her. Turning on her knees and reaching high, grinning.

Jean kicked hard as she swept down.

The toe of her shoe caught the bitch in the throat, lifted her off her knees and knocked her sprawling.

*Got her*!

Jean dangled by her hands, swaying slowly back and forth. She bucked and tried to fling her legs up to catch the limb. Missed. Lost her hold and cried out as the steel edges of the bracelets cut into her wrists. Her feet touched the ground.

The scalped girl rolled over and crawled toward her.

Jean leaped. She grabbed the limb. She pulled herself up to it and drove her knees high but not fast enough.

The girl's arms wrapped her ankles, clutched them. She pulled at Jean, stretching her, dragging her down, reaching higher, *climbing* her. Jean twisted and squirmed, but couldn't shake the girl off. Her arms strained. Her grip on the limb started to slip. She squealed as teeth ripped into her thigh.

With a *krrrack!*, the limb burst apart midway between Jean and the trunk.

She dropped straight down.

Falling, she shoved the limb sideways. It hammered her

shoulder as she landed, knees first, on the girl. The weight drove Jean forward, smashed her down. Though the girl no longer hugged her legs, she felt the head beneath her thigh shake from side to side. She writhed and bucked under the limb. The teeth kept their savage bite on her.

Then *had* their chunk of flesh and lost their grip.

Clutching the limb, Jean bore it down, her shoulder a fulcrum. She felt the wood rise off her back and rump. Its splintered end pressed into the ground four or five feet in front of her head. Bracing herself on the limb, she scurried forward, knees pounding at the girl beneath her. The girl growled. Hands gripped Jean's calves. But not tightly. Not with the missing fingers. Teeth snapped at her, scraping the skin above her right knee. Jean jerked her leg back and shot it forward. The girl's teeth crashed shut. Then Jean was off her, rising on the crutch of the broken limb.

She stood up straight, hugging the upright limb, lifting its broken end off the ground and staggering forward a few steps to get herself out of the girl's reach.

And saw the others coming. All but the rotted skeletal girl who had no arms and still lay sprawled between the Reaper's legs.

'No!' Jean shouted. 'Leave me alone!'

They lurched toward her.

The charred one held the Reaper's severed arm like a club. The breastless girl with runny skin wore both his boots. Her arms were raised, already reaching for Jean though she was still a few yards away. The rock-thrower had found a rock. The skinned girl aswarm with maggots picked at herself with the pliers as she shambled closer.

'NO!' Jean yelled again.

She ducked, grabbed the limb low, hugged it to her side and whirled as the branchy top of it swept down in front of her.

It dropped from its height slashing sideways, its bony fingers of wood clattering and bursting into twigs as it crashed through the cadavers. Three of them were knocked off their feet. A fourth, the charred one, lurched backward to escape the blow, stepped into the Reaper's torso and stumbled. Jean didn't see whether she went down, because the weight of the limb was hurling her around in a full circle. A branch struck the face of the scalped girl crawling toward her, popped and flew off. Then the crawling girl was behind Jean again and the others were still down. All except the rock-thrower. She'd been missed, first time around. Out of range. Now, her arm was cocked back, ready to hurl a small block of stone.

Jean, spinning, released the limb.

Its barkless wood scraped her side and belly.

It flew from her like a mammoth, tined lance.

Free of its pull, Jean twirled. The rock flicked her ear. She fell to her knees. Facing the crawler. Who scurried toward her moaning as if she already knew she had lost.

Driving both fists against the ground, Jean pushed herself up. She took two quick steps toward the crawler and kicked her in the face. Then she staggered backward. Whirled around.

The rock-thrower was down, arms batting through the maze of dead branches above her.

The others were starting to get up.

Jean ran through them, cuffed hands high, twisting and dodging as they scurried for her, lurched at her, grabbed.

Then they were behind her. All but the Reaper and the armless thing sprawled between his legs, chewing on him.

*Gotta get the handcuff key*, she thought.

Charging toward them, she realized the cuffs didn't matter. They couldn't stop her from driving. The car key was in the ignition.

She leaped the Reaper.

And staggered to a stop on the other side of his body.

Gasping, she bent over and lifted a rock from the ring around the fire. Though its heat scorched her hands, she raised it overhead. She turned around.

The corpses were coming, crawling and limping closer.

But they weren't that close.

'HERE'S ONE FOR NUMBER EIGHT!' she shouted, and smashed the rock down onto the remains of the Reaper's face. It struck with a wet crunching sound. It didn't roll off. It stayed on his face as if it had made a nest for itself.

Jean stomped on it once, pounding it in farther.

Then she swung around. She leaped the fire and dashed through the clearing toward the waiting car.

# DINKER'S POND

The prospector's yarn went like this. I just kept mum and listened him out.

From the start, she wouldn't have nothing to do with me. She was Jim's gal from head to toe – and all the goodies in between.

I told him, 'Jim, we don't wanta bring her along.'

'I sure do,' he allowed.

'She ain't good for nothing but spawning trouble and ruination.'

Jim said, 'She's right pretty.'

Well, I knew that, but it was off the point. 'She only just wants to fall in with us 'cause of the strike. She's after our gold, that's all. Why, she likely don't even *like* you.'

Jim got this drifty look in his eyes, and I could see his mind was back on last night when he'd sampled Lucy's wares. She'd met up with us yesterday afternoon when we come strutting out of the assay office, which made me suspicious right away. I guess she kept herself stationed there, just waiting for a couple of prospectors to come out grinning.

Right off the bat, she latched onto Jim.

He's the gullible one. That's how come she sidled up to him,

271

not me. Jim's got less sense than mule flop, and it shows all over his face.

You might say to yourself I'm peddling sour grapes when I tell you that's why she went for him, but it's not so. Jim's no younger than me. He wasn't any more sprucy, and he didn't smell any better, and I'm just as fine a specimen of manhood as him. In addition, we were equal partners, though Lucy couldn't of known that at the start.

Nope. Jim's just a stride short of idiot, whereas I've got a fair parcel of brains and common sense.

I'm not one to be led around by the pecker, but you can't say that for Jim, and Lucy knew it.

Next thing you know, I'm all by my lonesome in the saloon and he's got himself a fine room in the Jamestown Hotel getting convinced he's in love.

Which brings me back to that drifty look in his eyes while we're putting away steak and eggs the morning after.

'I reckon she likes me just fine,' he said. 'She's not real keen on you, though, George.'

'Now, there's a fine state of affairs. How long have you and me been partners?' I asked.

He scrunched up his brow, giving it a shot. 'I reckon it's been a spell.'

'It's been a right *long* spell, and now you're all set to ruin us. A woman at the digs is the worst kind of bad luck, you know that just as well as me. You recall what happened to Placer Bill and Mike Murphy over on the Kern.'

Jim puzzled over that, looking for the answer on the spikes of his fork.

'Let me refresh your memory, then. Why, Bill and Mike, they was thick. They was buddies more years than you got teeth.'

'I got most my teeth,' Jim allowed.

'Well, that's the point. It was a lot of years. You couldn't find better buddies than Bob and Mike . . .'

'Thought you said he was Bill.'

'Robert William, that was his name. Some called him Bob, some Bill. Thing is, Bob and Mike was like brothers till the black day a woman showed up at their digs. She took to Mike, right off, and treated Bob so bad you'd think he had the scabbies. Poor Bob, he was left out cold and lonesome. But did he complain and carry on? No, sir. He was too big a man for that. He bore his troubles in silence. And you recall what happened then?'

'What was the gal's name?' Jim asked.

'Greta.'

'I recall a Greta Gurney in Bible school. A redhead. Was this Greta that took up with Mike a redhead?'

'I don't believe she was.'

'Didn't you never see her?'

'Let me tell the story, will you? You're enough to drive the patience out of a hospital for the blind and crippled.'

'Well, I just . . .'

'This weren't your Greta. This was some other Greta. Now, the point I'm trying to stick you with is this – when she went strolling into the digs, she brought disaster and tragedy down on the luckless heads of Bill and Mike. It wasn't bad enough she spurned Bill and made a shambles of two fast pals. No, sir. That was bad, but it weren't bad enough.

'The way it turns out, she'd run off from her spouse. She didn't let on about that, however. No, she kept mum on the subject of her spouse. He was Lem Jaspers, a one-eyed smuggler from Frisco. And he went looking for her. And he found her out there on the Kern with Bill and Mike, and massacred the three of them.'

'Killed 'em?'

'He killed 'em mean and slow. I'd tell you all about it, but I don't want to spoil your breakfast. Let me just say it weren't pretty. He put out Mike's eyes with a burning stick to make him suffer for looking at Greta. And he cut off Mike's pecker with a Bowie knife and shoved it up Greta's whatsis. He told her, "You wanted it so bad, now you got it."'

Jim was starting to look a little gray around the lips.

'After they was dead,' I went on, 'he took the skin right off Greta. Peeled her raw. He tossed her face in the campfire. The rest of her skin, he tanned it. I won't tell you about the tobacco pouch. But Lem used some of Greta's hide to fashion himself a new pair of moccasins so he could have the pleasure of walking around on her all the time.'

'Mighty lowdown of him,' Jim allowed.

'That wasn't the lowest of the low, either. Lem didn't let it go with taking out his vengeance on Greta and Mike. He took poor Bill and gutted him like a trout. Here, Bill was just as innocent as a baby, never put a hand to Greta, but Lem slaughtered him just the same.'

'That weren't right.'

'Right or not, Bill met himself a grisly end, and it was all because his buddy turned traitor on him and took up with a gal. Like I said, a woman at the digs is the worst kind of luck.'

'What happened to Lem?'

'Well, I don't know. For all I know, maybe he got tired of being a widower and hitched up with your Lucy.'

Jim spent a long time pondering that, scowling down at his plate and wiping his hand around on it to get up the last of the egg yellow. After he was done licking his hand, he raised his eyes to me. I could see he was grateful for the warning. But what he said was, 'We'll keep our eyes sharp. If this Lem comes along, you and me we'll shoot him dead.'

A man only has so much breath to spare in this life, and I'd just wasted a good parcel of it. I might as well of told my story to the butt end of a mule.

Later on in the morning, just before the three of us headed out, Jim took me aside. 'I had a talk with Lucy,' he whispered. 'She don't know any Lem Jaspers, but she knew a Jasper Wiggens once. She claims she never married him.'

I figured Lucy was bound to warm up to me, once she got to know me better. She got to know me a whole sight better on our travels back to the Stanislaus where we'd made our strike, but she didn't warm up like I hoped.

The way she looked at me, one would think I had nasty stuff hanging out my nose.

The trip took longer than it should've. Every now and again, they'd leave me on the trail so I could keep the mules company, and Lucy'd take Jim off into the woods. She did it mostly just to torment me. Half the time, she'd come back half unfastened to give me a look at regions she never planned to let me scout around in.

Lucy was as cruel and cold-hearted as any woman that ever crossed my path.

Still, I tried to be friends with her. I wanted to get into her good graces, even if not her drawers. And who knows but that the former might lead up the trail to the latter?

No matter what I did, though, she spurned me.

She even spurned my stories. Jim liked to listen to them pretty near as much as I liked the telling. On the first night, she sat there by the cookfire sighing and rolling her eyes around while I told my best rip-snorter about the squaw with the two-headed baby. One head was partial to one of her tits, and the other hankered all the time for the other. Trouble was, the heads didn't match up with the tits they favored, so the squaw had to hold the child upside down at chow time. The little scamp liked that just fine. Only thing was, he got so fond of being upside down he never learned the use of his legs. He grew up walking on his hands with his feet in the air, and drowned himself one day when he tried to wade a stream that weren't even waist deep.

Well, Jim just nearly split his sides while I told that one. Lucy, she just sat there acting like she wished I'd either shut up or die.

Before I could start in with a new story, she said to me, 'George Sawyer, you're about as crude as the day is long. I'd rather be snakebit than listen to another one of your vile whoppers.'

'Why, that was a true story,' Jim said, sticking up for me.

She turned her eyes on him. They were pretty eyes that glimmered in the firelight, but there didn't seem to be much warmth inside them. 'If you believe that was true, Jimmy dear, why you've got dust in your brain pan.'

Jimmy dear looked at me, scowling from the effort of trying to piece a thought together. 'You been telling fibs?'

'A false word has never passed these lips. Why, I was there when the boy drowned, both heads down in the creek and his feet kicking like a hanged man.'

Jim turned to Lucy, raised his eyebrows and said, 'See?'

'All I see,' she opined, 'is one lying fool and one idiot. Makes me wonder why I ever took up with you in the first place, James Bixby.'

That let the air out of his sails something horrible to witness. He sat there, slumped over and speechless, while Lucy flounced her way into the shadows and crawled into her blankets.

I tried to cheer him up. 'How'd you like to hear about the time I got pulled under the quicksand and . . .'

'Never happened at all,' he muttered, looking as if he'd

caught me with a fifth ace in my hand. 'You'd of gone down in the quicksand, you'd be dead, George.'

'Well, I *would've* been dead, but there was such a heap of skeletons down there at the bottom that I was able to fashion myself a ladder and . . .'

I could see by his eyes that he was just starting to believe me again. I could see his doubts just melting away. But all of a sudden, Lucy called to him.

'Come on away from that lying, foul-mouthed nogood. Right this minute. I'm cold over here. Come on over and heat me up.'

Jim was mighty quick on his feet after he heard that.

I was left all by my lonesome, listening to the lively crackle and snap of the fire, the wind in the trees, and Lucy grunting and squealing like a sow getting stuck by a hot poker.

My own poker got mighty hot while I heard her carrying on that way.

Lucy weren't a sow, even if she did sound like one.

Sitting there on my rock, I felt like the two-headed boy. One of my heads thought it'd be a nice idea to poke her. The other would just as soon put a bullet in her noggin.

Neither one of my heads done a thing about it.

After that first night on the trail, I didn't tell no more stories. A couple of times, I made the offer. The offer caused Jim to shake his head sadly, and caused Lucy to spit in the fire.

Finally, we got to our digs on the Stanislaus. We got there just after dark. Lucy didn't express any great fondness for our shack. I allowed as how she might rather sleep under the stars, but she asked me to shut my yap.

She spent a good portion of the night bellyaching about

how she couldn't properly breathe in such close quarters, and how a woman requires some privacy, and how this was the one and only night she would ever spend beneath the same roof as George Sawyer, a lying man of such vile habits and temperament that he was no better than a plague of worms.

Lucy not only gnashed her teeth and bitterly complained about our 'hovel,' but she refused Jim her favors. 'My modesty won't allow it,' she protested. 'Not with *him* breathing down our necks.'

I considered her remark about modesty to be a joke, but neither Jim or me was happy with her decision, which come as a letdown to both of us. On the trail, I'd grown partial to the sounds she made. I'd started looking forward to the three of us in the shack. She was right about close quarters. If she and Jim went at it in the shack, I was sure to hear more than her wild grunts and groans. I was likely to see more, too. The way I had it figured, that would suit Lucy just fine. The more she could torment me, the better she'd like it.

But maybe she reckoned it'd push me too far and I might join in.

Maybe she was right.

At any rate, she didn't risk it. She just left Jim alone that night.

While I tried to get asleep, I figured up a few of the wrongs she'd done to me and Jim.

She'd stolen my pal. She cheated me and Jim out of the pleasure we took in my stories. Finally, she was holding out, robbing Jim out of the reason he'd brung her along in the first place and keeping me from the pleasures of being a witness when she got herself poked.

Like I said before, I never met a crueler, colder-hearted woman.

Come the next morning, Jim set out with an axe figuring to knock down some forest and put up a mansion for his lady. I figured I'd let him handle that on his own. I was here to dig gold. His lady could sleep in the dirt, for what I cared.

I took my pick out to the mine and set to work. However, I couldn't get the blamed woman out of my head. I kept pondering on her, wondering what she might be up to now that she was all by her lonesome. Pretty soon, I come to figure this'd be a fine chance to visit with her. Without Jim around to muddle up the works, maybe I could set things right with her. Or at least give her my angle on matters.

Well, I went looking for her. Lucy weren't in the shack, and she weren't at the river. I scouted some more, and pretty soon I come upon her.

The gal was down by the shore of Dinker's Pond, slipping off her duds. I ducked behind the big old tree at the top of the slope, and give my eyes a treat. I'd gotten looks at bits and pieces of her along the trail, but now I got to see the whole woman and it weren't any wonder Jim felt obliged to bring her along. She could knock the breath out of a dead man.

Me, I got caught up in looking, and she was up to her knees in the pond before I sung out.

'Get on outa there!' I yelled.

She jumped like I'd jabbed her with a stick. I reckon she forgot to be modest, for she turned herself around and rammed her fists into her hips without even trying to cover nothing. 'George Sawyer!' she railed. 'You son-of-a-bitch! You dirty, rotten, lowdown, leprous, claim-jumpin' son-of-a-whore!'

'I ain't no claim-jumper,' I informed the woman, and started on my way down the slope.

She aimed an arm at me and shook a finger. The finger weren't all the shook. 'Don't you come any closer! Get outa here! You bastard, don't you dare come down here!'

I kept coming, and she started backing up till the water crawled around her waist. About that time, she remembered her modesty and so she hunkered down till she was covered to the neck.

'Wouldn't do that, were I you,' I said. I sat myself down on a stump by the shore. Her clothes were heaped in front of me, but I kept my boots off them. 'You'd better listen to me, gal, and step outa that water pretty lively.'

'I most surely won't.'

'Should've gone over in the river, if you wanted to get yourself wet. Shouldn't of come here.'

'I go where I like. Sides, the river's so cold I'd freeze up solid.'

'You're in Dinker's Pond,' I informed her.

'Well, it's a good pond. It *were* a good pond till you showed up. Go on and get.'

'Used to be a good fishing hole,' I allowed. 'Up till around a year ago. Just ask Jim if you don't believe me. But the fishes, they all petered out after we strung up Clem Dinker.'

Lucy, she squinted her eyes at me. Then her hand come up with a rock. She kind of unsquatted there for a second and let fly. I got distracted, admiring her, or I could've dodged. The rock give me a good clip on the shoulder.

I jumped up, rubbing my hurt.

'Don't you come in here!' Lucy yelled, and fetched up another rock.

'Not me. I ain't a fool like some.'

'I'm a fool, am I?' She pitched the rock, but I ducked it.

'You're a fool for sure, you don't come outa there.'

'Jim, he's gonna shoot you dead.'

'Jim'll be mighty grateful I happened to come on down here and warn you off.'

'You just come here fixing to doodle me.' All of a sudden,

280

she lost her mean glare and found a smile. 'You're scared of the water, George Sawyer. Ha!'

'I'm scared of *that* water. You'd be scared of it, too, if you knew what I know.'

'Oh, dear me, yes. I'd be thrown into such a fright I'd hop right out and be ever so grateful. Oh, George, you're just pitiful.' She eased herself back and started floating, all sprawled out pale and shiny on the water, grinning up at the sky. 'You're just the most pitiful thing.'

'I'm half inclined to leave you to your fate,' I called.

She picked up her head, and the rest of her sank out of sight. 'Did you say something, poor George?'

'Maybe I'll just go off and leave you.'

'You can't leave, George.' She must've found the bottom, for she come up a little. The water was almost up to her shoulders. It was too murky to let me see anything worthwhile, unless you count her smile. That wasn't under water, but I wouldn't count it. It was too smirky and mean. 'Why, you haven't scared me witless yet,' she said. 'I 'spect, once I've heard your whopper, I'll just come out screaming and hurl myself into your manly arms.'

She reckoned I *couldn't* scare her out of the pond.

I took it for a challenge.

So I set myself down on the stump. 'Did you ever hear of a fella named Clem Dinker?'

'Why, no, George. Do tell me all about him.'

'Clem, he was a crazy man that used to live in a tree over across the river. He was so skinny, looked like he never ate nothing. But that weren't so. Clem used to eat everything he could get his teeth on.

'When it come to food, he was just about the most patient, sneaky fella you ever seen. He'd sit so quiet, up in his tree, that birds'd come along and settle on him. When they done

281

that, he'd grab 'em quick and pop 'em right into his mouth. Munched the tweeters up, wings, beaks, eyes and all. We used to hear him off in the distance, coughing up feathers.'

Lucy shook her head and rolled her eyes up at the sky. 'Well, George,' she said, 'I just got goosebumps running all up and down my body. You keep scaring me like this, I might just swoon dead away.'

'If you swoon, you're on your own. Now, do you want to keep on mocking me, or you want to hear about Clem?'

'Oh, I beg your pardon. Please, go on.'

'Clem, he'd eat just about anything. He just weren't particular. If he could get his teeth on it, he'd chow it down. Did I tell you he had pointed teeth?'

Lucy laughed.

'Yes, ma'am. You may not care to believe it, but Clem filed all his front teeth so they come to points. They was so sharp, he couldn't talk much without ruining his lips. You'd be talking to the fella, and he'd no sooner answer back than the blood'd start flying at you. He'd act like he didn't even notice, and you'd be standing there getting rained on. It was enough to make you lose your train of thought.'

'If your mama'd had a lick of sense,' Lucy said, 'she would've strangled you at birth.'

'I'm only just telling you how it was. I ain't making up any of this. You don't believe me, ask Jim. He'll tell you same as me. Why, I laid down for a snooze one day after chatting a spell with that man, and Jim come upon me and I was so bloody he took me for dead and had a grave half dug before I woke up.

'But that's off the point,' I said before Lucy could start in again. 'Thing is, Clem Dinker was crazy mad, and he'd eat anything he could get his pointy teeth into. Not just birds. We seen him eat a beaver, once. And there was a trapper over yonder had a hound till Clem got hold of it. He gobbled up squirrels, coons, coyotes, butterflies, spiders, slugs and worms.'

Lucy wasn't smiling any more. She was giving me a hateful look, and her upper lip had crawled up above her gums. I could see she was ready to start yelling, and I might never have a chance to finish my story. So I got to the point quick.

'Clem finally ate one of our mules. Her name was Jane, and we come upon Clem with his face buried in her innards. So we strung him up.' I twisted around and pointed up the slope at the same tree I'd hidden behind to watch Lucy strip off her duds. 'See that branch there? The one sticks out this way? That's where we hung him from.'

'You didn't hang nobody,' Lucy said. She didn't say it spunky, though. Seemed like she'd lost some of her starch.

'I put the noose around his scrawny little neck, myself. We stood Clem smack on the edge, up there under the three. The plan was, we'd give Clem a push, and he'd swing out over the bank and strangulate.

'But he was our first hanging. The mistake was, we should've made the rope tight between Clem's neck and the branch. Way it turned out, it had a mite too much slack in it. So when we nudged him off the edge, he didn't swing so much as he dropped. Plucked his noggin right off his shoulders.

'Well, we carted Clem's body off into the woods and planted it. All but his head. Being round like it was, it rolled on downhill and plopped into the pond here. We never could find hide nor hair of it. That's how come we call this place Dinker's Pond. His head's still in there, far as we know.'

Lucy, she just sort of stared at me.

'After a spell, the fish in there started to peter out. Pretty soon, there wasn't none to be caught at all. Oh, you'd get nibbles pretty quick. Bring up your hook, and your bait'd be gone. But you never had a fish for your troubles. Me and Jim went through a whole parcel of worms before we give up on our old fishing hole.'

Lucy, standing real still, slanted her eyes down at the water. Then she jerked them up at me real quick. I could see she was riled that I'd caught her looking at the water. 'Weren't a breath of truth in that yarn, George Sawyer. It didn't tell me nothing I didn't already know – just that you're vile trash that ain't fit for human civilization.'

'I ain't no liar,' I said.

I caught her eyes checking around some more.

Then they darn near popped out and Lucy threw a holler that made my hair stand up. She commenced to thrash around considerable. The water around her churned and bubbled and got kind of red.

I give some thought to splashing in to try and save her. Would've been mighty heroic.

That was the end of George's yarn, and the end of the whisky bottle sitting between us on the saloon table.

'And you didn't even lift a finger to save her?' I asked.

'She didn't amount to much, anyhow,' George said.

'Now you want *me* going out to the digs with you?'

'Gets mighty lonesome out there. It surely does. I reckon I'd risk some bad luck for the company of a sweet thing like you.'

'You've got Jim, don't you?'

'Well, he come at me with his axe when he saw what happened to Lucy. Couldn't talk him outa it. He got it into his head it was me killed Lucy and chewed her up that way. So I had to shoot him.'

'Did you do her that way, George? Was it you?'

'Why, Mabel, bite your tongue. I ain't that kinda man. And you ain't lowdown like Lucy was. That gal was pure poison.

She was such poison I run across Dinker's head next morning in the pond there, afloating face up with his lips turned black.'

# MADMAN STAN

The TV screen went blank.

Billy, sitting on the floor in front of it, felt his mouth sag open. He twisted his head around. Agnes gave him a mean smile from the couch. She had the remote control in her hand, aimed like a gun at the television. 'Hey, that's no fair,' he said. 'The show wasn't even over.'

'It is now,' Agnes said. 'Time for beddy-bye, children.'

Billy turned his eyes to Rich, looking for help.

The boy's arms were folded across his plaid robe. He was frowning. 'We're allowed to stay up until eleven on Saturday nights,' he informed the woman. 'It isn't even ten yet.'

Billy nodded, proud of his older brother.

'Children your age belong in bed at a decent hour,' Agnes said.

'If I may speak my mind,' said Rich, 'that really bites.'

Agnes smiled at him. 'Aren't you the little darling?'

'Well, it does. And Mom and Dad are going to hear about this. *They* let us stay up. So does Linda.'

'Linda isn't here,' Agnes said in her sweet, nasty voice. 'And frankly, I'm more than a little sick of hearing about that twit.'

'Linda isn't a twit,' Billy said, gaining courage from his brother's stand against this dumpy old creep. 'She's a lot nicer than you are. And besides, you don't even know her.'

Agnes peered at her wristwatch. 'I'm losing my patience, children. It's off to bed with you, now.'

'You're a really rotten babysitter,' Rich said.

'Why, thank you. And you, my dear, are a really rotten child.'

Rich's face turned red. He stood up. 'Come on, Billy. Let's get out of here.'

'Yeah.' He got to his feet.

'Don't go away mad,' Agnes said, and chuckled.

They headed for the other end of the living room, glancing at each other. Rich looked steamed.

'No, I mean it,' Agnes called after them. 'Come back here. I've got a little surprise for you. Something to cheer you up.'

They turned to face her. 'What?' Rich asked.

The lamplight gleamed on Agnes's glasses. Her chubby face widened with a grin. 'A bedtime story. A *scary* one.'

Billy felt a quick flutter in his stomach.

He looked at Rich. Rich looked at him.

'I'll just wager your precious Linda never tells you spooky stories.'

'Sure she does,' Rich said, and Billy nodded.

'Not as spooky as mine.'

That wouldn't be too hard, Billy thought. Linda was great, but her stories were just okay. Billy figured *he* could tell scarier stories than Linda.

'You want to hear it, don't you?

Billy blurted, 'Sure.'

Rich shrugged. 'Yeah, I guess so.'

'Should I . . .?' Billy stopped himself.

'Should you what?' Agnes asked.

'Nothing,' he muttered.

He had almost said 'turn off the lights.' That's what they did when Linda told stories. Made the living room dark and sat on the couch, Linda between them. Even if her stories weren't so hot, it was wonderful. She would put her arms around them. Even in winter, she always seemed to smell like suntan oil.

'Why don't we turn off the lights?' Agnes suggested.

Rich shook his head. 'Billy's afraid of the dark.'

You lying sack, Billy thought, and nodded and tried to look worried.

He wasn't afraid of the dark. Not usually, anyhow. But he certainly did not want to be in a dark room with Agnes.

'Leave the lights on, then.' She patted the cushion on each side of her.

Billy pretended not to see that. He sat down on the carpet, facing her, and crossed his legs. Rich sank to the floor beside him.

Agnes laughed softly and shook her head. Her cheeks wobbled. 'You're not frightened of *me*, are you?' she asked.

'Huh-uh.' That was the truth, too. He wasn't frightened of Agnes. Not much, anyhow. But the idea of sitting close to her on the couch was revolting. The woman was not only fat and ugly, but she had some kind of sour smell like a washcloth that had sat around damp too long.

For the zillionth time, Billy wished Linda didn't have that date tonight. He sure liked sitting up there with her.

'This is how we always sit,' Rich lied again.

'I didn't relish the idea myself,' she said, 'of you two darlings up here with me.'

'Are you going to tell us the story?' Rich asked. He sounded good and impatient.

'Are you ready for it? Maybe you need to wee-wee first.'

'We'll urinate later,' Rich told her.

Billy almost laughed, but held it in. He didn't want to make Agnes mad, or she might call off the story.

The woman scooted back on the couch. She grunted softly

as she brought her legs up and crossed them on the cushion. Billy was surprised she *could* cross them, they were so thick. He was also surprised her pink sweatpants didn't split open. The way they bulged, they looked as if they might burst at any second and let Agnes's flesh flop out all over the couch.

She folded her arms across the front of her sweatshirt in a way that made her look like she was trying to hide a couple of footballs and sneak them past the defensive line.

The idea of that made Billy smile.

'Would you like to tell us what you find amusing, young man?'

He felt his face go hot. 'Nothing. Huh-uh. I was just daydreaming, that's all.'

'Don't daydream during my story.'

'We're both going to fall asleep if you don't get on with it,' Rich said.

'All right.' She cleared her throat. She squirmed a little as if trying to work her fat rump deeper into the cushion. 'This is the story of why nobody goes to bed at night without making sure to lock the house up tight.'

'I know, I know,' Rich said. 'So the boogeyman can't get in.'

'Save your sarcasm for that Linda twat. And don't interrupt me, or I won't let you hear the story.'

'C'mon, Rich,' Billy said. 'Don't interrupt.'

Rich made a quiet huff.

'In some towns,' Agnes said, 'people don't lock their doors at night. But we always do, here in Oakwood. There's a very good reason for that. It's because of the madman.' Agnes bobbed her round head. 'Madman Stan,' she said, her voice lower, almost a whisper. 'Nobody knows where he comes from. But I've heard it said he hangs around the cemetery, especially on hot summer nights when he likes to take off all his clothes and get up against the tombstones. They're cool, you know. They feel good when it's so hot at night you can't sleep. Remember that, come summer.'

Rich glanced at Billy and rolled his eyes upward.

But Agnes didn't seem to notice. She was gazing straight ahead, swaying gently back and forth.

'Myself,' she said in that same low voice, 'I've never seen him in among the graves. But I've been told by others. I've been told that's where he takes his victims. Nobody'll even whisper what he does with 'em. But I've got my own ideas on that.'

'What?' Rich whispered.

Agnes stopped swaying. She stared down at him. 'You don't want to know.'

'You're just making this up, anyway,' he muttered.

She smiled. 'The Madman Stan will settle for men and women. And he likes little girls very much. But more than anything else in the whole wide world, he likes little boys. They're his favorite.'

'Sure,' Rich said.

Billy nudged him with an elbow. Rich elbowed him back, harder.

'Like I told you, I don't know what the madman does with them. But they're never seen again. Ever. Folks who live over by the graveyard say they hear screams, sometimes. Horrible screams. And sometimes, they hear digging sounds out there.'

'Like fun,' Rich muttered.

'Not much fun for those he snatches,' Agnes said. 'Not much fun at all, I should think. That's why we all lock our doors up tight, here in Oakwood. Like I told you, I've never seen Madman Stan over by the graveyard. But I've seen him other places. Plenty of times. Always late at night. I'll be looking out a window at the street, or I'll be walking home after a sitting job, and I'll see him. I've even seen him right here on Fifth Street. Do you know what he's doing?'

Rich didn't make any crack. Billy felt a little breathless and sick.

'The madman is walking from block to block, from house to house, going up to each and every door and trying the knob. He's looking for a door that isn't locked. And when he finds one, in he goes. And that's the last of someone.' Agnes nodded and grinned. 'Off to bed, children.'

'That's all?' Rich asked. 'That's no story.'

'That's my story. Now, to bed with you. I want you to go straight to sleep, children.' Her grin suddenly grew so large that her cheeks pushed against the bottom of her glasses and the round lenses drifted upward. 'If I hear so much as a peep out of either one of you . . .' Unfolding her arms, she pointed past the end of the couch toward the front door of the house. 'I'll unlock it.'

'Rich?'

'Shut up,' Rich whispered.

Billy braced himself up on his elbows and squinted through the darkness. His brother's bed, just on the other side of the night table, was a dim blur. He thought maybe the small pale area near the headboard might be Rich's face. 'It wasn't true, was it?' he asked.

Low on the pale area, a dark spot moved when Rich said, 'Don't be a dork.'

Billy was seeing Rich's face, all right. That was a relief. He said, 'It kind of sounded like it might be, you know?'

'She was just trying to scare us.'

'Are you sure?'

'There's no madman going around trying doorknobs. Are you kidding? The cops'd be all over a guy like that.'

'Yeah, I guess.'

'So forget about it and . . .'

The bedroom door flew open, slamming the wall. Billy flinched. He jerked his head toward the light.

Agnes filled the doorway, fists on her hips. 'What did I tell you children about talking?'

'We weren't,' Rich argued.

'I'm not deaf, sweetie-pie. I told you what I'd do, didn't I? You bet I did! And that's just what I aim to do.'

She jerked the door shut, cutting out the light.

Billy clutched his pillow to his face. He clamped his lower lip between his teeth. He tried not to cry.

He listened.

Listened for the quiet clack of Agnes unlocking the front door.

He didn't hear it. That was awfully far away.

But soon he heard quiet sniffing, gasping sounds. They came from the other bed.

'Rich?' he whispered.

'Shut up.'

'Are you crying?'

'None of your business. It's all your fault, you little crud.' He made a wet, slurpy sniffle. 'Why'd you have to go and open your big mouth?'

'I'm sorry.'

'Now she's gone and unlocked the door.'

'You said you didn't believe in Madman Stan.'

'I don't.'

'Then what are you crying about?'

'I'm not. It's just she's such a bitch.' Another loud sniff. 'How could Mom and Dad leave us with a bitch like that?'

Billy shrugged, even though he knew Rich couldn't see it. 'Linda had that date.'

'Hope she had a rotten time.'

'Don't say that, Rich.'

'She should've been with us.'

'You're telling me.'

'Shut up before *she* comes back.'

'Okay.' Billy rested his head against the pillow and shut his eyes.

He heard soft, muffled sobbing.

Jeez, he thought. Rich is even more scared than me, and he doesn't even believe it about the madman.

Bet he *does* believe it.

'Mom and Dad'll be home pretty soon,' he whispered.

'Oh, sure. Pretty soon. Like two or three hours.'

'I bet she didn't unlock the door, anyway.'

'Like fun she didn't. Shut up, huh?'

'Okay.'

Billy rolled onto his back. He stared at the ceiling. He listened to his brother cry.

After a while, the crying stopped.

'Rich?' he whispered.

No answer.

'You asleep?'

It seemed impossible. How could *anyone* fall asleep with the front door unlocked and everything?

Soon, Rich started to snore.

Billy felt deserted. It wasn't fair. Rich shouldn't leave him alone like this.

He wished *he* could fall asleep. But his eyes felt locked open.

My bed's closest to the door, he thought. When Madman Stan comes, he'll get me first.

He had an urge to watch the door. But fear stopped him.

What if he turned his head to look and just then the madman smashed the door open?

So he kept on staring at the ceiling.

He wished Rich would wake up.

I could wake him up, he thought. We could sneak out the window and get out of here.

If we do that, we'll be outside where *he* is.

Billy considered hiding under his bed.

That's probably the first place a madman would look.

Besides, what if I hide and he gets Rich instead of me?

For a while, he wondered how things would be without his brother around. Rich teased him a lot and started fights. But sometimes he was okay. Billy sure didn't want the madman to get him and take him to the graveyard and do things to him that even a rotten bag like Agnes wouldn't talk about.

Rich called her a bitch.

He'd get in trouble if Mom or Dad found out.

Well, she *is* a bitch.

Billy suddenly had a thought that made him smile.

If Madman Stan comes to the house and the door is unlocked and he comes in . . . won't he get Agnes first?

Doesn't she know that?

Is she a stupe, or what?

Billy had another nice thought.

The bitch didn't unlock the door, at all.

He knew positively that Agnes had lied about unlocking the door.

He just wished he could be sure.

Heart slamming, Billy eased open the bedroom door until a strip of light came in. He peered through the crack. The coast was clear.

He slipped into the hallway. Getting down on his hands and knees, he made his way to the dining room. He crawled between a chair and a table leg.

What'll I do if she sees me? he wondered.

Sometimes, Mom and Dad caught him under the table. But plenty of times they hadn't. He and Rich had both gotten away with watching late TV shows from under here while their parents watched from the couch, just out of sight because the edge of the doorway blocked them out.

Billy halted when he could see the television. It wasn't on.

What's she doing anyhow? he wondered.

Maybe reading a magazine, or something.

If she was reading, he might be able to sneak by and get to the front door.

He crawled slowly toward the far end of the table, turning his head and gazing out through the bars of the chair and table legs. Finally, the bottom of the couch came into view. He inched upward, leaned forward, and peered around a chair back that was in the way.

Agnes was lying down on the couch.

A big mound of pink, hands folded on the hill of her stomach.

Her eyes were shut. She didn't have her glasses on.

Billy spotted her glasses on the lamp table between the end of the couch and the front door.

Okay, he thought.

He didn't *feel* okay. He could hardly catch his breath and his heart was thundering and he felt like he needed to use the bathroom bad.

But this was his chance.

He crept out from under the table. Staying on his hands and knees, keeping his eyes fixed on Agnes, he crawled into the living room.

*Wait'll I tell Rich*, he thought.

'You what?' Rich would say.

'Yeah, I just crawled over to the door and made sure it was locked.'

'And Agnes was there?'

'Yeah, right on the couch.'

'Wow, Billy. I didn't know you had that kind of guts.'

'Wasn't any big deal.'

'How did you sneak by without her seeing you?'

'Indian style.'

'Was she asleep or something?'

'I don't know. She could've been playing possum.'

Billy's fantasy fell apart. *What if she is playing possum*? He halted and stared at Agnes.

Her eyes were still shut. Her mouth hung open. Her chin looked like a golf ball someone had shoved into a pile of raw dough that was heaped up where her neck was supposed to be. The front of her sweatshirt slowly rose and fell.

She *is* asleep, Billy told himself.

But he wasn't sure of that, any more than he was sure she had lied about unlocking the door.

If only she would snore.

Billy forced himself to start crawling again. He was halfway to the door when a floorboard creaked under his knee. He cringed. A hand slid down the slope of Agnes's stomach. It fell off the edge of the couch, taking her arm with it. Billy scurried forward, knowing she would wake up, praying he could get past the head of the couch before she opened her eyes.

His spine froze as she mumbled something.

Her eyes stayed shut.

At last, the stuffed arm of the couch blocked Billy's view of her head. He slowed down, and crept past the lamp table.

When he was even with the front door, he turned to the right and crawled toward it.

Staring at the lock.

It had an oblong brass gizmo that you turned between your thumb and forefinger. It was straight up and down. But it always was. By looking, you couldn't tell whether or not the door was locked.

Billy would have to try the knob.

Bracing himself up with his left arm, he raised his right hand toward the knob.

*What if Madman Stan's right outside?* he thought.

*What if he's reaching for the knob right now?*

Billy's fingers fluttered as if he were having a spaz attack. He closed them around the doorknob. The knob rattled. He heard a soft whimper slip out of his throat.

Holding his breath, he turned the knob.

He pulled.

The door wouldn't budge.

The dirty pig hadn't unlocked it, after all.

Behind the dining room table again, Billy got to his feet. He pressed a hand against his chest. His heart was kicking like a wildman.

I did it, he told himself.

*I did it and she didn't catch me.*

He stared at Agnes, still sleeping on the couch.

He felt a smile stretch his mouth.

Then he tiptoed toward the bedroom, hoping Rich might be awake so he could tell him about it.

Billy woke up in the dark, terrified, hot urine shooting down his leg as something bashed the bedroom door again and again and Rich shrieked, '*Yaaaaaaaah*!'

More bashing. The door opened wider with each bash as the straight-backed chair under its knob scooted a bit more on the carpet.

'Boys!' Dad shouted.

Billy had never heard him sound so scared.

'Boys! What's going on!'

Billy hurled himself out of bed. He rushed toward the door, wet pajama pants sticking to his groin and left leg. He pulled the chair out from under the knob and backed away.

Dad came in. He hit the light switch. He was out of breath, eyes bulging as he looked quickly from Billy to Rich. 'They're okay!' he called over his shoulder.

'Oh, thank God.' Mom lurched through the doorway, weeping.

'What's been going on around here?' Dad asked. 'Jesus! Where's the babysitter? Why was the door blocked? What's going on?'

Rich had stopped screaming a few seconds ago. Now, he was sitting up in bed, crying and shaking his head.

'Agnes was *horrible*,' Billy blurted.

'Well where is she? How could she go off and leave you guys? What the hell . . .?'

Mom, Billy noticed, was holding Agnes's glasses down by her side.

'We come home,' Dad went on, 'and the Goddamn babysitter's gone and the front door's standing wide open! What the hell happened?'

'Madman Stan got her,' Rich whimpered through his sobs. 'Oh geez! She unlocked the door so he'd get *us*, but . . .' Then, he was crying too hard to say more.

Billy looked up at his parents and shook his head. He decided not to tell who had really unlocked the door.

# BAD NEWS

The morning was sunny and quiet. Leaving the door ajar, Paul crossed the flagstones to his driveway. He sidestepped alongside his Granada, being careful neither to tread on the dewy grass nor to let his robe rub against the grimy side of the car.

As he cleared the rear bumper, he spotted the *Messenger*.

Good. Nobody had beaten him to it.

Every so often, especially on weekends, somebody swiped the thing. Not this morning, though. Getting up early had paid off. The newspaper, rolled into a thick bundle and bound by a rubber band, lay on the grass just beyond the edge of Paul's driveway.

On Joe Applegate's lawn.

Crouching to pick it up, Paul glanced at his neighbor's driveway and yard and front stoop.

There was no sign of Applegate's paper.

Probably already took it inside, Paul thought. Unless somebody snatched it.

Hope the damn redneck doesn't think *this* is his.

Paul straightened up, tucked the paper under one arm, and made his way up the narrow strip of pavement between his car and the grass.

Inside the house, he locked the front door. He tossed the

newspaper onto the coffee table, started away, and thought he saw the paper wobble.

He looked down at it.

The *Messenger* lay motionless on the glass top of the coffee table.

It was rolled into the shape of a rather thick, lopsided tube. The wobble he'd noticed out of the corner of his eye must've been the paper settling from the toss he'd given it.

It shimmied.

Paul flinched.

A rat-like, snouted face poked out of the middle of the folds. Furless, with white skin that looked oily. It gazed up at him with pink eyes. It bared its teeth.

'Jesus!' Paul gasped as the thing scurried out, rocking the paper, and rushed straight toward him, claws clicking on the table top, teeth snapping at the air.

Paul staggered backward.

*What the fuck is it*!

The creature left a slime trail on the glass. It didn't stop at the edge of the table. It tumbled off, hit the carpeted floor with a soft thump, and sped toward Paul's feet.

He leaped out of its path. The thing abruptly changed course and kept coming.

Paul hurled himself sideways, lurched a few steps to his easy chair and jumped up onto the seat. His feet sank into the springy cushion. He teetered up there, prancing for balance as he turned around, then dropped a knee onto the chair's padded arm.

He watched the thing rush toward him.

Not a rat, at all. It had a rodent-like head, all right, but beyond its thin neck was a body shaped like a bullet: a fleshy, glistening white cylinder about five inches long, rounded at the shoulders, ending just beyond its hind legs without tapering

306

at all as if its rear was a flat disk. It had no tail.

At the foot of the chair, it dug its claws into the fabric and started to climb.

Paul tore a moccasin off his foot. A flimsy weapon, but better than nothing. He swept it down at the beast. The limp leather sole slapped against the thing's flank, but didn't dislodge it. It kept coming up the front of the chair, eyes on Paul, its small teeth clicking.

He stuffed his hand into the moccasin and shoved at the thing. Its snout burst through the bottom, a patch of leather gripped in its teeth. He jerked his hand free, losing the moccasin, and sprang from the chair. Glancing back as he rushed away, he saw the creature and moccasin drop to the floor.

At the fireplace, he grabbed a pointed, wrought-iron poker. He whirled to face the beast. It worked the rest of its body through the hole in the slipper and charged him. He raised the poker.

Something brushed against Paul's ankle. A furry blur shot by. Jack the cat.

Jack slept in Timmy's room, curled on its special rug beside the boy's bed. The commotion out here must've caught its attention.

'Don't!' Paul blurted.

The tabby leaped like a miniature lion and pounced on the creature.

*Stupid cat! It's not a mouse!*

Paul's view was blocked by Jack. He bent sideways, trying for a better angle, and saw the blunt rear and tiny legs of the thing hanging out the side of Jack's mouth.

'Nail the bastard!' he gasped.

Jack worked his jaw, biting down. His tail switched.

'Paul? What's going on out there?' Joan's groggy, distant voice.

Before he could answer, the cat squawled and leaped straight up, back hunching.

'PAUL!' Now alarmed.

Jack went silent. All four paws hit the floor at once. The cat stood motionless for a moment, then keeled over onto its side. Its anus bulged. The bloody head of the beast squeezed out.

Paul stared, numb with shock, as the thing slid free of Jack's body. It came at him, a tube of red-brown mush flowing out of its stubby rear.

'Christ!' he gasped, stumbling backward. 'Joan! Don't come in here! Get Timmy! Get the hell out of the house!'

'What's going . . .?' The next word died in Joan's throat as she stepped past the dining room table. She saw Paul in his robe dropping to a crouch and whacking the floor with the fireplace poker. The hooked end of the rod nearly hit a yucky thing that she thought for a moment was a rat. It scooted out of the way.

It wasn't like any rat that Joan had ever seen.

She saw the cat, the carpet dark with gore near its rump.

'Oh dear God,' she murmured.

Paul gasped and leaped aside as the creature darted toward his foot. It chased him across the carpet.

Joan took a step forward, wanting to rush in and help him. But she stopped abruptly. She had no weapon. She was barefoot, wearing only her nightgown.

'Shit!' Paul jumped onto the sofa, twisted around and back-stepped, the poker raised overhead. The thing scurried up the upholstery. 'Do like I said! Get Timmy out of here. Get help, for Godsake! Call the cops!'

The little beast suddenly halted.

It looked back at Joan.

Ice flowed up her back.

She whirled around and ran. Straight to Timmy's room. The boy woke up as she scooped him out of bed. 'Mommy?' He sounded frightened.

'It's okay,' she said, rushing out of the room with Timmy clutched to her chest. Hanging onto him with one arm, she snatched her purse off the dining room table. She raced into the kitchen, putting him down while she opened the back door, then hoisted him again and ran outside.

'What's wrong, Mommy?' he asked. 'Where's Daddy?'

'Everything's fine,' she said, easing him down beside the Granada. 'A little problem in the house. Daddy's taking care of it.' She fumbled inside her purse, found the car keys, unlocked the driver's door and opened it. 'You just wait here,' she said, lifting Timmy onto the seat. 'Don't come out. I'll be back pretty soon.' She slammed the door.

And stood there at the edge of the driveway.

*What'll I do?*

Go back inside and help him?

He's got the poker. What'm I gonna do, go after the thing with a carving knife?

*She cut off its tail with a carving knife.*

That was no damn mouse.

He said to call the cops. Oh, right. Tell them a *thing* is chasing my husband around the house. And then when they get here in ten or fifteen minutes . . .

Joan snapped her head toward Applegate's house.

Applegate, the red-neck gun nut.

She crouched and looked through the car window at Timmy. The boy wasn't stupid. He knew that, somewhere in the house, shit was hitting the fan in a big way. His eyes looked huge and scared and lonely. Joan felt her throat go tight.

At least you're safe, honey, she thought.

She managed a smile for him, then whirled around and rammed herself into the thick hedge beside the driveway. Applegate's bushes raked her skin, snagged her nightgown. But she plunged straight through and dashed across his yard.

She leaped onto his front stoop.

The plastic sign on Applegate's door read: THIS HOUSE INSURED BY SMITH & WESSON.

What an asshole, she thought.

Hoping he was home, she thumbed the doorbell button.

From inside came the faint sound of ringing chimes.

Joan looked down at herself and shook her head. The nightie had been a Valentine's Day present from Paul. There wasn't much of it, and you could see through what there was.

Applegate's gonna love this, she thought. Shit!

Where *is* he?

'Come on, come on,' she muttered. She jabbed the doorbell a few more times, then pounded the door with her fist. 'Joe!' she yelled.

No answer came. She heard no footsteps from inside the house.

'Damn it all,' she muttered. Being careful not to slip again, she hurried to the edge of the concrete slab. She stepped down, took a few strides across the dewy grass, then made her way into the flower bed at the front of Applegate's house. He must be home and up, she thought; his curtains are open. He always kept them shut at night and whenever he was away.

Joan pushed between a couple of camelias, leaned close to his picture window and cupped her hands around her eyes.

She peered into the sunlit living room.

Applegate was home, all right. But not up. He lay sprawled on the floor in his robe and a swamp of blood.

\* \* \*

Paul leaped off the end of the couch. He landed beside the front door.

*Get the hell out*! he thought.

Sure, and leave the thing in here? You come back and can't even find it.

I've gotta kill the bastard.

He lurched sideways as the creature sprang off the arm of the couch. He was almost fast enough. But he felt a sudden small tug on his robe, and yelped. The thing was hanging by its claws near the bottom of the robe, starting to climb. Paul threw open his cloth belt. He twirled to swing the beast away from his body, and jerked the robe off his shoulders. It dropped down his arms.

He let go of the poker so his sleeve wouldn't hang up on it. The poker thumped against the carpet. With one hand, he gave the robe a small fling. It fell to a heap, covering the beast.

He snatched up the poker. For just an instant, he considered beating the robe with the iron bar. But the rod was so thin, he'd be lucky to hit the beast.

Squealing 'SHIT!' he sprang onto the cloth bundle with both feet. He jumped up and down on it. Shivers scurried up his legs. He felt as if cold fingers were tickling his scrotum. The skin on his back prickled. He thought he could feel the hair rising on the nape of his neck. But he stayed on the robe, dancing on it, driving his heels at the floor.

Until his right heel struck a bulge.

He screeched, 'Yaaaah!' and leaped off.

He whirled around, poker high, and bent down ready to strike.

The robe was too thick, too rumpled, for Paul to locate the lump he'd just stomped.

*Gotta be dead*, he thought. *I smashed it. Smashed it good.*

Then realized he hadn't actually felt it squish.

311

He whacked the robe with his poker. Stared at it. The rod had left a long, straight dent across the heap. Nothing moved. He struck again. The second blow puffed up the old dent and pounded a new one close to where it'd been. He struck a few more times, but never felt the rod hit anything except the robe and the floor.

Paul stepped a little farther away, then leaned forward and stretched out his arm. He slipped the tip of the poker under a lapel, jostled it until a heavy flap of the robe was hooked, then slowly lifted.

The blanketed area of carpet shrank as he raised the robe higher.

No creature.

Then the end of the robe was swaying above the carpet, covering nothing at all.

Still no creature.

It came scurrying down the slim rod of the poker toward his hand.

Paul screamed.

He hurled the weapon and ran.


Racing up Applegate's driveway toward the rear of his house, Joan wondered if she should try next door. An older couple lived there. She didn't actually know them. Besides, they might be dead, same as Applegate.

And what if they didn't have a gun?

Applegate had plenty. That, she knew. She and Paul had been in his house just once – enough to find out that he was not their kind of person. A Republican, for Godsake! A beer-swilling reactionary with the mean, narrow mind of his ilk. Anti-abortion, anti-women's rights, big on capital punishment and the nuclear deterrent. Everything that she and Paul despised.

But he did have guns. His home was an arsenal.

Dashing around the corner of his house, Joan spotted a rake on the back lawn. It had been left carelessly on the grass, tines upward. She ran into the yard and grabbed it up, then swung around and rushed across the concrete patio.

She skidded to a halt at the sliding glass door. With the handle of the rake, she punched through the glass. Shards burst inward, fell and clinked to the floor, leaving a sharp-edged hole the size of a fist. Reaching through the hole, she unlatched the door. When she pulled her hand out, a fang of glass ripped the back of it.

She muttered, 'Fuck.'

Not much more than a scratch, really. But blood started welling out.

I'm ruining myself, she thought. But then she remembered how Applegate had looked, remembered Paul scampering over the couch with that little monster on his heels.

He could end up like Joe if I don't hurry, she told herself.

Why doesn't *he* get the fuck out of the house?

Deciding to ignore her bleeding hand, Joan wrenched open the door. It rumbled on its runners. She swept it wide, and entered Applegate's den to the left of the broken glass.

There was the gun rack on the other side of the room. She hurried toward it, holding the rake ready and watching the floor.

What if Applegate hadn't been killed by one of those horrible *things*? Just because we've got one . . . Maybe he was murdered and the killer's still . . .

One of those horrible *things* scurried out from under a chair and darted straight for Joan's feet.

She whipped the rake down.

Got it!

The tines didn't pierce its slimy flesh, but the monster seemed to be trapped between two of the iron teeth.

Joan dropped the rake.

She rushed to the gun rack. A ghastly thing with the weapons resting on what appeared to be the hooves of deer or stags. Wrinkling her nose, she grabbed the bottom weapon. A double-barreled shotgun?

She whirled around with it just as the monster slithered free of the rake tines.

Clamping the stock against her side, she swung the muzzle toward the thing, thumbed back one of the hammers, and pulled the front trigger.

The blast crashed in her ears.

The shotgun lurched as if it wanted to rip her hands off.

The middle of the rake handle exploded.

So did the monster. It blew apart in a gust of red and splashed across the hardwood floor.

'Jesus H. Christ,' Joan muttered.

Then, she smiled.

Paul slammed the bathroom door. He thumbed in the lock button.

An instant later, he flinched as the thing struck the other side of the door.

Just let it try and get me now, he thought.

Then came quiet, crunching sounds. Splintering sounds.

'Bastard!' he yelled, and kicked the bottom of the door.

He pictured the beast on the other side, its tiny teeth ripping out slivers of wood.

If only he hadn't lost the poker, he could crush its head when it came through.

Rushing to the cabinet, he searched for a weapon. His Schick took injector blades. They'd be no use at all. He grabbed a pair of toenail scissors. Better than nothing. But he knew he couldn't bring himself to kneel down and ambush the thing. Not with scissors four inches long.

If only he had a gun.

If only the cops would show up.

He wondered whether Joan had managed to call them yet. She'd had plenty of time to reach a neighbor's phone. Applegate himself might come charging over with one of his guns, if she went to his place.

The door rattled quietly in its frame as the creature continued to burrow through.

There must be something useful in here!

The waste basket! Trap the thing under it!

Paul crouched for waste basket. Wicker. Shit! They'd had a heavy plastic one until a couple of weeks ago when Joan saw this at Pier One. The bastard would chomp its way out in about a second.

He looked at the bottom of the door, and two tiny splits appeared. A bit of wood the width of a Popsicle stick bulged, cracked at the top, and started to rise.

He heard a faint boom like a car backfiring in the distance.

The flap of wood broke and fell off. The snout of the beast poked out.

Paul whirled. He rushed to the bathtub and climbed over the ledge. The bathmat draped the side of the tub. He flipped it to the floor.

The shower curtain was bunched at the far end, hanging inside.

With no rug or shower curtain to climb, the thing couldn't get at him.

He hoped.

I don't care how good it is, he thought, it can't climb the outside of the tub.

'Just try,' he muttered as the thing scurried across the tile floor. It stopped on the bathmat and looked up at him. It seemed to grin. It sprang and Paul yelped. But the leap was short. The beast thumped against the side inches from the top. Its forelegs raced, claws clittering against the enamel for a moment. Then it dropped. Its rump thumped the mat. As it keeled backward, it flipped over and landed on its feet.

Paul bit down on the scissors. He crouched. With both hands, he twisted the faucets. Water gushed from the spout. As it splashed around his feet, he stoppered the drain. He took the scissors from his mouth, stood up straight and looked at the floor beside the tub.

The beast was gone.

*Where . . .?*

The waste basket tipped over, spilling out wads of pink tissue. It began rolling toward the tub.

'Think you're smart, huh?' Paul said. He let out a laugh. He pumped his legs, splashing water up around his shins and calves. 'BUT CAN YOU SWIM? HUH? HOW'S YOUR BACKSTROKE, YOU LITTLE SHIT?'

The waste basket was a foot from the tub when the beast darted up from the far side. It landed atop the rolling wicker. Paul threw the scissors at it. They missed. The creature leaped.

He staggered backward as it flew at the tub. It landed on the ledge, slid across on its belly, and flopped into the water. It splashed. Then it sank.

'GOTCHA!' Paul yelled.

He jumped out of the tub. Bending over, he gazed at the beast. It was still on the bottom, walking along slowly under a few inches of water.

He jerked the shower curtain over the ledge so it hung outside.

The beast came to the surface, glanced this way and that, then spotted Paul and started swimming toward him.

'Come on and drown,' he muttered.

It reached the wall of the tub. Its forepaws scampered against the enamel. Though it couldn't climb the smooth wall, it didn't seem ready to drown, either.

Paul backed away from the tub.

On the counter beside the sink was Timmy's smurf toothbrush standing upright in its plastic holder. He rushed over to it and snatched it from the Smurf's hand.

He knelt beside the tub.

The beast was still trying to climb up.

Paul poked at it. The end of the toothbrush jabbed the top of its head and submerged it. But the thing squirmed free. It started to come up. Before its snout could break the surface, Paul prodded it down again.

'How long can you hold your breath, asshole?'

It started to rise. He poked it down again and laughed.

'Gotcha now.'

Again, the beast escaped from under the toothbrush and headed for the surface.

Paul jabbed down at it. His fist struck the water, throwing a splash into his face. As he blinked his eyes clear, something stung his knuckles.

He jerked his hand up.

He brought the creature with it.

Screaming, he lurched away from the tub and shook his arm as the thing scampered over his wrist. It held fast, claws digging in.

He swiped at it with his other hand. It came loose, ripping flesh from his forearm, and raced up *that* hand.

Raced up his left arm, leaving a trail of pinpoint tracks.

Swinging around, he bashed his arm against a wall. But the beast merely scampered to its underside. Upside-down, it scooted toward his armpit.

\* \* \*

'PAUL!'

Joan twisted the knob. The bathroom door was locked. From beyond it came a horrible scream.

She aimed at the knob and pulled the trigger.

As the explosion roared in her ears and the shotgun jumped, a hole the size of a fist appeared beside the knob. The door flew uopen.

Paul, in his underpants, stood beside the bathtub shrieking. His left arm was sheathed with blood. In what remained of his right hand, he held the monster.

He saw her. A wild look came to his eyes.

'Shoot it!' he yelled, and thrust his fist toward the ceiling. Blood streamed down his arm.

'Your hand!'

'I don't care!'

She thumbed back one of the twin hammers, took a bead on her husband's upraised bleeding hand, and pulled a trigger. The hammer clanked.

'My God! Shoot it!'

She cocked the other hammer, aimed, jerked the other trigger. The hammer snapped down. The shotgun didn't fire.

'RELOAD. FOR GODSAKE RELOAD!'

'With *what*?' she shrieked back at him.

'IDIOT!' He jammed the monster into his mouth, chomped down on it, yanked, then threw the decapitated body at her. It left a streamer of blood in the air. It slapped against Joan's shoulder and bounced off, leaving a red smear on her skin.

Paul spat out the thing's head. Then he dropped to his knees and buried it in vomit.

In the living room, he put on his robe. They hurried outside together.

Timmy was still in the car, his face pressed to the passenger window, staring at the woman in curlers and a pink nightgown who was sprawled on the sidewalk, writhing and screaming.

From all around the neighborhood came the muffled sounds of shouts, shrieks and gunshots. Paul heard sirens. A great many sirens. They all seemed far away.

'My God,' he muttered.

He scanned the ground while Joan opened the car door and lifted Timmy out. She kneed the door shut. She carried the boy around the rear of the car.

'Where're you going?' Paul asked.

'Applegate's. Come on. We'll be safer there.'

'Yeah,' he said. 'Maybe.' And he followed her toward the home of their neighbor.

# THE TUB

'Hello?'

'Guess who, Kenny.' She spoke into the phone using her very most sultry voice and that, she knew, was exceedingly sultry.

'All *right*!'

'Whacha doin'?'

'Nothing much. Hanging around. How about you?'

'I'm languishing in bed.'

'Yeah?' Joyce heard his husky laugh. 'You sick?'

'I'm sure running a fever,' she said. 'I'm hot. I'm just so hot I had to strip myself stark naked. I don't know *what* could be the matter with me.'

'Have you got a temperature?'

'I just don't know, Kenny. I don't have the strength to get up and fetch the thermometer. Why don't you come over and bring yours? That big one you've got between your legs.'

Silence for a moment. Then Ken asked, 'What about Harold?'

'Oh, don't you worry about him.'

'That's what you said the last time, and he almost caught us at it.'

'Well, it's absolutely safe tonight. I can guarantee it. He went off to New York, New York and he won't be back till Sunday evening.'

'When did he leave?'

'You *are* a nervous nelly.'

'I just don't want any trouble.'

'Well, he left this morning. And you needn't worry that he missed his flight. He phoned me just a few minutes ago from his room at the Marriott. He's three thousand miles away, so I'm sure there's no danger whatsoever of him popping in on us.'

'How do you know he didn't call from a pay phone a mile away and *say* he's at the New York Marriott? Maybe he's at the Brentwood Chevron.'

'My, aren't we paranoid?'

'Why don't you phone the hotel? Just make sure he actually did check in, then call me back. If he's there like he says, I'll come right over.'

Joyce sighed. 'Well, if I must, I must.'

'I'll wait right here.'

She rolled sideways, cradled the telephone, swung her legs off the bed and sat up.

What a nuisance.

Harold was in New York, just as he'd said. He had been nominated for a Bram Stoker award for that disgusting novel of his, and he certainly wouldn't miss his chance to bask in the glory. Tonight, he would be sopping up liquor in the hospitality suite with Joe and Gary and Chet and Rick and the others, yucking it up and having a ball. Joyce would be the farthest thing from his mind.

Even if he did have his suspicions about her – even if he didn't care a whit about chumming around with those other writers – even if he weren't nominated – he *still* wouldn't have the balls to pretend he'd gone to New York so that he could sneak back to the house and catch her with Ken.

Such a gutless wonder.

Such a wimp that even if he walked in on her by accident and caught her in full rut with Ken, he would probably do no more than blush, say nothing, and walk away.

Silly of Ken to worry about him at all.

What did he think, Harold might shoot him? Harold was terrified of guns. He probably wouldn't use one to save his own life, much less to blow away his wife's lover. And without a gun, Harold wouldn't stand a chance against Ken.

Ken, a 290-pound giant, all hard bulging muscles, could take care of little Harold without breaking a sweat.

She waited a while longer, then picked up the telephone and tapped Ken's number. He answered after the first ring.

'Hello?'

'Hello yourself, big man.'

'Is he there?'

'According to the front desk, he checked in at six o'clock this evening.'

'All *right*. I'm on my way.'

'I'll leave the front door unlocked. Just come right in and see if you can find me.'

'*Ciao*,' he said.

'Yuck. Don't say that. That's what Harold always says. It's sooo pretentious.'

'See you in ten minutes.'

'Much better. See you then.'

She hung up, stepped to the closet and reached for her satin robe. Then she decided not to bother with it. She *was* feeling hot. Though she would have to walk past windows to reach the front door, it was unlikely that anyone would see her. There were no other houses within viewing range, and hedges made it impossible to see her house from the road.

She left the bedroom, walking swiftly, enjoying the soft feel of the air stirring against her skin and the way her breasts jiggled just a little when she trotted down the stairs.

At the bottom, she saw her dark reflection in the window beside the front door.

She imagined a peeping Tom gazing in at her, and felt a small tremor. Not a tremor of fear, she realized. For the benefit of the imaginary voyeur, she brushed her thumbs across the jutting tips of her nipples. The touch made her breath tremble.

She unlocked the door.

Her heart thumped and she trembled even more as she considered opening the door and stepping out onto the stoop. Waiting there for Ken. In the moonlight, in the open, the warm night breezes licking at her.

Some other time. Maybe later tonight, they could go outside together. But not now. She had already decided on her method of greeting Ken and she didn't have much time.

She hurried about, turning off all the downstairs lights before rushing upstairs. At the top, she shut off the hallway lights. Now, the entire house was dark except for the master bedroom.

She entered, flicked a switch to kill the bedside lamps, then made her way carefully over the carpet to the bathroom. She put the light on, but only for the moment she needed to find the matchbook and strike a match.

She shut the door and fingered the switch down. Then she touched the flame to the wick of the first candle. That was enough for now. She shook out the match. The single remaining flame was caught by mirrors that covered every wall and the ceiling. The bathroom shimmered with fluttering, soft light.

Joyce smiled.

Harold has his damned tub, I have my lovely mirrors.

When they'd remodeled the bathroom, she had wanted a spacious sunken tub. Harold had insisted on his white elephant. It was a hideous ancient thing that stood on tiger feet in the middle of the floor. Like a showpiece. And he did enjoy showing it. He would bring his friends upstairs to the master bathroom so they could admire the monstrosity while he told them the whole long boring story of how he'd gotten it at an estate sale in Hollywood. Some bimbo actress from the silent screen days had supposedly slit her wrists while she was in the thing. *Cashed in her chips*, Harold liked to say. *In this very tub.*

What a schmuck, Joyce thought as she bent over the tub and turned on its faucets. Water gushed from its spout. When it felt good and hot, she plugged its drain with the rubber stopper. She straightened up and wiped her wet hand on her thigh.

At least I got my mirrors out of the deal, she thought.

She had let him have the stupid haunted tub, and he'd let her have the mirrors.

She admired herself in them as she made her way around the bathroom, lighting more candles.

The wavering mellow glow made her eyes shine, her russet hair sparkle and gleam. Her skin looked dusky and golden. When the last candle was burning, she set down the matches and stretched, turning slowly, arms high.

She was surrounded by Joyces, all of them shimmering and mysterious. She gazed at their sleek, arched backs curving down to the perfect mounds of their buttocks. She gazed at the velvety backs of their thighs, legs tapering down to soft calves, delicate ankles. Still turning slowly, she lowered her arms and interlaced her fingers behind her head. All the Joyces did the same. They had such long, elegant necks. Shadows were pooled in the hollows of their throats and above the bows of their collar bones. Their breasts were high, the color of honey, tipped a deeper hue of gold. Below them, the rib cages were maybe a little too prominent. Harold certainly thought so. *Why don't you eat!*

The bastard.

I'm perfect the way I am.

She brought her hands down, savoring their touch and excited by the view of all the Joyces caressing their breasts, gently squeezing their nipples, sliding their hands down their ribs (which are just fine, thank you), down the slim smoothness of their bellies, lower until their thumbs pushed into soft, gleaming coils of hair.

If Ken walks in and sees me like this, she thought, he'll never let me make it to the tub.

She hurried over to it. The water was high. She shut off the faucets and listened, wondering if he might already be in the house. She heard only her own quick heartbeat, her own ragged breathing, and quiet plops of water dripping from the spout.

But Ken could be just outside the bathroom door.

Gripping the high rim of the tub, she swung a leg over. Hot water wrapped her foot. Almost too hot. In the mirrors, she watched other Joyces climb into the tub, hold onto both sides, and slowly lower themselves. Then only their heads and the tops of their shoulders still showed.

Joyce slid herself forward. Her rump squeaked once against the porcelain. When she was submerged to the chin, she stopped her slide by raising her knees and pressing her feet flat against the bottom of the tub.

The damn thing was too long. She could never just stretch out in it, feet against the far end to keep her head out of the water. Which meant she could never truly relax. She had to keep her feet planted. Either that, or brace herself up by spreading her legs wide enough to brace her against the sides of the tub.

A royal pain.

But this is one damn cloud with a silver lining, she told herself. The fucking tub's just the right size for fucking. Big Ken would be able to fit right in.

'Gonna do it right in your precious tub,' she muttered. 'How do you like *them* apples, Harold?'

She waited, savoring the water's heat, caressing herself. The ceiling mirrors reflected candlelight down into the tub. She watched her hands move, her body writhe as she squirmed with pleasure.

She flinched at the sound of a floorboard creaking.

He's here!

In the bedroom?

She scooted backward, sliding herself up the rear of the tub until she was sitting. She rested her arms on the edges. She wanted to look just right when he entered, and the mirrors showed that she did. The water covered her like a sheer blanket from the belly down. Her arms, shoulders and chest were wet and shiny.

She turned her eyes to the bathroom door.

What's taking him so long? she wondered . . . and heard a faint, muffled footstep.

Definitely a footstep.

*What if it isn't Ken?*

A shiver crawled up Joyce's body. She felt her skin tighten and tingle with goosebumps.

*Anybody might've walked into the house.*

It had seemed like such a grand plan – leaving the front door unlocked, making the house dark, secluding herself in the bathroom so he would find her in candlelight, naked and gleaming in the tub.

Stupid!

But it has to be Ken.

It doesn't *have* to be.

Christ!

But if it's a stranger out there, maybe he thinks the house is deserted. Maybe he won't find me. Maybe . . .

The door flew open.

Joyce gasped and flinched.

Ken strode into the bathroom as if parading onto the stage at a body-building contest.

He had removed his clothes. He had oiled his skin.

'It's you,' she whispered.

He began to pose. He turned this way and that, moving and pausing and flexing with slow, graceful elegance. His muscles bulged and rippled and bounced. Joyce watched, breathless. She had seen him do all this before, but never in the fluttering gold of candlelight.

He looked magnificent and strange. A gorgeous, hairless monster of dancing mounds and slabs.

When he strutted to the rear of the tub, Joyce didn't have to turn her head. She watched him in a mirror, watched him bend and reach down and slip his hands down her breasts. They touched her only for a moment. Then he pranced backward, curling his arms and twisting his torso.

He twirled around. With coy glances over his shoulder, he came to the side of the tub. He raised his arms and flexed, displaying the bands of muscle criss-crossing his back, the hard mounds of his rump. Joyce smiled when he made the buttocks bounce. One side at a time. She reached up and stroked one slick cheek.

He gently swatted the hand away as if offended, strutted away from the tub, then whirled around and sashayed back to her. Hands on hips, he bent his knees. His rigid penis, inches from her face, jerked up and down. He hopped closer. Joyce twisted toward him, rolling onto one hip, clutching the rim of the tub with both hands. Her breasts pushed against the cool porcelain wall. She opened her mouth. He brushed against her lips, teasing her, not entering. Then he pranced backward.

'Quit it,' she gasped. 'Get in here. I want you *in* me.'

He returned to the tub. Peering down at her, he whispered, 'You look delicious.'

'You look pretty good yourself.'

'You seriously want me in the tub?'

'There's plenty of room.'

'The bed would be more comfortable.'

'But not as exciting.'

He shrugged his massive shoulders. Bending over, he clutched the side of the tub and climbed in. He stood at her feet, glanced down at her, then turned his head slowly, surveying his images in the mirrors.

'Quit admiring yourself and fuck me.'

He sank slowly to his knees, flinching a bit when the hot water met his scrotum. Joyce slipped down into the warmth. As it wrapped her to the neck, her feet met the slippery skin of Ken's thighs.

'You don't want me on top, do you?'

'Of course I do.'

'You want to drown?'

'I want to be crushed.' She lifted a foot out of the water and stroked him. 'I want to feel you on me, that whole gorgeous body pounding me senseless.'

He moaned. He nodded. He muttered, 'Let's lose the water.'

'Hurry. Just hurry.'

He reached down behind his rump. Joyce heard a quick

sucking gurgle, then the soft rush of water flowing down the drainpipe.

She spread her legs. Ken crawled forward slowly. His hands glided up her thighs, caressed her hips and belly, moved up the slope to her ribcage. They cupped her breasts. As they squeezed, she lifted a hand out of the water and curled her fingers round his penis.

'In,' she whispered.

His hands slid away and down her sides. Bracing himself above her, he lowered his face into the water. His tongue flicked her right nipple, swirled and pressed. His mouth opened, and she felt his lips around her breast. He sucked. He sucked it deep into his mouth.

'God!' she cried out. She let go of his penis and clutched his back.

He let go. He came up, gasping. His dripping face smiled at her, then plunged down again. She felt lips on her other breast. They were like a soft, plaint ring encircling her nipple, making a tight seal. This time, they didn't suck. They blew. Blew like a kid making fart sounds on his arm. Lips and air and water vibrated against her nipple. Bubbles erupted on the surface.

Gasping, she pushed his head away.

'Did it hurt?' he asked.

'No. Just . . . quit it and fuck me . . . *now*!'

He struggled, trying to reposition himself. Joyce realized that their differences in size were causing him problems. That, and the water. He was still worried about drowning her.

Suddenly, he reared back onto his haunches, dragging her up out of the water by the armpits, lifting her, planting her down on him, impaling her.

A club shoving high up into her.

332

She cried out and shuddered and clamped herself tight to his chest as spasms quaked through her body.

Spasms also quaked Ken.

He dropped forward, driving her down. Her back splashed, then slammed the bottom of the tub. Her head snapped down and thunked. Lights exploded in her vision as water rained down on her face.

When the exploding lights went away, she realized she was sprawled beneath Ken, her chin resting against the top of his shoulder.

'Christ,' she gasped. 'You hurt me.'

He didn't apologize.

He didn't say a thing.

She realized that he couldn't. His head, next to her own, was face-down in the water. The level was lowering, but slowly. The heat enclosed Joyce's head like a warm hood, only the front of her face in the air.

So Ken's face had to be submerged.

*He's going to drown*!

'Ken!'

He didn't stir.

He wasn't making bubbles. He wasn't breathing.

His chest was mashed tight against Joyce's chest. She felt a raging heartbeat. Whether *his* was beating, she couldn't tell.

Though she was pinned down by his weight, her arms were free. They'd been around him at the moment of the fall. So she made fists and pounded on his back.

'Ken! Ken, wake up!'

*He's not sleeping, you idiot*!

'Ken! Get your head up! Ken!'

She kept hammering her fists down against his back. They made meaty thuds. She had no idea whether pounding on him would do any good, but she'd seen it done on doctor shows. Also, in a way, it felt good. Each blow sent quick little tremors through his body. Like rapping a water melon at the grocery store. The tremors made him vibrate on top of her. They gave Joyce a tingle.

The blows even jostled his penis a little.

It was still buried in her. Still erect.

'I *know* you're faking,' she said. 'Now, come on. Dead guys don't have boners.'

He didn't move.

'Come on, Ken. This isn't funny. I bumped my damn head. Besides, you scared me. I thought you were dead or something.'

He still didn't move.

'All right. You're asking for it.' She jabbed the long nail of her forefinger into his back. She felt it pop into his skin. He didn't flinch.

A sick, icy chill snaked through her bowels.

'Oh, my God,' she muttered.

She nudged his head with the side of her face. It moved easily. She bumped her cheekbone against his ear. His head swung away, then flopped back and hit her as if trading blows.

'Shit!'

He's dead! The bastard's *dead*!

Joyce squirmed under his terrible weight.

This won't be easy, she thought.

She took a deep breath, then attacked. She bucked, she twisted, she shoved and tugged at Ken, she kicked and thrust at the bottom of the tub with her feet, she clawed at the sides with her hands. But she couldn't roll him off. She couldn't lift him. She couldn't writhe her way out from under him.

All her efforts hardly moved him at all.

Finally, she was too exhausted to continue the struggle. She lay beneath him, limp and sweaty, arms at her sides, fighting to breathe.

Calm down, she told herself.

Right. Calm down. I've got a fucking *stiff* on top of me. Not to mention . . .

Don't even think about that.

There has got to be a way out of this.

A way out of it *fast*!

Use your head, use your head.

The problem – the *major* problem, is the damn tub. The way it's holding us in. Of course.

If only we'd done it on the bed! I could've just rolled him off me . . .

If only. A lot of good that'll do you.

If only he hadn't *fallen* on me, that's what.

What happened to him? A heart attack? An aneurism? Who knows? Who cares? The jerk was pumped up with steroids, probably fucked up his system.

And now *I'm* the one who's fucked.

For the first time since she'd landed on her back under Ken, Joyce noticed the overhead mirror. She stared up at it.

No wonder she was trapped. She could hardly see herself. Only her face and legs were visible. The rest of her was hidden beneath Ken's massive body. She raised her arms. They came up into view below Ken's armpits. They looked so small.

Her legs looked useless. Beautiful, useless legs, with their knees in the air – legs spread wide and painfully apart and jammed against the walls of the tub by Ken's thick thighs.

She tested them. She was able to unbend her knees. She could straighten her legs, lower them, and raise them high.

When she moved her legs at all, Ken seemed to shift position deep inside her, probing and exploring.

She didn't let that stop her. She watched her legs in the mirror and kept on testing their maneuverability. She found that she could kick around pretty well, but mostly just from the knees down. What she couldn't do was bring her legs together. Though she tried, they remained tight against the walls of the tub.

Maybe . . .

She lifted her right leg high, hooked its calf over the edge of the tub, shoved her right elbow against the bottom, and struggled to raise and turn herself, hoping to roll Ken off. She couldn't budge him.

Okay. This doesn't work. *Something* has to work.

She lowered her leg. She tried to relax.

I can't actually be *stuck* here.

But I'm certainly *being* stuck.

At least I should be able to do something about that, she thought.

She slid her open right hand into the tight crevice between her belly and Ken's. His skin was slippery against the back of her hand. She shoved downward. Their pelvises, locked together, stopped her fingertips. She tried getting to him from the side of her groin. No way.

'Great,' she muttered.

Then she screamed and kicked and pushed and twisted and squirmed, determined to get him off her, out of her, knowing she could do it – she had to do it and she could – mothers picked up cars, didn't they, when they had a kid trapped under a wheel? – and she could lift Ken. She would. She would hurl him aside and scamper out of the tub.

When she found that she couldn't, she wept.

* * *

Sometime later, the candles began to die. One by one, they fluttered, flared brightly and went out. She was left in darkness.

Just as well, she thought at first. Nothing to look at, anyway, but a dead guy pinning me down.

She didn't feel that way for long.

Terror began creeping through her.

A dead guy. A *corpse*. I'm trapped by a corpse.

What if it starts to move?

It's only Ken, she told herself. It's not any fucking ghoul or zombie or spook, it's just Ken. And he's dead, kaput. He isn't about to start *moving*.

But suppose he does? Suppose he wants revenge? I'm the one who killed him.

He threw a heart attack or something. Wasn't my fault.

Maybe he doesn't see it that way.

Shit! He doesn't see anything. He's dead! Besides, he died happy. What a way to go, right? He came and went.

She heard a laugh. It sounded a trifle mad.

He didn't come, she reminded herself.

*Coitus interruptus croakus.*

She laughed again.

It went silent, frozen in her throat as she imagined Ken lifting his head, kissing her mouth with his dead lips, whispering 'I've got some unfinished business,' and starting to thrust.

It took the light of morning to ease her terror. She slept.

She woke up aching and sweaty, her rump numb, her legs lifeless. She flexed her muscles, kicked and squirmed as much as she could. Soon, circulation came back. Her buttocks and legs burned. They felt as if they were being pricked by thousands of needles.

When she felt better, she noticed the odor.

The overhead mirror revealed its cause. Down between Ken's feet, a turd was hanging over the edge of the drain.

'Shit,' she muttered.

She closed her eyes.

Don't sweat the small stuff, she told herself.

Think, *think*.

Okay, it's Saturday. If he doesn't miss his flight or something, Harold will be getting back tomorrow evening. Around seven. That gives me better than a full day to get out of here. Or hubby'll get the surprise of his life.

How's *this* for a horror story, Harold? Write this one up, why don't you? Maybe you'll win a fucking award!

Won't happen. I'll be out of this mess long before he gets home.

Right. How?

*I can float Ken off me!*

She thought about that for a while. If she filled the tub, wouldn't the rising water lift him? Sure it would.

I might drown in the process.

But if I can hold my breath long enough . . .

She raised her legs, stretched them out, tried to squeeze them closer together. And came nowhere near the bathtub's faucets.

So much for great ideas.

There has to be a way. There . . .

'Get off me!' she shrieked, and fought the body. It was rigid with rigor mortis. It felt even heavier than before. Finally, exhaustion made her quit.

There *is* no way, she realized.

I'm gonna be trapped under this Goddamn stiff until Harold gets home.

After that, she spent a long time crying. Later, she dozed. When she woke up, her butt and legs were numb again, but she no longer felt the horrible desperation. She felt resigned.

'When rape is inevitable,' she muttered, 'relax and enjoy it.' What asshole thought up that one? she wondered.

This isn't the end of the world, she told herself. It may be the end of my marriage, but that's no great loss. Harold will come home tomorrow and get me out of this.

It's awful and disgusting, but I'm not going to die from it.

Later in the day, the stench got worse as her own excretions joined Ken's.

When darkness returned, so did her terror.

She lay motionless, hardly daring to breathe, waiting for Ken to stir. Or to speak.

*Joyce.*

*What?*

*I'm hunnnngry.*

She imagined his head turning, nuzzling down against the side of her neck, biting.

When she finally did feel him move, she shrieked. She screamed until her throat felt raw and burning.

Later, she convinced herself that Ken hadn't come back to life. The motion had probably been caused by something natural. Like decomposition. Shifting gasses. Tendons or muscles turning soft. Gross. Disgusting. But he wasn't coming back to life. He wasn't going to start talking to her. He wasn't going to bite her. He wasn't going to start humping her.

Just make it through the night.

Later, as she was starting to drift off, Ken moaned.

Joyce gasped. She went rigid, goosebumps squirming over her skin.

It's just escaping gasses, she told herself.

He did it again, and she whimpered.

'Stop it,' she whined. 'Stop it. Get off me. Pleeease.'

She exploded into another frenzy of struggles, then lay sobbing under his bulk and prayed for daylight.

When the first gray light of dawn came into the bathroom, Joyce's panic subsided and she closed her eyes.

It's Sunday.

Harold will come. He'll be here around seven. Before dark.

There won't be another night under Ken.

Exhausted, she drifted into sleep.

The jangle of the telephone startled her awake.

Who is it? Maybe someone had heard her screams in the night and was calling to check on her. When I don't answer . . .

Fat chance.

Nobody had heard the screams. Probably just a friend calling to chat. Or a salesman.

Or Harold. Harold calling to say he'd missed his flight, or he'd been bumped, or he'd decided to stay on another day or two in New York to meet with his agent, his editor.

'No,' she murmured. 'No, pleeease. Harold, get back here. You've got to.'

*I can't go through another night*!

It's all right, she told herself. He'll come. He'll come.

A few more hours, and he'll be here.

She wondered if Harold would be able to get her out from under Ken. Probably not. Such a weakling. He might have to call the fire department. *I hate to bother you folks, but I'm afraid my wife is stuck in the bathtub. It seems she was screwing this muscle-man and the fellow pitched a coronary or something.*

The idea of it made her laugh. The laughing made her chest hurt. Worse, it jostled her insides and jiggled Ken's penis.

She groaned.

There's nothing funny about this, she thought.

But if Harold can't get me out, the fire department will. It'll be a little embarrassing, but so what? I'll be free.

She imagined herself running down the corridor, butt naked, the firemen gaping in shock and maybe just a bit turned on. Running to the other bathroom, the big one, the one with a shower.

First, she would drink cold water. Fill her parched mouth with it. Drink till her belly bloated. Then she would take the longest shower in history. Sudsing and scrubbing until there was not a trace left of Ken's foul dead touch. Douching, too. Getting rid of his death.

Afterwards, cocktails. Vodka and tonic. Ice clinking in her glass. A twist of lemon. Drinking until her head was full of soft, cozy cotton.

Then, a steak dinner. A thick slab of rare filet mignon, charcoal broiled.

I'll have to broil it myself, she thought. Harold isn't likely to be in any mood to cook for me. If he sticks around at all.

Thinking about the steak, her mouth watered. Her stomach growled.

I'll be eating soon, she told herself. In just a few more hours . . . if that wasn't Harold on the phone, calling to say he wouldn't be home.

It wasn't.

Please, it wasn't.

He'll be here. He'll come.

He came.

Joyce, lost in daydreams about his arrival, heard nothing until the bathroom door swung open.

'Harold!'

'Joyce?'

She heard his quick footsteps. Then he was gazing down at her, at Ken. His face turned a shade of gray almost the same color as Ken's back. His mouth drooped open.

'Get me out of here!'

He frowned.

'My God, quick! I've been pinned under him since Friday night!'

'You can't get up?'

'Would I be here if I could?'

'Jeez, Joyce.'

'Get your thumb out of your ass and get me out of here!'

He kept staring down into the tub, shaking his head slowly from side to side.

'Harold! Get me out of here!'

'Uh-huh. Right.'

He turned and walked away.

'*Ciao*,' he said. The bathroom door bumped shut.

Harold flew to Maui and spent a week relaxing on the beach, reading horror novels written by his friends, dining at fine restaurants. He ogled some beautiful women, but he stayed away from them. He didn't need any more traitorous bitches in his life.

Upon his return, he stepped into the house and called out, 'Joyce, I'm home.'

She didn't answer.

Grinning, Harold trotted upstairs.

The smell was not good. It made him gag. It made his eyes water. With a handkerchief over his nose and mouth, he hurried across the bedroom and entered the bathroom.

He went numb.

He dropped the handkerchief.

He stared.

The tile floor near the bathtub was strewn with body parts.

A bloody orb that he recognized as a head. Part of a head, anyway. It was missing its jaw. The ragged stump of its neck looked *chewed*.

He saw an arm. Another arm. Big, muscular things. So much missing from around their tops. The knobby ends of the humerus bones looked as if they'd been licked clean.

The floor was littered with other pieces. Curving slats of rib bones. Chunks of flesh. Slabs of stringy muscle. Slimy gobs that might have been interior organs – parts of lungs, maybe, or kidneys – who knows?

Harold *did* recognize a heart among the assortment of litter.

Over the rim of the tub hung coils of intestines.

Harold threw up.

When he was done, he approached the tub, careful not to step on any mess.

Joyce wasn't in it.

Her boyfriend was. Some of him. From the ass down, he appeared to be in fine shape. Excellent shape.

Most of his torso, however, had been hollowed out. He was an armless, headless husk sprawled in a swamp of blood and puke and floating bits of God-knows-what.

'Welcome home, honey.'

Harold whirled around.

Standing in the bathroom doorway was Joyce. Clean and fresh and smiling. Wearing her red satin robe.

'My God,' was all he could say.

She grinned and clacked her teeth together. Then she brought her right hand around from behind her back. It was holding a jawbone. 'Ken has good, sharp teeth. He was of enormous benefit.'

'My God,' Harold muttered.

She tossed the jawbone, caught it with her forefinger behind the front teeth, and twirled it. 'Let's talk settlement,' she said. 'I get the house. The tub is yours.'

## *A selection of bestsellers from Headline*

| | | | |
|---|---|---|---|
| A HEROINE OF THE WORLD | Tanith Lee | £5.99 | ☐ |
| THE HUNGRY MOON | Ramsey Campbell | £5.99 | ☐ |
| BEWARE | Richard Laymon | £4.99 | ☐ |
| THIS DARK PARADISE | Wendy Haley | £4.99 | ☐ |
| THE PRESENCE | David B. Silva | £5.99 | ☐ |
| BLOOD RED MOON | Ed Gorman | £4.99 | ☐ |
| WIZRD | Steve Zell | £5.99 | ☐ |
| ROAD KILL | Jack Ketchum | £4.99 | ☐ |
| RED BALL | John Gideon | £5.99 | ☐ |
| COVENANT WITH THE VAMPIRE | Jeanne Kalogridis | £4.99 | ☐ |
| THE SUMMONING | Bentley Little | £5.99 | ☐ |
| WINTER MOON | Dean Koontz | £5.99 | ☐ |

*All Headline books are available at your local bookshop or newsagent, or can be ordered direct from the publisher. Just tick the titles you want and fill in the form below. Prices and availability subject to change without notice.*

Headline Book Publishing, Cash Sales Department, Bookpoint, 39 Milton Park, Abingdon, OXON, OX14 4TD, UK. If you have a credit card you may order by telephone – 01235 400400.

Please enclose a cheque or postal order made payable to Bookpoint Ltd to the value of the cover price and allow the following for postage and packing:

UK & BFPO: £1.00 for the first book, 50p for the second book and 30p for each additional book ordered up to a maximum charge of £3.00.
OVERSEAS & EIRE: £2.00 for the first book, £1.00 for the second book and 50p for each additional book.

Name ..................................................................................................

Address ..............................................................................................

.............................................................................................................

.............................................................................................................

If you would prefer to pay by credit card, please complete:
Please debit my Visa/Access/Diner's Card/American Express (delete as applicable) card no:

| | | | | | | | | | | | | | | | | | | |
|---|---|---|---|---|---|---|---|---|---|---|---|---|---|---|---|---|---|---|

Signature .................................................... Expiry Date ..............

Richard Laymon was born in Chicago in 1947. He grew up in California and has a BA in English Literature from Willamette University, Oregon, and an MA from Loyola University, Los Angeles. He has worked as a schoolteacher, a librarian and as a report writer for a law firm. He now works full-time as a writer. Apart from his novels, he has published more than fifty short stories in magazines such as *Ellery Queen*, *Alfred Hitchcock* and *Cavalier* and in anthologies, including *Modern Masters of Horror*, *The Second Black Lizard Anthology of Crime* and *Night Visions 7*. His novel *Flesh* was voted Best Horror Novel of 1988 by *Science Fiction Chronicle* and also shortlisted for the prestigious Bram Stoker Award, as was *Funland*. He lives in California with his wife and daughter.

*Also by Richard Laymon*

**The Cellar**
**The Woods are Dark**
**Night Show**
**Beware!**
**Allhallow's Eve**
**The Beast House**
**Flesh**
**Resurrection Dreams**
**Funland**
**The Stake**
**One Rainy Night**
**Darkness, Tell Us**
**Blood Games**
**Dark Mountain\***
**Savage**
**Alarums**

\* previously published under the pseudonym of Richard Kelly
*Dark Mountain* was first published as *Tread Softly*